BREAK IN CASE OF EMERGENCY

BRIAN FRANCIS

Break IN CASE OF EMERGENCY

inkyard
press

Recycling programs
for this product may
not exist in your area.

ISBN-13: 978-1-335-07061-6

Break in Case of Emergency

First published in 2019 by HarperCollins Canada Ltd.
This edition published in 2020.

For questions and comments about the quality of this book, please contact us at CustomerService@Harlequin.com.

Inkyard Press
22 Adelaide St. West, 40th Floor
Toronto, Ontario M5H 4E3, Canada
www.InkyardPress.com

Printed in U.S.A.

For Sergio, my lighthouse

The day I lost my mom, I turned left instead of right. If I had listened to her instructions, if I had turned right, she would still be here.

That morning, I knew something was wrong. While I was eating my breakfast, my mom said she wasn't going to work.

"The women of Tilden and their fat feet can wait." She pulled her frayed pink robe tighter around her. "I am unwell."

I looked down at my bowl of Cheerios. My mom didn't have the sniffles or a fever. She didn't have a headache or a sore throat. But I knew what she meant. There was a storm brewing inside her head, inside the walls of our two-bedroom apartment. My school wasn't far from where we lived, so I told my mom that she didn't need to pick me up at the end of the day like she always did. It would be easier. For both of us.

"I can walk home with Trisha," I said.

"What if Trisha isn't at school today?" she asked.

"Then I can walk home on my own. I'm ten now. That's old enough."

This felt like both a lie and the truth.

"Maybe you are," my mom said, but she wasn't looking at

me. Instead, she was studying Henry, our goldfish, who kept rising up and diving down, over and over again. "Don't stop, Toby. Come straight home. Or I'll worry."

"Okay," I said. "I won't stop."

But when the end of the day came, I didn't say anything to Trisha about walking home. I slipped my arms through the straps of my backpack and pretended it was just another day.

"Do you want to come over this weekend?" Trisha asked as we walked out. "My mom wants to teach me how to knit, but if you come, I'll say you're allergic to yarn."

"I don't think I can," I said. "I'm supposed to visit my grandparents."

"Did I tell you my grandmother had her vagina taken out when she turned sixty?"

"Yes," I said. Sometimes it felt like Trisha said these kinds of things just to shock me. Or maybe to shock herself. Maybe I was easier to shock back then.

"Mike says they took it out through her belly button," Trisha said. "But have you ever heard anything so stupid? And how would he know? He doesn't have a vagina."

I said goodbye to Trisha at the edge of the schoolyard and then I walked toward the parking lot like I did every day, pretending to look for my mom's silver car and her blank face staring out from the windshield. I walked through the parking lot and kept going in the direction of our apartment. When I got to the corner of Kathleen and East, I should've turned right and gone down Kathleen, which would've led to my apartment building, to my front door, to my mom.

But I didn't turn right. Instead, I stopped and looked down our street.

It was October and the branches were letting go of their leaves. They tumbled through the air like hopeless birds. I wanted to forget, even for a moment, about my life. Just for one day. So I swung my body around and started to walk down East Street.

I went to Greer's, a variety store in a plaza that had a drugstore (where my mom would pick up her medication) and a bank and a restaurant called the Horse's Feather that no one ever seemed to eat at except old people and "confirmed bachelors," as my mom would say. Halloween was around the corner and Greer's went all out. The air smelled like waxed teeth and makeup. There were vinyl vampire capes with cardboard collars and foam clown noses and pieces of rubber made to look like scars and open wounds. Costumes hung from the ceiling like bodies with no bones. There were masks, too, staring back from their hollowed-out eyes, small slits between spray-painted lips so that a person could breathe.

I had wanted to be a gypsy that year. I had a picture in my head of what I'd look like in my makeup and head scarf and big, gold hoop earrings. My ears weren't pierced, but Trisha said we could take care of that with a safety pin and a candle.

"Why a candle?" I asked.

"You hold the pin in the candle's flame to sterilize it," Trisha said. "Safety first, Toby. Oh, and we'll need ice. Lots and lots of ice."

But my mom had said no, that I was going to be a pirate

because she saw it in a magazine and I could put Vaseline on my face and smear coffee grinds onto my cheeks.

"I'll even make you a hook out of a coat hanger and tin-foil," she said as she sliced open a package of ground beef.

As if that would change things.

I didn't want to be a stupid pirate. I didn't want to put coffee on my face. And I didn't trust my mom to do a good job with the hook. But I also knew I couldn't say anything. If there was one thing I had to do every day, it was to make sure I didn't say or do anything that would upset my mom. When she got upset, when the dark thoughts started running around inside her head like angry squirrels, the entire world turned upside down. It was my job to keep things right-side up.

I wanted to be a gypsy that Halloween because I wanted to be beautiful that year. I wanted to see what was possible.

"I think a gypsy would be easier," I said. "And you wouldn't have to waste all that coffee."

My mom said she'd think about it and turned around to fry the ground beef. But the answer, to me, was already clear.

So I went to Greer's to see if they had any girl pirate costumes. That's what I told myself, anyway. But the real reason was that I didn't want to go home. I didn't know what my mom would be like when I got there. If the voices would have taken over. When that happened, they were the only voices my mom listened to.

I took a Frankenstein mask down from its hook and tried it on. There was a hand mirror tied to a long string and I held it up in front of me. The eyes looking back were still mine, but the face wasn't. It made me feel better to not be recognizable, to know that I could be someone else, someone besides Toby Goodman, the girl who lived in apartment 211 with her mom, Heather, and a goldfish named Henry.

The girl who wanted to hide, even though she never could.

"Those masks aren't for trying on," the woman behind the counter said. "That's how germs get spread, you know."

I put the mask back on its hook and bought a pair of red wax lips. The woman put them into a paper bag and gave me my change.

"Don't eat the lips," she said. "They'll constipate you."

I said okay, even though I'd never even think to eat wax.

By the time I got home, my mom was dead.

CHAPTER 1

GOODMAN DAIRY FARM, 1992

C'mon, girls! Giddy up. Giddy up now."

I wake to the sound of Grandpa Frank's voice every morning, along with a dull, rhythmic thudding. His plastic bucket and wooden spoon.

"C'mon now. Get up."

The girls are lazy this morning. Now that it's late June, they don't want to come into the barn for their morning milking. It will be like this until the cold weather comes.

"Get up, you stupid things! For the love of Christ!"

The kitchen window screeches open.

"Keep up that hollerin' and you'll wake the entire county!"

Grandma Kay.

"Won't be me who wakes up the county," Grandpa Frank yells back. "You're doing just fine on your own. And you left them bedsheets on the line overnight again. Now they're going to smell like cow shit."

"If anything around here smells like cow shit…" The window slams shut.

I look up at the pink-glass light shade on my ceiling with the little Raggedy Anns. Grandma Kay bought it for me when

I first moved to the farmhouse five years ago. They had turned the sewing room into a bedroom for me. Painted the walls lilac. Grandma Kay made curtains with a butterfly pattern. They even brought in a little table to set Henry's fishbowl on, although he died not long after. All traces of my life with my mom officially disappeared. My grandparents had tried, as best they could, to make me feel welcome. But no amount of paint was going to cover everything. Some cracks always push through, no matter how many coats you apply.

The light shade is embarrassing. I'm fifteen years old now. But I can't tell Grandma Kay to replace it. It would hurt her, and that's the last thing I want to do, even though I always end up hurting everyone, whether I mean to or not.

I won't be able to get out of bed today. Every day is harder, like my pyjamas and bedsheets are made of Velcro. Even putting one foot on the floor seems impossible. But I have to get up. I can't let my grandparents suspect anything. I have to be very careful these next few days, how I go about things. I can't make anyone—my grandparents, Trisha, Mr. Whitlock—suspicious in any way.

There's a light rap at my door.

"Toby, time to get up," Grandma Kay says.

I won't be able to do it, I tell myself. Another day, making small talk at the breakfast table, trying to focus at school, listening to Trisha go on about her latest crush. I can't keep pretending to care, to be in the same world as everyone else. To keep up the lie.

My only comfort is that the lie will soon be over.

"I'm up," I say.

"You don't sound up," Grandma Kay says. "You sound horizontal. Don't make me come in there. Unless you want me to sic your grandpa and his bucket on you."

I pull the quilt back. It's a lead apron. "I'm up," I say, this time more loudly.

One foot on the floor, Toby. Just get one foot on the floor.

I grasp my thigh between my hands and move my leg off the side of the bed. The wood floor is cool beneath my foot. Then I take the other leg in my hands and swing it over the edge as well. I'm lying here, twisted, half on the bed and half off, still staring at the Raggedy Anns.

"Giddy up, girls. Giddy up!"

Somehow, I manage to haul myself up. I slowly walk over to my bedroom door. My bathrobe hangs from a hook. It's pink. Grandma Kay gave it to me for my birthday last year. She didn't know my mom had a pink bathrobe as well.

Open the door, Toby.

I can't.

Open the door.

No. I won't do it.

If you don't open the door, they'll find out what you've got planned. And then everything will be ruined.

I can't.

Open the door.

It's always this way. I'm afraid of what's on the other side. Sadness. Black sludge. The world. My hand reaches for the handle. I feel like I'm going to throw up.

Open. The. Door.

what stays shut stays hidden

Open the—
what's hidden can't hurt
—door!

I close my eyes and twist the handle. It feels like every bone in my arm is breaking, snapping and splintering. Pencils in a vice.

I hear the cracking.

Just a few more days, I remind myself.

CHAPTER 2

The first thing that greets me when I enter the kitchen is Grandma Kay's butt, flat and wide, the seams of her jeans pulled tight.

"Cleaning the baseboards," she says before I can ask. "I took a good look at them this morning and realized how filthy they were. A farmhouse is impossible to keep clean. The outside is always coming inside."

Our dairy farm has fifty cows, a half-dozen hens and an old, dandruff-ridden border collie named Ladybug who mainly just walks in circles because she's senile.

"Surrounded by too many females," Grandpa Frank often says, and I feel bad for him because it's true, although the hired hands are all men. Well, except for Mike. He's not really a man. Not at seventeen. Even though he'd say otherwise. The milking gets done twice a day, rain or shine, 365 days a year. Even Christmas Day. When I first came to the farm, Grandpa Frank said that was the only day of the year the cows produced eggnog.

Our dairy farm is small compared to some of the others in the area. I know we don't make much money, even though my grandparents don't talk about it. But it's the little things I notice. The sighs when Grandpa Frank does his paperwork. And how Grandma Kay never buys any new clothes, even though she says she doesn't need any.

"The cows don't care what I look like."

As I watch her, down on all fours, her worn jeans, her running shoes with the broken laces tied and re-tied, I can't help but wonder if this is the life she imagined for herself when she was my age, when she was young and full of dreams. Not that all young people have dreams. Some of us can't even imagine what our dreams would be.

"What did you want to be when you grew up?" I asked her once.

She paused for a long time, her mouth scrunched over to one side. "I don't know," she eventually said. "I'm not sure I ever thought about it, and no one ever asked me. I used to play the piano. I was pretty good, all things considered. I had a flair for musicality, you could say."

There's a Lesage piano, the colour of milk chocolate, in the living room. Grandma Kay never plays it. It's nothing more than a piece of furniture, a place for her to prop my embarrassing school photographs or her copper trinkets or the nativity scene at Christmas time, which she always sets on a layer of cotton batten.

"Why didn't you pursue music?" I asked.

"No money in that," she said and swatted the air. "And I wasn't good enough. Not enough to make someone of myself."

"You should still play."

"With these knobby things?" She held up her hands. "I can't even open a jar of pickles without calling in the Armed Forces." She sighed in a way that made me instantly sad. "There were a lot of plans in those days. But things don't always go the way you want them to. I was very young when I got married. The first time, anyway. I picked love over music, or what I thought was love. And love limits a girl's options."

Babies limit a girl's options too, I thought. My mom had me when she was only eighteen.

I watch as Grandma Kay dips a brush into a small bucket and brings it back out, drops of sudsy water hitting the linoleum floor.

"Do you need help?" I ask.

"No, you've got school," she says. "You don't have time to deal with my foolish whims. But can you give an old gal a hand getting back up? I need to get breakfast ready for the crew."

As I take her extended hand, I realize I can't remember the last time I touched her.

"You're not old, Grandma. You're only fifty-eight."

"Fifty-eight going on ninety-four," she says. Her eyes scan my face and body. "Have you lost weight, Toby?"

I look down. "No."

"It sure looks like it to me. You're not on any diet, are you? You know how I feel about that."

"I'm not dieting."

"It's a good thing I made a big lunch for you today."

"I'm not bringing my lunch. Trisha passed her history exam, remember? I said if she did, I'd buy her lunch in the cafeteria."

"You likely did. But I forget everything if it's not written on a piece of paper and stapled to my forehead."

"How could you read it then?"

"That's what mirrors are for, smarty-pants. Anyway, Trisha is lucky to have a friend as kind and supportive as you, Toby."

She smiles at me, and for a moment I realize how what I'm planning will affect her. She'll blame herself at first. But she'll be fine. She'll understand why it had to happen. Why I had no choice. And why both of my grandparents are better off. Without the burden of me. She'll convert my bedroom back into her sewing room. I can almost hear the whirr of the sewing machine.

"There's toast and peanut butter on the plate over there," she says. "Don't even think about not eating it. Have a glass of orange juice too."

"No time for juice," I say, taking the toast. I won't eat it. I'll give it to Ladybug. "Remember that I'm babysitting for the Whitlocks tonight. Grandpa will need to give me a ride. I'm supposed to be there for 7 p.m."

"Right," Grandma Kay says. "I knew that."

We both know she's lying.

I grab my knapsack and head out the side door. I see Mike then, just outside the barn. I know that he sees me too, but it's awkward, so we both pretend the other is invisible. It's easier that way.

* * *

Most of my memories of my mom are like snapshots or mini movies about our lives before she died. I remember when she first told me about my father. I was seven. We had gone for chili dogs in downtown Tilden. We didn't go out to eat very much on account of my mom not making much money working in the shoe department at Sears. I'm not sure if it was a special occasion, but it wasn't my birthday or hers. Maybe she took me out because she wanted to tell me about my father in public. Maybe she felt safer with other people around. I don't know, and she's not here to answer my questions. Which means I'm left to figure out puzzles, only I'm always working with the wrong pieces.

The restaurant was called Tops and their speciality was hot dogs served with a sweet chili sauce. We each ordered one and the chili dogs came in red plastic baskets with noisy paper and crinkled fries that were thick and hot and the colour of butter. I remember there was a pressed-tin ceiling above us and pendant lights like glowing peppermints and an air conditioner wedged in the tiny window above the door. My mom had her gloves on, the light blue ones, my favourite. They had a small pearl button that fastened at the wrist. My mom had many pairs of gloves. She wore them all the time, even indoors and in the summer. The gloves made her look like a church lady, even though she wasn't religious. She wore the gloves because she didn't like her hands. Or, I mean, the veins in her hands. Sometimes she'd say they were worms crawling beneath her skin, and she'd scratch them until her hands were raw and red and bleeding. Then she'd have to rub them with the special cream she got from Mr. Whitlock, the pharmacist.

I remember it was a nice fall day. Sunny with pulled-apart clouds. The kind of day that made you think summer was back. But it wasn't. You'd feel the chill the minute you stepped out of the sun and into the shadows.

The hot dog tasted weird to me. I was used to ketchup. There were these little seeds in the chili sauce that popped in my mouth when I bit down.

My mom said she used to come to Tops as a teenager.

"Feels like ages ago," she said, dipping a french fry into a puddle of ketchup. "That was in the seventies. I wore bell-bottoms. Does that make me sound old? I don't look old, do I, Toby? I'm only twenty-five, after all."

I shook my head. I thought my mom was the prettiest mom in the world. She had shoulder-length brown hair, and I loved her freckles. We used to lie on the couch together and I'd count them, my fingertip touching each one as I went along. I kept eating my hot dog, even though I didn't want to. I knew I'd ruin the day if I didn't. The sun would slip behind a cloud and all the leaves would blow away and the sidewalks would be bare except for black dots of gum.

After the waitress took away our baskets, my mom looked at me and sighed. "I think it's time. But I'm not sure. I can never be sure."

"Time to go?" I asked.

"No." My mom reached over and grabbed my hand. Her glove was smooth against my skin. "Time I told you about your father, Toby."

My face went hot. There was a seed inside my mouth, and I started to roll it around and around with my tongue.

"You need to know," my mom said, reaching into her purse. "Every girl needs to know about her father." She pulled out a white square and gently unfolded it, as if she were pulling back the petals of a flower. I could just make out the faint lines of handwriting, like ribbons, on the other side of the paper.

"This is a letter he wrote to me," my mom said. "Just after he moved away." She cleared her throat and began to read.

Dearest Heather. How for art thou? Is your hair up or down? I liked it best down. Bone straight. I was always envious. I look as though a hairy octopus has fallen asleep on my head. Are you sane, dear Heather? Are you keeping the voices at bay or are they keeping you at bay? It's a fine, fragile line. Myself, I'm all ground up like hard dust. This business will kill me if I let it. So much falling down and getting back up. But I must never doubt myself. I need to return a hero. I want them to see me, Heather. As I am. All I want is a parade in my honour. Oh, and a key to the city. Is that too much to ask? Will you come and visit? I'll pick you up in a limousine. We'll throw banana peels at people from the windows and demand the driver drive fast. I can smell the burning rubber now. Write soon.

All my love, Arthur

"That," my mom said with a soft sigh that made the paper flutter and seem like it was about to fly away, "is your father. And one day, when he stops being a child, he'll come back to us. And we can be a family."

I went back to Tops not too long ago. The tin ceiling was

still there. But the pendant lights were gone. The air conditioner wasn't there either. It's an antique store now.

Everything inside is from another time.

CHAPTER 3

"Could you ever date someone with a colostomy bag?"

Trisha and I are sitting in the cafeteria. The voices of the other students around us sound to me like garbage can lids banging against each other. I'm picking at the remnants of a half-baked oatmeal cookie. It's one of the cafeteria specialities, which tells you how crappy the rest of the food is. The only reason anyone gets them is because they're so big.

"What's a colostomy bag?" I ask.

Trisha rolls her eyes. "Oh my God, Toby. You're so rural. You've never heard of a colostomy bag? When you can't poop, there's a tube attached to your stomach and instead of crap coming out your butt, it comes out the tube and into a bag that's taped to your abdomen."

"That's disgusting," I say. Now I have a good reason to not finish my cookie.

"Could I date someone with one?" Trisha asks. She's not looking at me but at some point beyond my shoulder. "Could I love him so much that I wouldn't care if he had a colostomy bag?"

"Why do you think these things?"

"Because you don't know who you are until someone takes his shirt off and there's a Ziploc bag full of poop taped to his stomach. It's a test, Toby. To see how good and true you are. How unconditional your love is. For example, could I love someone who had murdered another person, even if it was in self-defence? Could I love someone who had no legs, just stumps? Could I love someone who had a cleft palate? Kissing, though. Just imagine."

Her eyes focus on me. "Did you wash your hair today?"

"Yes," I lie.

"It's looking a bit greasy. You might want to consider switching conditioners. My mom buys this expensive brand and forbids me from using it. But I never listen to her."

Trisha runs her hand along the side of her hair. She has red hair, like Mike, only she straightens it every day.

"Otherwise I'd look like Orphan friggin' Annie."

I watch as her eyes scan the cafeteria. Unlike me, Trisha has other friends. Normal friends, like Angela and Claire. She only spends time with me because we've known each other for so long. And she feels sorry for me. Her mom does too. Whenever I'm over there, Mrs. Richardson looks at me like I'm a flower with a bent stem. The Richardsons live a few blocks away from my old apartment building. Sometimes it's hard to visit them, because it feels like I'm visiting a part of my life where I'm not welcome. It's too complicated to explain.

I remember the first time I slept over at Trisha's after my mom died. She took a carton of eggs out of the fridge. I told her I wasn't hungry. She said they weren't for eating.

We walked to the park behind her house. There was a

swing set and metal slide that our thighs would stick to in the summer and a creaky see-saw that no one ever went on. Behind this were the tennis courts, which is where Trisha took me.

"Here," she said, handing me the eggs. "Throw these against the wall."

"What for?" I asked.

"It will be good for you," she said. "I'd be really angry if my mom died."

"I'm not angry," I said. In truth, I didn't know how to feel. It was easier to feel nothing. Five years later, it still is.

"How do you know until you throw an egg?"

I was scared at first—and it was a waste of an egg—but I did it. I remember the sound of the splat as the egg slammed against the wall. It felt good in a way I couldn't describe. Just to destroy something. She kept handing me the eggs and I kept throwing them, each one a little harder than the last. Finally, I threw the last egg. The wall was a mess of egg guts and shells. I was panting and sweating. And tired.

"Do you feel better?" Trisha asked.

I nodded.

"Good. Let's go back to my house and make popcorn."

So, while Trisha has been a good friend to me, eggs or not, I know that if my mom hadn't died, Trisha and I wouldn't be friends. Not that I wouldn't want to be friends with her, but it'd be the other way around. I'm not good at being friends with anyone.

"Toby?"

I look up from my cookie and realize Trisha has been saying my name.

"What?"

She leans across the table. "Is everything okay?"

"Yes. Why?"

"You seem a little down lately." Her eyes scan my hair again, which I know is greasy and should be combed. There are lots of things about me that should be another way.

I could tell Trisha how I really feel, my plans, what I'm going to do. The words are right there, a cloud in my mouth. All I'd have to do is open my lips just a little bit and let the words slip out and fill the space between us.

I'm ending it, Trisha.

But I know I can't. I can't let Trisha know because then she'd try to stop me. Her poor, sad little friend. Her charity case. She wouldn't understand how it would be better for her without me in the cafeteria. She'd be able to sit with her other friends and not feel guilty. I can almost hear Trisha laughing, tossing back her conditioned hair.

"I'm fine," I say. "Just stressed out. I have a couple of exams coming up."

"We should get high," Trisha says. "I'm totally ready to explore my marijuana years. I could steal some from Mike. He keeps a stash in his night table. Along with those drawings." She shudders.

Trisha told me once that she found a pile of pornographic pictures that Mike had drawn. Mike never mentioned anything about drawing to me, pornographic or not. Why wouldn't he tell me he drew? What other things was he keeping a secret from me?

"They were all women with gigantic tits and wearing superhero costumes," she said. "The costumes were so tight, you could see everything. I mean *everything*." Trisha said the word like it had fourteen syllables.

That's another thing I can't tell Trisha. About what happened between me and her brother. She'd never speak to me again.

"I'll pass on the pot," I say.

"You really need to break out more," Trisha says over a yawn. "You're in this box, Toby. You worry about school, you worry about your marks, about your grandparents. I mean, when do you do something that makes no sense? When would you ever do something completely irrational?"

If she only knew.

"But thanks again for lunch," she says. "And for helping me study for my history exam. I'd fail everything if it wasn't for you."

I feel a sudden rush of emotion. I'll miss Trisha. She's been a good friend to me. Better than I've ever been to her.

"I think you'd still love him," I say quietly.

"Who?"

"The guy with the colostomy bag. You're not the type of person who'd walk away from someone just because there's something weird about them."

I keep my eyes down so Trisha can't see the swell of my tears.

CHAPTER 4

That day, in the restaurant, after the waitress had taken away the empty plastic baskets and my mom had put the letter my father had written back inside the secret folds of her purse, she lit a cigarette.

"You should've had two parents at home," she said, looking up at the glowing pendants. "And I tried, Toby. God, did I try. But you can only try for so long before your head starts to hurt from banging it against the wall."

I searched my mom's forehead for bumps. I was too young then to understand figures of speech.

"But even if you don't have a normal family," my mom said, "you are loved all the same. By me, by Grandma Kay and Grandpa Frank. And even though you've never met him, your father loves you too, Toby. I know he does."

How could you love someone and never meet them, I wondered? How could my father love me without knowing me? Without knowing what my favourite food was? How could he love me without even knowing the colour of my hair?

The waitress came by and refilled my mom's coffee cup. I shifted in my seat. She wasn't supposed to drink too much coffee. It made her nervous. We hadn't been to the pharmacy lately. I hoped she had enough pills. When the waitress walked away, my mom inhaled deeply and leaned back in her chair.

"He. Was. Magic."

I felt something cover me when my mom said those words. Something settled over my head. Not a cloud. It was finer. A cloth that sparkled, but one that was heavy all the same. I felt it brush the top of my head and I knew that it would stay there forever, that it would always be there, hanging over me, whether I wanted it to be there or not.

"Where did you meet him?" I asked.

"In grade nine," she said, tapping her cigarette into the ashtray. "He performed in a talent show. Your father is a singer. I still remember what he wore. He came on stage wearing this hat, a plaid sort of thing, what a golfer might wear, and a denim pantsuit. It was 1973, after all, but it was still brave, in that high school. Clogs too." My mom laughed. "Oh, God. Those clogs! They were ridiculous. You could hear him coming a mile away. Clomp! Clomp! Clomp! He wore them to make himself taller. His eyes too, Toby. Emerald green and fringed with lashes that would make any girl envious. You have his eyes, you know."

My fingers lightly touched the skin around my eyes. I had never really paid attention to them before. Now there was something special about them. They were my father's eyes.

"He sang 'Delta Dawn' by Helen Reddy that day," my mom said. "I was mesmerized the whole time. I'd never heard anything like that voice. It was so pure. Not what you'd expect from a boy. But not a girl's voice either. It was gloriously in the middle. Like what an angel would sound like."

I saw someone with wings. A white robe. This was my father.

"He had a way of holding you with his voice. Cradled. It's hard for me to explain, but it was like his voice grabbed onto me, my heart and all my pain and made me forget everything that was wrong about me. When he sang his final notes he stretched his arms out, like he was trying to grab the curtains on either side of the stage, and threw his head back. I remember his Adam's apple, poking out from the white skin of his neck. It seemed like such a vulnerable spot on a boy."

"Did he win the talent show?" I asked.

My mom shook her head and stubbed out her cigarette. "Of course not. You think people living in this city celebrate difference? They only reward the familiar, what talks like them and acts like them and thinks like them. It made me sick. Arthur was a bright light in a pile of darkness and no one, except for me, appreciated that. That's why he had to move away after high school. I hate Tilden for that. These people." Her eyes scanned the tables around us. "They ruined my life."

We were the only ones in the restaurant.

* * *

"What time do you need me to pick you up?" Grandpa Frank asks me. We're sitting at a red light on the outskirts of Tilden. I keep playing with the truck's radio, trying to find a song I like, but it's impossible.

"You don't need to pick me up," I say. "Mr. Whitlock will drive me home."

"Didn't you say they were going to a party?"

"Something like that."

"Well, I best pick you up, in that case."

"Mr. Whitlock isn't an alcoholic. He's a pharmacist."

"Alcoholics take on all shapes and sizes."

I glance over at Grandpa Frank. His baseball hat is perched high on his head. It reads, "I Didn't Wake Up Grumpy This Morning. I Let Her Sleep." He's had it for years. Grandma Kay threw it in the garbage once, but Grandpa Frank fished it out.

"Your grandma has the humour of a wart," he said.

Grandpa Frank is Grandma Kay's second husband. Her first husband, Jack, abandoned her when my mom was a little girl. We never talk about Grandma Kay's first husband, just like we never talk about my mom. Being in a family is learning how to not talk about certain things.

Even though Grandpa Frank isn't my blood relative, I still think of him that way. He's the only grandpa I've ever known. I don't know anything about my father's side of the family, although they must be living here, in Tilden. Do they know about me? Do they know I even exist? They probably don't care. Just like my father. Even when my mom died, I never heard from him. He pretends like I was never born. What did I do that was so wrong? Why didn't he ever want to get to know me?

"Frank was a good man for stepping in like he did," Grandma Kay said once. "A woman with a small child is a tough sell on the best of days. So I give him credit for that. Many men would've turned and run the other way."

"You smell alcohol on that pharmacist's breath, you call me, okay?" Grandpa Frank says. "I'll be there lickety-split."

"Okay," I say.

* * *

Mrs. Whitlock tells me there's a German chocolate cake on the counter and to help myself.

"But nothing for April and June after eight o'clock. And no eating in the living room." She wags a finger at them, but the girls aren't listening. They're too absorbed in a television show that's all studio laughter and rubbery people tripping over furniture.

"If the Whitlocks ever have a boy," Trisha asked once, "are they going to call him November?"

"We should be home before midnight," Mr. Whitlock says.

He's wearing a nice shirt. Light blue. I think most men look good in light blue. Mr. Whitlock has broad shoulders too. And large hands. His hair is combed back, and I don't think I've ever seen him look more handsome.

"You have the hots for him," Trisha said once. "I can tell. That's gross."

"I don't," I said, but what Trisha said wasn't a lie. Only it's weird to think of him like that. I don't want to make out with Mr. Whitlock or anything. I just want him to hold me. I want to feel his hand stroking my hair and his heart beating against mine.

"I'll always be here, Toby," he'd say. "I'll never leave you."

"See you in the morning, girls," he says.

After the Whitlocks leave, I cut three pieces of cake and let the girls eat in front of the TV.

"Don't tell your parents," I say. It's important for them to have this last memory of me. I want them to look back on me fondly. To remember that I was a girl who broke the rules sometimes. We watch TV for a while and then I tell them it's time for bed.

"Do you have a boyfriend?" April asks when I'm tucking her in.

"No," I say. "I used to. Kind of."

"Why don't you still have one?"

"It got a little complicated. Do you have a boyfriend?"

She makes a face. "Boys are gross."

"You might change your mind," I say. "One day."

"No way. Never."

After they're in bed, I go back downstairs and watch the last bit of *Unsolved Mysteries*. After what seems like a reasonable amount of time, I get back up and make my way down the hall and check in on the girls. They're both asleep, so I continue down the hall toward the Whitlocks' bedroom. Even though it's dark, I know my way around; this isn't my first time in their bedroom. I turn on the lamp next to the night table. Then I run my hands along the bedspread. It's beige with brown and orange flowers. They ordered it from the Sears catalogue; I know because I saw it in there. I think about the things that happen in this bed. The sex. The quiet conversations. Maybe they fight sometimes. The bed is like a secret, and now that I'm here, I'm part of that secret too.

But I remind myself to hurry up. I'm not here to touch the Whitlocks' comforter, and one of the girls could wake up and find me in here.

I walk over to the dresser on the opposite side of the room and pull out the top left-side drawer. Inside are tidy triangles of Mr. Whitlock's underwear. They're all red, black and blue. Trisha once told me that men buy dark underwear so the skid marks don't show. In the far corner of the drawer, buried beneath pairs of old underwear, there's a pill bottle. I take it out and try to count the pills. I can't remember, but it looks about the same as the last time I babysat. I snap off the lid and take out the last two pills I'll need.

I've been stealing pills every time I babysit for the Whitlocks. I don't know if Mr. Whitlock knows about the bottle in his dresser or if he forgot about it. Sometimes I think he knows it's there and he knows that I'm taking the pills and he's okay with that. He understands he's helping me. He remembers my mom, how I'm her daughter, that it's my destiny to do what my mom did. We'll always be joined.

I slide the two pills into my jeans pocket. This is the last time. I have enough now. Twelve of them. That should do it. I snap the lid back on, tuck the bottle back to where it was and gently slide the drawer shut.

My plan is set. I'm taking the pills tomorrow night. I'm going to sneak out in the middle of the night through the basement window and go to the far corner of the farm, where the tall evergreens are. There's a spot, a clearing in the tall grass, where I'll lay down a blanket, take my pills and say goodbye to the world, the starlit sky, the trees, my grandparents, all my jagged-glass memories. I'll slip into nothingness and the sad, pathetic life of Toby Goodman will be no more.

No one can leave you if you leave them first.

I go back to the living room, to a TV show that's half over. The light from the television bounces off the walls and my face.

Ice blue.

* * *

The thing that bothers me most is that Mike will assume he's the reason I killed myself. Boys always think it's about them. But my reasons have nothing to do with Mike. Maybe some of them do. My mind feels like a tangled ball of string these days and when I try to pull out one strand, it's no use. The tangled ball just gets tighter and tighter.

Mike and I dated, if you can call it that, for a couple of months. He was the one who first approached me back in the late winter. I was dipping the cows' teats in iodine one morning and he came up behind me.

"Been noticing you're going through some significant changes, Tobe-ster," he said.

"What are you talking about?" I asked.

"You're looking pretty damn fine these days."

I told him to get lost, that I didn't have time for jokes, but he said he was serious.

"Maybe we can catch a movie some time," he said, before walking away. "Or something."

Or *something*? What did he mean by *that*?

Afterwards, I couldn't stop thinking about him, even

though I'd never really given Mike much thought before. I'd only ever thought of him as Trisha's annoying older brother. The guy who put bugs in my bed when I went to the Richardsons' summer cabin. The guy who drew dirty pictures of female superheroes. The guy who smoked and had acne scars and a moustache that looked like a caterpillar. The guy who, at sixteen, dropped out of school because he said it was "stupid" and took a job working full-time on our dairy farm. Mike was hardly a Prince Charming. But when he showed interest in me, something went off in my brain. It was like a spell, and once that door opened, I couldn't shut it. I had to step through to the other side and see what was there. I had to keep it a secret from Trisha, though, and that made me feel like a horrible person. What kind of friend dates their best friend's older brother? Behind her back even? I knew she'd never forgive me if she found out.

We went to the movies a couple of weeks later and made out for a bit in his car. It was the first time I'd kissed someone. His mouth was like a wet flower and his moustache tickled. I told him to drop me off at the end of the lane. If Grandpa Frank or Grandma Kay knew I was out with him, they'd have a fit.

"There's something about that boy I don't trust," Grandma Kay told me once. "Boys with no ambition can be the most dangerous. They have nothing to lose."

So we kept things quiet. Not that we had a choice. I begged Mike to not tell Trisha.

"Who cares if she knows?" he asked.

"I do," I said. "You wouldn't understand." I knew if Trisha

found out, our friendship would be over. She thinks Mike is the biggest loser. Even worse, I betrayed her trust. How could I do something like that when she's been such a good friend to me?

Mike and I met in the fields, or in his car, sometimes at this old diner on Highway 7, but even that was risky. I was always turning my head whenever the diner door opened, expecting to see someone I knew. And how would I explain to anyone why I was alone with Mike? At a restaurant? On the outskirts of Tilden?

"Why didn't you ever tell me that you liked me?" I asked him once.

"A man's gotta hold his cards close, Tobe-ster."

"Adding 'ster' to the end of a girl's name isn't going to win you any romance points," I said. "Just so you know."

We never went very far with the sex thing. I mean, I never saw his penis. I felt it through his pants and I let him feel my breasts, but I couldn't go further than that, even though Mike wanted to. All my life, I've been ashamed that my mom got pregnant when she was a teenager, that she let a boy have sex with her without protection, and how that boy, my father, abandoned her. I hated my mom for being so stupid, for not being smarter. When people find out you're the daughter of a single teenage mom, they look at you a certain way.

When they find out your mom also killed herself, they don't look at you at all.

Mike never brought up my mom or made me feel strange. Maybe that's because he's a bit strange himself. That's why he says he left school.

"Couldn't stand it," he told me once. "All those jocks and cheerleaders and kiss-asses. Just because you're not like them, they make you feel like you're less than them. I don't need an education if it only makes me feel stupid."

He has an interesting way of looking at things, I suppose.

After a while, I started to have feelings for Mike. I mean, I thought I did. I have a hard time really understanding what feelings feel like, if that makes sense. I knew that I *should* have feelings for him, that I was supposed to fall in love. That's what happens with everyone else. But every time I thought about love, I felt sick to my stomach. Even the word itself caused a crack to open in the ground, and all of this horrible stuff came oozing out. I had to keep everything closed. I knew it was the only way to be safe. I stuffed and crammed everything back inside, where it belonged. So while I *wanted* to fall in love with Mike, I couldn't. It's dangerous for me to feel anything about anyone. Why would I care for anyone when all they'll do is leave me one day?

I knew I had to end things with Mike. He deserved someone better. Someone who could love him back.

"I can't do this anymore," I said to him a few weeks ago at the diner.

"Fine," he said. "We'll find someplace else to eat."

"I don't mean this," I said. "I mean *this*." I waved my hand in the space between us.

His face looked like it was about to melt, but he cleared his throat and sat up straighter in his chair. "What do you mean by that?"

"You're a nice guy," I said. "But I'm just not ready."

"Ready for what?"

"A relationship."

"Is that what this is?"

"I thought so. Didn't you?"

"I didn't think that much about it." He slid a cigarette out and tapped the end on his pack. "No harm done on my part."

"I don't want it to be awkward when we see each other."

"Too late for that." He bent his head down to light his cigarette. I noticed the straight line of his part, his pink scalp. It seemed so delicate.

So I ended things with Mike for no good reason. Which he knew, of course. And that's what makes things harder. Seeing him every day on the farm since then hasn't been easy. But it's for the best. He'll understand that, in the days ahead. Why I had to break it off. Some people aren't built for love.

* * *

The inside of the Whitlocks' car smells like hamburgers.

"Sorry about that," Mr. Whitlock says. "You go to these dinners and all you get is a chicken breast and two mini potatoes. How's that supposed to fill anyone up? So we went through the drive-thru. I should've asked if you wanted anything."

"That's okay," I say. "I don't eat late at night."

"Neither do I," he says. "I have a feeling I'm going to have a severe case of heartburn."

I like being in Mr. Whitlock's car, the glow of the dashboard, the quiet song on the radio that I can't remember the name of, the darkness outside. I feel safe inside his car, especially when I think of what could be out there, in the dark night around us. Animals waiting to pounce. People hiding. Ghosts, maybe, even though I'm not sure if they exist. Trisha asked me once if I thought my mom was a ghost.

"Have you ever seen her?" she asked. "Like, in a fog? Or really quickly? Like you turn to look at something and catch just a glimpse of her wearing a petticoat before she disappears?"

"Why would she be wearing a petticoat?"

"All female ghosts wear petticoats. And their hair is always in a bun."

But there's been nothing from my mom. No sign. No foggy appearance. She's dead and she's forgotten about me. I'll forget everyone too. Even Mr. Whitlock, although this makes me sad. I glance over at him and wonder: If I reached for him right now, at this moment, what would he do? What would he say?

"How were the girls tonight?" he asks.

"Good," I say. "They always are."

"They have their moments."

I see the half-smile on his face and I realize, for the first time, how much he loves his daughters. How much he cares about them. A father's love. It's something I've never known.

* * *

That day at Tops would play over and over in my head for years. The strange smile on my mom's face as she told me the story, the swirl of smoke from her cigarette. The first image I had of my father, standing on the stage in his hat and clogs, a voice that sounded like an angel. What did that sound like,

I often wondered. I'd try to imagine it in my mind, but I couldn't. Once, I heard a man sing in a movie, one of those old black-and-white ones that Grandma Kay watches on Saturday afternoons, and his voice seemed to fit the space my mom had described, somewhere between male and female. But I couldn't be sure.

He. Was. Magic.

Those words too. I imagined their letters bordered by light bulbs. My father was a singer. What kind of songs did he sing? Had I ever heard him on the radio and not realized it? Did he have albums? (I checked once at the record store in the mall but didn't see anything.) Was he ever on television?

My father, this hole in my life, was someone real and unreal at the same time. After hearing my mom speak about him, I wanted to meet him more than ever, more than when he was just a faceless mist, before I knew his name ("Arthur, Arthur, Arthur," I'd whisper in my bed at night, as though saying his name was going to make him materialize). Before I knew what he wore. Before I knew we had the same eyes. I wanted my father to return. He'd come back one day, dipped in gold with swaying, snow-coloured wings, at first a trick, but then, not a trick, because he was real and warm and there, right in front of me, so close I could feel his breath on my face.

After that day at the restaurant, my father took on a new shape. The few details my mom shared gave me something to work with. Bits and pieces that could help me build him. To create him as the father I wanted him to be. To fill the space that I always kept for him, hoping he'd fill it one day.

A singer. The plaid hat. His green eyes, which, when I imagined them, shimmered like jewels, my own face reflected in them.

* * *

Mr. Whitlock turns into our driveway. The living room light is on. Grandma Kay is likely asleep in her rocking chair, her mouth open. She'd be so embarrassed if she knew what she looked like sleeping.

"We'll likely need you in another week," Mr. Whitlock says as he puts the car in park. "Anne has some kind of concert. I'm not sure what it is. She'll let you know."

"Okay," I say. "Do you have anyone else who babysits for you? Just in case I can't make it sometime."

Mr. Whitlock frowns. "Hmm. That's a good question. I don't think we ever thought about it, on account that you're always free."

"But I might not be," I say. "It would be good to have a backup. Just in case. You never know."

"I'll mention it to Anne. I'm sure there's someone. And I agree, a backup plan is always smart."

My fingers touch the pills inside my pocket.

"Thanks again," I say and get out of the car. I'm halfway up the driveway before I hear Mr. Whitlock calling my name. I walk back to the car.

"You forgot your money," he says, handing me a twenty through the open window.

"Right," I say. "Thanks."

"Toby, is everything all right?" he asks. "You don't really seem yourself."

"Oh?" I blink back at him, trying to look calm.

"You just seem a little…distracted. Anything going on that you want to talk about?"

"No, there's nothing. Just the usual."

"I can only imagine what 'the usual' must be," he says. "Especially for teenaged girls living in this day and age. If you ever start feeling down, or if you're having thoughts that don't seem right, can you promise me you'll tell someone? It doesn't have to be me. It could be anyone. Your grandparents. Or a teacher at school. Even a friend. I'd feel better if you promised me that."

There's something that he's not mentioning. My mom. But both of us know she's there, sitting in the back seat, watching us have this conversation. Maybe there are ghosts, after all.

I need to put Mr. Whitlock's worries aside. I can't have him calling my grandparents. I can't have him questioning me, wondering if I've gone searching for things inside his drawers.

"I promise," I say. And then I do something I probably shouldn't, but given everything, I don't really care. This is our last moment together.

I lean through his open window and give him a kiss on the cheek.

"Good night, Mr. Whitlock," I say, and before he can say anything back, I hurry up the driveway.

I stand there, at the front door, blinking back at the pair of headlights. I wave and hold my smile in place until I see the lights slowly make their way down the driveway and onto the road and disappear into the night.

I hope he remembers me. I hope he tells stories about me when June and April are older. In case they forget about the sad girl named Toby Goodman who used to babysit them.

When I open the door, Grandma Kay isn't sleeping like I thought she'd be. Instead, she's sitting on the sofa, her eyes red and raw.

"What's wrong?" I ask her.

"I've been waiting for you," she says in a shaky voice. "I have some news. It's about your father."

I stare at her blankly. What did she just say?

"Toby, he's coming back."

CHAPTER 5

I can't move. I'm stuck in the doorway. This can't be real life. But there's Grandma Kay in her blue housecoat, the one I bought her for Christmas. Her red eyes, her hands squeezing together, like one hand is trying to strangle the other.

"What did you say?" I ask.

"I wasn't expecting this. Not after all these years. I wasn't even sure if I should tell you. I didn't know what to do."

"Why wouldn't you tell me?"

"There I was, in the middle of watching *Wheel of Fortune* when Shirley called. Out of the blue. It was a regular Friday night. Then everything flipped upside down. I haven't been able to settle out since."

Shirley was my mom's best friend. *Is* my mom's best friend. I'm never sure what tense to use when it comes to my mom. *Was* I her daughter? *Am* I her daughter? *Was* she my mom? Is she still?

"Why would Shirley call you about my father?" I ask.

"*He* called *her*," Grandma Kay says. "To say that he was coming. He knew better than to call here. I'd give him a piece of my mind, that's for sure. I'd tell him that he wasn't—"

"When is he coming? And why?"

"In a few days. He's going to Toronto. To do a show of some kind. And he asked Shirley if it would be all right if he came for a visit. Why, after all these years, I have no idea."

Grandma Kay gets up from her chair and starts pacing back and forth. She seems to be talking more to herself than to me.

"Didn't even come back for Heather's funeral. That tells you the kind of person he is. Selfish. Said something about doing a run of shows. That he couldn't get back in time. A lie if I ever heard one. I knew why he wasn't coming back. The real reason he was staying away. He couldn't own up to it. What he did. What he left behind."

Grandma Kay stops suddenly and looks at me, her mouth a small, dark circle. It's as though she's just realized I'm in the room with her. She walks over and places her hands on my arms.

"Toby, I'm not in my right mind. I'm all wound up. Frank told me to go to bed, to talk about this in the morning, once I had a chance to calm down. But I couldn't sleep. My mind was going a mile a minute. I'm sorry to do this to you, so un-expectedly. My emotions got the better of me. It's late. Let's go to bed and, in the morning, we can talk."

"Okay," I say, even though I don't want to go to bed. How can she drop a bomb like this and leave me hanging? I have so many questions, but I already know she won't give me the answers. Not tonight, anyway.

"We'll see you in the morning," Grandma Kay says. "Have a good night's sleep."

Tomorrow, I was going to sneak away and take my pills. All

my weeks of planning. Every last detail of my death imagined and sorted out. But now this. This news. About my long-lost father, finally coming home. I don't have much choice but to put my plans on hold. For a couple of days, anyway. Until my head sorts this out. Until I see my father, finally, face to face.

The only thing I know for certain is there won't be any sleep tonight.

✳ ✳ ✳

I haven't seen Shirley in over a year. I used to hear from her more in the years following my mom's death, mainly because she was worried about me, I guess. She'd invite me over for Chinese food whenever I saw her, but then she'd never follow up on it. I think, that way, if anything were to happen to me, she'd be able to say, "I used to invite her over all the time," and not feel bad.

Shirley is the age my mom would be now—thirty-three. Even though it's only been five years, I can't imagine what my mom would look like if she were alive today. Or maybe I can but it hurts too much to think about it. Shirley lives in a basement apartment in the south end of Tilden. Not the south side, as you'd think it'd be called, but "the end." Like something has finished. There's a sign outside her apartment building that reads "Carnation Acres" in faded black script, but I've never once seen a carnation anywhere near the building. I don't understand why people give pretty names to ugly things.

Shirley isn't married and doesn't have any kids. She has diabetes and works at Merle Norman, the cosmetics store, in the mall. Sometimes she goes around to people's homes to do makeup demonstrations. She used to take me along as her makeup model.

"Never tell your grandma," she'd say as she wiped my face clean of lipstick, blush and eyeshadow. "We're at a Disney movie as far as she's concerned."

Shirley would come over and babysit me when my mom was having one of her spells. My mom used to lock herself in her bedroom. She said it was the only way she could get the voices to go away.

"Call Shirley," she'd say, pressing her fingers against her forehead. It always sounded like she was fighting to get the words out. "Ask if she can come over for a few hours. Tell her there are a couple of TV dinners in the freezer."

Shirley would show up with chocolate bars or chips and we'd watch TV until my mom came out of the bedroom. She'd be in there for a couple of hours, sometimes longer. A few times, she was in her bedroom overnight and into the next day.

"Don't be scared, sweetie," Shirley would say. "Your mom is just fine."

"I know that," I'd say, trying to sound nice, but I never could. The truth was that I hated Shirley. I didn't like her coming into our lives like that. I didn't like anyone seeing the private world I shared with my mom. The closed bedroom door.

what stays shut stays hidden

Why, after all these years, is my father coming back? And

why did he tell Shirley? Why didn't he call the one person he *should've* called?

His daughter.

* * *

In the morning, I wait patiently for Grandma Kay to say something, but she doesn't. Instead, she only mutters to herself while getting breakfast ready for the hired hands. This morning, it's toasted Western sandwiches, along with coffee and orange juice. Since it's Saturday, I help. I think about saying something while I'm chopping the onions, but I don't. We work in silence. But it's the loudest silence I've ever heard. I both want to talk about it and I don't. It's complicated.

"Let's get these out," Grandma Kay says, grabbing the platter of Westerns. "They'll be coming to the back porch soon enough."

We set the toasted Westerns, orange juice and coffee onto the picnic table on the back deck just as the hired hands start walking over. I glance up and see Mike, lifting his ball cap to reveal an explosion of red hair. My knees wobble. I hurry back inside before he gets any closer.

While we're doing the dishes, Grandma Kay clears her throat.

"We'll need to have a talk after this," she says. "I asked Grandpa Frank to be here. To keep me in control."

"Why do you need control?" I ask.

"Your father has a certain...effect on me. I don't want to get all wound up. That won't help."

I go to my room after we've put away the dishes. Inside

my closet, there's an old suitcase. Inside the suitcase, there's a zippered pouch. Inside the zippered pouch, there's a pink sock. Inside the pink sock, there's a folded-up piece of aluminum foil. Inside the folded-up piece of aluminum foil are the pills. I take them out and count them, touching each one gently with my fingertip.

Twelve.

I'll still go through with it, once all of this has died down. Once things go back to being normal.

CHAPTER 6

A few months after my mom had shared my father's letter, I asked if we could send him my grade two school photo.

"So he'll know what I look like," I said. "That way, if he ever sees me on the street, he'll come over and hug me."

My mom sighed. "I don't think you'll be passing your dad on the street anytime soon, pudding. He doesn't live around here. He lives in Europe."

"Where's Europe?"

"A long way away. Across a big ocean." She stretched her arms out. "The Europeans are more accepting of him. Of his craft. Your father is very famous over there. He's a celebrity."

Inside my head, flash bulbs popped.

"Arthur has a very strange and wonderful talent," my mom said. "I'll tell you more. One day. When you're older. He'd come over all the time when we were in high school and sing songs in the living room. He didn't get along well with his own family, so I think it was an escape for him. Your grandma would play the piano. They'd tear the roof off, those two got along so well. Strange to think how things have changed. For all of us. Sometimes that seems like it happened a lifetime ago. Maybe, in some ways, it did."

"Does he know about me?" I was afraid to ask the question, but I needed to know.

"Of course he does," my mom said. "He knows your name and everything."

"If he knows about me, why doesn't he ever come to see me?"

My mom was quiet for a few minutes and looked down at her gloved hands. "I think he wants to. But he's afraid. Sometimes, when you go away, it's hard to come back. Sometimes people don't want to think about what they left behind. So it's easier to just stay away and pretend. Your father is very good at pretending."

"Did he write any other letters to you?" I asked, trying not to show my disappointment.

"A couple. Though nothing recent. Nothing in a long time. Do you want me to read you another?"

I said yes, so my mom went to her room and came back with a card with daisies printed on it.

"Arthur knew daisies were my favourite flowers," she said. "He remembered the littlest details about me, things I didn't give a second thought to."

Dearest Heather, the card read:

Here I sit in a stinky bar. I have two more shows to do before I move on to the next stinky bar. I am tired tonight, of not being good enough. Of always having to prove myself. I want to be seen the same as everyone else. Is that too much to ask? I thought I could escape, but it's followed me here and everywhere I go. I feel it on my shoulders, pressing me down when

all I want to do is float. I think of you often. I miss our talks.
You always made me feel better. I hope you're well and the
voices are delicate whispers that hover above your head like an-
gels, protecting you.

xo
Arthur

My mom closed the card and there were tears in her eyes.
I was both sad and angry. My father needed to be here, in
Tilden. He needed to find a regular job like all the other fathers and come home at the end of the day with an empty
lunch box. He needed to ask, "How's my little girl?" and tuck
me in and read bedtime stories. He needed to lean over and
kiss my cheek and leave my skin smelling like his aftershave.

He needed to be a dad, like all the other dads on television and in movies and the ones I saw holding their daughters' hands in the grocery stores or along the sidewalks. Those
were the dads that hurt the most—the ones who didn't even
realize how the smallest things could mean so much to someone who never even had the tiniest thing.

I asked my mom if she had a photo of my father. She said
only one. She kept it in an envelope in her dresser drawer.
She brought it out and handed it to me.

"It was taken at a fair," she said. "The kind they set up in
mall parking lots in the summertime. There was a Tilt-A-
Whirl and a small Ferris wheel and games. We only went to
laugh at people, which is how we usually spent our week-

ends. It made us feel better about who we were. About our difference."

In the photo, my mom was standing on the right. Her hair was down, and she was wearing jeans and a pink V-neck blouse. Standing next to her, and not much taller, was a boy. He was wearing a sweater that was the colour of green salt-water taffy and looked too big. He had curly hair and an expression on his face like he had just sucked on a lemon. His body was turned toward my mom and one leg was up. I remember thinking it seemed a funny way for a boy to stand.

This was my father. Seeing him made me feel funny inside. I was looking at a stranger, but also someone who was a part of me. And I was a part of him.

"Arthur won me a big stuffed dog that day," my mom said. "Then we got sick from eating candy apples and corn dogs."

The photo went back into my mom's dresser, but I looked at it every chance I could. I'd take out the magnifying glass and go over it, searching for any little clue, some sign of myself. But I was nowhere, of course. I was still in darkness. I had yet to be.

The day my mom died, the photo was the first thing I took. It was the only thing I had left.

✳ ✳ ✳

After what seems like a long time, I hear Grandma Kay's voice calling from the kitchen.

"Toby! Can you come here for a minute?"

The two of them are sitting at the kitchen table. Grandpa

Frank is playing with a fork, running the tines along his fingertips over and over.

"Have a seat," Grandma Kay says in a tight voice. I pull out a chair across from them.

"I want to talk to you about last night," she says. "I'm sorry for how I acted. And what I said. I'm sure it was shocking to you. I wasn't in my right mind. I should've just gone to bed and waited until this morning to tell you."

"It's all right," I say. "I don't know what difference it would've made. He's still coming."

"Yes, he is," Grandma Kay says with a sigh. She starts scratching a crusty spot on her apron. Grandpa Frank keeps playing with his fork. I don't know why they're acting so weird. I mean, I get why this is strange, but it feels like there's something else going on. Something they're not telling me.

"How much do you know about your father?" Grandma Kay asks.

"Not much," I say. "My mom said that he was a singer and that he lived in Europe."

"That was all she said about him?" Grandpa Frank asks.

"Maybe a few other things," I say. "That he used to come over here and you'd play the piano while he sang songs."

"That's true," Grandma Kay says. "Although it's hard to believe now, given everything. Did Heather say what kind of singer your father was?"

"No," I say.

"Your father is a troubled man," Grandma Kay says, scratching harder on the spot.

"Troubled how?" I ask.

Grandma Kay turns to Grandpa Frank. "How will we put this, Frank?"

"Don't look at me," he says. "You're the one with the gift of gab."

"I should've known I couldn't count on you for this," Grandma Kay says, her voice rising. "It's not fair of you to leave this all on me. You know just as much as I do."

"I'd sooner not know anything."

What are they talking about?

Grandma Kay turns back to me. "Heather loved Arthur. She was always so protective of him. They had a strong connection, I guess. When he left Tilden, it wasn't on the best of terms. He didn't tell anyone. Only Heather. Shortly after he left, she found out she was pregnant. With you. And we thought, naturally, that Arthur would come back home. To make things right. Because that's what men are supposed to do. The good ones, anyway. But he didn't. He didn't come back at all. There were other things, over the years. Stories we heard. Things we read in those gossip magazines. About his life. The people he associated with. Sometimes, there were calls in the middle of the night."

"He called here?" I ask. "At the house?"

"Yes, but that hasn't happened for a long time," Grandma Kay says. "Anyway, I called Shirley and told her that Arthur isn't welcome here. Your grandfather and I think it's best if you don't meet him. He needs to stay away. From you."

I can't believe this. "Why would you tell Shirley that? And why wouldn't you want me to meet him? He's my father."

"Because he has no business coming back," Grandma Kay

says. Her face looks as hard as a rock. "You can't stay away for all these years and show up at the doorstep and expect to be invited in for tea and cookies. You don't get to have that. Not after everything."

"What's done is done," Grandpa Frank says.

"No, Frank," Grandma Kay says, her voice rising again. "What's done is never done. It carries on. Things don't fall off a cliff. They keep circling back and causing more damage. I said good riddance to that man a long time ago. I won't open my door to that chaos again."

"But this isn't about you," I say. "This is about me." The tone of my voice surprises me. I've never spoken to my grandparents this way before. But anger fills me, head to toe. I have a right to meet him. Even if he pretended that I didn't exist. Even if he abandoned me, and my mom, when we needed him most. I keep thinking about those three words my mom said.

He. Was. Magic.

I deserve to look at him, face to face, and tell him all the things he did to us. How he hurt my mom. How he hurt me by never trying to contact me, not even one birthday card in fifteen years. I want to hear his excuses, what reasons he could possibly give for turning his back on his own flesh and blood.

"There are things you don't know, Toby," Grandma Kay says.

"Then tell me," I say.

She glances over at Grandpa Frank. "I don't even know how to begin."

"Arthur is...feathery," Grandpa Frank says.

"What are you saying?" I ask. "That he's a bird?"

"What I mean to say is that he walks lightly."

"You mean he's skinny?"

"He marches to the beat of a different drummer."

I'm so confused. "I don't know what you're talking about."

"Frank, you're only making things worse," Grandma Kay says. "What your grandfather means to say, in his convoluted way, is that Arthur is different from other men. At least the ones you see around these parts."

"I already know he's an entertainer," I say.

"It's more than that," Grandma Kay says. She takes a deep breath and her words come out like a sneeze.

"I'msorrytotellyouthisbutyourfatherisahomosexual."

I can't decide what's more shocking—what my grandma just said about my father or that she said the word "homosexual." It's like hearing another language come out of her mouth.

"What?" I ask, because it's the only word I can think to say.

"A homosexual," Grandma Kay repeats. "A man interested in other—"

"I know what a homosexual is!" I interrupt. "But I don't understand what you mean. He's my father. I mean, my mom and him…"

"I don't know what turned Arthur that way," Grandma Kay says with a slow shake of her head.

"I'll tell you what," Grandpa Frank says. "That stupid piano. It's no goddamn wonder."

"Don't you blame this on me," Grandma Kay says, slapping the table. "It's too easy for everyone to point fingers."

There's a moment of silence before Grandpa Frank speaks.

"Well? Aren't you going to tell her the rest?"

"There's *more*?" I ask. I don't think I can take it. I'm feeling claustrophobic, only from the inside, like I'm trapped in my body.

"We don't need to get into all that," Grandma Kay says. "Not today."

"He's a fella that gets *all* dressed up," Grandpa Frank says.

"Frank!"

"Puts on dresses."

"Stop it!" She turns to me. "I don't know if he still does. He did, at one time. I'm sure things are different now. Maybe. I just wish I could believe that."

Before either of them can say another word, I get up from the table and run out the front door. I grab my bike from the side of the house and start pedalling away as fast as I can, Grandma Kay's voice calling after me.

"Toby! Toby! To-beeeee!"

CHAPTER 7

As usual, I have nowhere to go, but I can't go back home. Not yet. Not for a long time. Not until my mind settles out. I keep thinking about my grandparents' words. And what was it Grandpa Frank said about dresses? By that point, I had mostly tuned everything out. All I knew was that I needed to get away.

I keep expecting Grandpa Frank's truck to pull up behind me, but every time I glance back, there's nothing. Maybe they've decided to let me be. For once.

Then I see a sign that tells me Tilden is ten kilometres away, so I keep pedalling because at least it's a destination. I decide to visit Trisha, but then second-guess that. The last thing she needs is me showing up on her doorstep with my screwed-up problems. And even though Mike is at the farm today, it would feel weird being inside his house. But where am I going to go in Tilden? Mr. Whitlock's? That's not even an option, especially after I kissed him last night. My old apartment building? Why? So I can stand outside and look up at our old window and feel like a stranger in my own life? To replay over and over again the guilt I feel about my mom's death? Why do I need the apartment building for that when it's something I already do every single day?

Then I think: Shirley.

She's the one who spoke to my father. She knows why he's coming. And maybe she'll have the answers I'm looking for, even if I'm not sure I know the questions. So even though my legs are burning, I keep going. Because if I stop, something will catch up to me.

* * *

One night, a few weeks after my mom told me about my father, we were sitting on the couch, watching a TV movie about a woman dying of cancer. The actress, who was bald and had dark circles under her eyes, reunited with her high school sweetheart just before she died. The actress cried a lot and the music swooped and swooned like giant waves. At the end of the movie, I looked over at my mom and saw that she was crying, even though there weren't any waves in our living room.

"I still remember that day so vividly," she said, reaching for the tissue box.

"What day?" I asked.

"The day your father told me he was leaving."

My mom said he swore her to secrecy. The night before he left, they arranged to meet at a playground. My mom wore lipstick.

"Something bright and pink," she told me. "I thought he'd like that. He always said I never wore enough makeup. He'd say, 'Heather, God gave you good bone structure. Start using it.' Of course, I didn't consider that it would be dark outside, that he wouldn't even see my face. I felt so stupid afterwards, standing at the bathroom sink and scrubbing my lips with a washcloth until they were raw."

My mom said my father asked if she'd visit him. He planned to get a big apartment. They'd go dancing until dawn. My mom told him she was already saving her money. My father said he'd buy her a bus ticket. My mom asked if he'd write to her and he promised he would. A letter a day. She asked if he'd come back, especially for Christmas.

"Say what you want about Tilden," she told him, "but the downtown is always so pretty with all the lights. There's nothing that a fresh layer of snow can't hide."

He promised he'd return.

"But even as he said those words," my mom said to me, "I knew he wouldn't."

She turned to look out our window. I remember that was the first time I felt my mom was far away from me. It was important to remind her that I was still there, a few feet away. I took a drink from my glass and crunched down on an ice cube. The noise startled my mom.

"Don't do that, Toby," she said. "It grates on my nerves."

I felt better knowing that she knew I was there, so I slowly sucked on the ice cube until my tongue felt numb and thick.

"I told Arthur that Shirley said he'd never come back," my mom said. "He called Shirley a twat."

"What's a twat?" I asked.

"Never mind. It's not a nice word. Shirley and Arthur never got along. She said he was fake, that he only ever thought of himself and no one else. Maybe that was true, but I loved him all the same. He promised me he'd come back. He said he'd bring me expensive chocolate and fill me with scandalous stories about life in the big city. I started to cry then because I realized what I was losing. Inside my head, the shadows were already taking shape. Arthur was the only one who made me feel normal, who made me feel right. We were freaks together, he used to say. But now that he was leaving, who would I have?"

I watched my mom's eyes travel to the window again. I felt the same loneliness as before, but I didn't touch my ice. I held it on my tongue, waiting for my mom's next words.

"I was sitting in a swing, like a big baby, and he came over to me and knelt down in front. He wrapped his arms around me and said, 'Heather, my little daisy. You'll be fine.' I asked him what I'd do when the voices came back. Who would help me chase them away? He just hugged me tighter."

I imagined that scene, my mom on a swing, my father's knees in the sand, for many years. Then, my mom said, something happened. A very beautiful thing.

"We became one person, there in the darkness of that spring evening, the stars a sparkling canopy above us. Afterwards, we lay there, in each other's arms, looking up at the sky for what seemed like a long time, both of us wishing for something we couldn't have."

My mom kept looking out the window. I kept looking at her.

"That was the night we made you, Toby," she said.

* * *

Grandma Kay doesn't know my mom told me this story. So how can my father be…what she said he was when I know for a fact what happened that night? Grandma Kay is confused, that's all. She's thinking of someone else. Someone who isn't my father. There's no way I could have a father like that. It's impossible.

Carnation Acres is even more depressing than usual. The grass out front is brown and flat. It looks like someone ironed it. The empty flowerbeds in front of the basement apartment windows are sad shoeboxes. The awnings are droopy eyelids. There are dog turds everywhere.

I made a mistake coming here, I think. But I still lock up my bike against a No Parking pole. It's close to 11 a.m. I don't even know if Shirley will be home.

Her apartment building is so old there's no buzzer to get inside. I walk right in and down the steps to the lower floor. Shirley's apartment is at the far end. The hallway smells like frying meat, bleach and baby-powder freshener. I pass a door with a cardboard bunny taped to it with "Please Stop Here" written beneath. Easter was two months ago. I hear television laughter coming from behind one of the doors and a man coughing behind another. It sounds like he's trying to bring something up.

I reach apartment 7, still wondering if I've made a mistake, but I knock anyway. I take a step back and wait.

"If it's Jehovahs again, I'm not interested," Shirley's voice calls out from behind the door. "I already sold my soul to the devil."

"It's not a Jehovah," I say. "It's Toby."

"Toby?" I hear her repeat, more to herself.

I hear the chain sliding off the lock and instinctively wince at the sound. It reminds me of the door at my old apartment, of that day, when my mom died. I remember going to our door, sliding the chain across and opening it to the hallway, the outside world. I remember the black sludge sliding past the doorway, across our parquet floor, inching toward my feet.

The door swings open. "Well, what a surprise!"

Shirley's hair is a different colour. It used to be blond. Now it's reddish-brown. It reminds me of a crayon. Her hair makes her face look whiter. More exposed. Older. She's wearing an oversized T-shirt that's slipping down one shoulder and purple leggings that make her legs look like grape Popsicles.

"I was passing by," I say. "I hope I'm not catching you at a bad time."

"Not at all," Shirley says. "I was just about to contemplate my sad existence over a cup of tea."

She sweeps her arm across and I step inside. Every wall is painted a different colour. The hallway is green and blue. The living room is red, yellow, purple and cream. There's an orange glow coming from the kitchen, as though the sun is setting behind her appliances.

"I'm a bit cuckoo for colour, I know," she says. "I used to have everything white. White walls, white rug, white wicker furniture. But it felt too much like a doctor's office. Like I should be telling people they had gonorrhea. Plus, I've always been afraid of going blind on account of my diabetes, and it seemed like colours were that much more important. Isn't that the way life is sometimes, Toby? It's only when you lose something that you understand what it meant to you."

I watch as she becomes aware of her words, how she wants to pull them back, like they're attached to a string. But she can't. It's always this way with people. They're always so careful around me, as though I'm bits of a mirror that need to be stepped around.

"Were you really in the area?" Shirley asks.

I shake my head.

"Your grandmother called. She suspected you might come here. I'll call her to let her know you're safe. Then we'll have a talk. About why you're here."

CHAPTER 8

She asks me if I drink tea and I say I do, even though I don't. I just want something warm to hold.

"I can order Chinese food," Shirley says. "You like Chinese food, right?"

"Don't bother," I say. "It's too early and I'm not hungry."

"You sure? There's a place not far from here. Although it's not very good. The chicken balls are more ball than chicken. And I don't think they change the oil very often. It's not real Chinese food, anyway. The best Chinese food I had was in Toronto, where there's a Chinese community. Chicken balls aren't real Chinese food. You know that, right, Toby? The difference between something that's real and something that's fake?"

The kettle starts to whistle.

"That's the problem living in this shitty hellhole of a city. Everyone has to conform. It must make the three Chinese people who live in Tilden sick to their stomachs." She takes the kettle off the stove and fills the cups. Steam rolls upwards.

"There's a Chinese girl at school who eats Pop-Tarts and peanut butter sandwiches every day for lunch," I say. "And

I'm pretty sure there are more than three Chinese people in Tilden."

Shirley drops the tea bags into the cups. "Not much more, I'll tell you that. This city's all about sameness, never about difference."

She brings a mug in each hand and sets them down at her dining room table, which is really just a card table with a purple tablecloth over it and some green, plastic fold-out chairs.

"Speaking of fake," she says, "how much did your mom tell you about your father?"

"A little," I say, shifting in my seat. The plastic is hard and uncomfortable. I have a feeling I'm not going to like whatever it is Shirley has to say. "That they met in high school. That he moved away. He's a singer."

Feathery. Was that the word Grandpa Frank used? There was a smirk on his face. It's clear Grandpa Frank thinks my father is a joke. A punchline. The complete opposite of what my mom thought. How can two people have such different opinions about the same person? And whose opinion are you supposed to believe?

"An entertainer," I say. Suddenly, I feel so stupid and embarrassed, but I'm not sure why.

"An entertainer," Shirley repeats with a snort. "That's one way of looking at him." So she thinks of him the same way as Grandpa Frank. She fishes her tea bag out of her cup. "I suppose he had his good qualities. Heather certainly saw them. She was so protective of Arthur. Of his 'gift,' as she called it." Her fingers hook around the word. "You couldn't ever criticize Arthur. Not when Heather was around, anyway. 'He's easily broken,' she used to say. Oh, God. That was rich. If anyone was broken…"

She stops and looks at me. "I'm sorry. I'm getting carried away. It's just that, with your mom, I was always so worried for her, you know? I knew that she was different, that she needed care. But all I could ever do was just be there, next to her, a friend. Because I didn't know what else to do. I remember one Christmas, when we were teenagers, she made me come with her into the woods to chop down a tree. She brought this crappy old saw. I mean, that thing wouldn't cut string, let alone a tree trunk. I remember her swearing and puffing and how her arm looked like a piston as she worked on that stupid tree. But she never gave up. That tree came down. I can still see the smile on her face. That was the way your mom was. Determined. She wouldn't stop until she finished something. She was like that with Arthur too. She set her sights on him. But there was no way *his* tree was falling."

She rolls her eyes.

"Your father had a way of getting under my skin. He still does, all these years later. I felt my blood boil the minute I picked up the phone and heard his voice again." She clears her throat, her eyes back down to her tea. "It's just that, when he didn't come back, not even for your mom's funeral, he crossed a line. He had some lame excuse, something about touring and managers and breaking contracts, but it was one plane ride. That's all it would've taken. To make up for everything."

"Why is he coming back?" I ask. "Why now?"

She's quiet for a long time. "I'd like to say for forgiveness. But knowing your father, I'm not sure."

"Grandma Kay told me he's gay." Even as I say the words, I feel so ashamed. I look down, unable to make eye contact with her. "And Grandpa Frank said something about him wearing dresses."

"Wow, your grandparents didn't hold back, did they? I'm surprised, given how conservative they are." She reaches over and takes my hand. I see the veins underneath her skin. I think of my mom. How she thought her veins were worms. How she wore gloves to hide her hands. Why would she ever think something like that? Why didn't I ever tell my mom she had nothing to be afraid of? That they were only veins? Pumping blood to her heart. Keeping her alive. Maybe if I had told her that, even just once...

"Sweetie, your father is a drag queen."

I feel my plastic chair fall through the floor.

* * *

"He's *what*?!?"

A couple of little kids turn their heads toward the sound of Trisha's voice. We're at the playground, the same one where Trisha told me to throw the eggs. Only we're not at the tennis courts and we don't have eggs. We're sitting on the rickety see-saw. Trisha keeps trying to push herself off the ground, but it's not working. My legs dangle in the air.

"Please keep your voice down," I say, glancing over at the kids.

When I left Shirley's, she offered to put my bike in her Chevette and drive me home, but I told her I was fine.

"I need the exercise," I said.

"You're sure you're okay, sweetie?" Shirley asked. "I know it's a lot of information for you."

"I'll be fine," I said, trying to sound convincing. I just needed to get away.

"I keep asking myself what Heather would want you to do, but I'm not sure. Anyway, I'm picking him up at the airport. Wish me luck. I'm not good with highway driving. The last time I drove on the highway, I got diarrhea. Not *while* I was driving. But I had to pull over at the side of the road. Sorry if this is too much information."

I couldn't go back to the farm. Not yet, anyway. I needed my mind to settle out. So I biked to Trisha's because I couldn't decide anyplace else I wanted to go. Mrs. Richardson answered the front door.

"Toby," she said. "This is a nice surprise. I was just taking some cookies out of the oven. Trisha is in her room."

I wondered what it would be like to have a normal mom, one who made cookies and invited my friends inside. But it's impossible to imagine another version of my life.

"Okay, let me get this straight," Trisha says from her perch on the see-saw. "Your dad is coming—"

"Not my dad," I interrupt. "Don't call him that. He's not my dad. He's my father."

Trisha's face scrunches up. "Dad, father. What's the difference?"

"You wouldn't understand, but trust me. There's a huge difference."

"Okaaay… So your father, who you've never met, is coming in a couple of days. He's an entertainer who lives in Europe. Not only is he an entertainer, he's also a big 'mo. And not only is he a big 'mo, he's also a wig-, sequin-and stiletto-wearing drag queen." She shakes her head and tries to push off from her end of the see-saw. "This is the most screwed-up thing I've heard this week."

I want to ask what kinds of screwed-up things she heard last week to compete with my news, but I hold back.

"You can't tell anyone," I say. "You have to swear to me." None of this can get out. Not only would I be known in school as the girl with the dead mom, but I'd also have a new crown of thorns to wear: the girl with the gay father. Even the thought of people finding out makes me sick with shame.

"On one condition," Trisha says.

"What's that?"

"You have to introduce me to him. Imagine, a real-life drag queen, right here, in Tilden. These kinds of opportunities only come once in a lifetime. Just think, Toby. They're going to make a movie out of your life. I can see it now. Only who would play you? And, more importantly, who would play your drag queen father?"

✳ ✳ ✳

She insists that we take the bus to the mall to get something for me.

"A new top to wear when you meet him," she says. "Something sparkly."

"I'm not wearing anything that sparkles," I say, flipping through the racks of clothes. "I don't even know anyone… like *that*."

"You mean a drag queen?" Trisha asks.

"I mean gay."

"Oh, God," Trisha says. "You are so naive. Of course you know gay people. There are lots of them."

"In Tilden? Who?"

"Evan Gray, for one."

Evan is in our grade.

"How do you know Evan is gay?"

"He listens to En Vogue. Duh." She holds up a red top. "What about this? Very dramatic. Daddy might steal it off you."

She starts to laugh.

"Stop making jokes, Trisha," I say. "This is humiliating for me. You have no idea."

"Hi, ladies."

We turn to see Claire and Angela standing next to us. My heart stops. How much of our conversation did they hear?

"Hi, ladies," Trisha says back. They call one another that all the time. It's so annoying.

"What are you two up to?" Claire asks, giving me the once-over. She makes me feel stupid.

"A little shopping," Trisha says. "Toby has a big event coming up." She winks at me.

I give her my best death stare. If she says anything, I swear—

"A date?" Angela asks. Is that a smile on her face or a smirk? It's hard to tell.

"No," I say, pretending to be preoccupied with my clothing search. "Nothing important."

"Well, don't let us keep you," Claire says. "We're just on our way to the movies. You should join us."

"Maybe," Trisha says, before glancing at me. My expression must say how I'm feeling. "On second thought, maybe another time."

Trisha's tried to get me to hang out with her, Claire and Angela before. She says they're nice, but I don't believe her. And I know she's only extending the invitation out of obligation, not because she wants us all to hang out together. It'd be so much easier for her if I wasn't around.

"Suit yourself," Claire says, giving me a quick glance. "See you around."

The two of them saunter off. I can only imagine what they're saying about me.

"You should've gone," I say. "I wouldn't have minded."

"Toby, I'm not going to leave you here alone."

"You don't have to think of me as your charity case," I say. "I can get by on my own. I always have."

"How's that for gratitude?" Trisha asks. "That's no way to talk to someone who's trying to help you be your glamorous best."

"Sorry," I say. "I'm just tense. How about this?" I hold up a grey top with pink hearts.

"I guess," Trisha says with a shrug. I can tell she's annoyed at me. I don't blame her. It's hard being friends with someone like me.

CHAPTER 9

We go back to Trisha's house so I can pick up my bike. It's getting late and I know Grandma Kay will be getting more and more worried with each passing minute. As we approach their driveway, I stop. Mike's car is there. I check my watch. He should still be at the farm. Why is he here? I tell myself to calm down. I don't want Trisha to suspect anything.

"You want to stay for dinner?" Trisha asks. "My mom is making lasagna. It's one of her relatively edible recipes. Way better than that stew she makes with the V8 juice. So disgusting."

"Thanks, but I need to get back home," I say.

My bike is leaning against the side of the house, so I grab the handlebars and start walking away. My legs can't move fast enough.

"Toby! Wait!"

I turn around to see Mrs. Richardson standing on the porch. "Do you want to stay for dinner? I've got lots."

"Thanks, Mrs. Richardson," I say. "But I should get going."

"You sure? Oh, before I forget. Are you around this summer?"

"I think so."

"Make sure you pick a weekend to come up to the cabin. Trisha, you organize it with Toby. And Toby, make sure it's okay with your grandparents."

"Oh my God, Mom," Trisha groans. "She's not four, for crying out loud."

Mrs. Richardson invites me to their cabin every summer. I know she's only doing it because she feels bad for me. Whenever I'm there, I feel like I'm ruining everyone's good time. I haven't been for the past couple of years and have no intention of going this summer either. Especially if Mike will be there.

"Thanks, Mrs. Richardson," I say. "I can't wait."

"You're not biking all the way back to the farm, are you?" Mrs. Richardson asks, putting her hands on her hips. Her forehead gets wrinkled. "It'll be dark soon."

"Mom, it's only four o'clock," Trisha says. "It doesn't get dark until, like, 10 p.m., for God's sake."

"Watch the attitude, Trisha. Toby, you wait there. I'll get Mike to drive you back."

"No, that's okay, Mrs. Richardson. Really. It's not that far. I could use the exercise."

"Nonsense. You wait right there while I get him."

Panic sets in. I'm going to cry. Can this day get any worse?

"Make sure he doesn't try to put you in a superhero costume," Trisha says. "You may have a big homo for a father, but I've got a pervert for a brother. I can't tell which of us has the shorter end of the stick."

I think about cycling away before Mrs. Richardson and Mike come back out, but it's a lost cause. Mrs. Richardson would only send Mike tearing after me. And that would make things worse.

"Remember, Toby," Trisha says. "I get a front-row seat for Daddy Drag Show."

"Don't say it like that," I say, glancing around. I'm still scared that Claire and Angela overheard us.

"I wonder if he can give me tips for my hair," Trisha says, curling a strand around her finger. "I'm just so sick of straightening it every day. There's got to be something else I can do."

The screen door opens, then slaps shut. The next thing I know, Mike is standing on the front porch, looking like he just woke up. We make eye contact and then quickly look away. He covers a yawn with his hand.

"I'm sending Mike to the grocery store anyway," Mrs. Richardson says. "I forgot to get garlic bread. Are you sure you can't stay, Toby? It's the one meal no one complains about. Which must mean they love it."

"I'm good," I say. How am I going to sit next to Mike for the fifteen minutes it will take to get to the farm? What on earth are we going to talk about?

"Okay, no pressure," Mrs. Richardson says. "Mike can put your bike in the back of his car. And no loud music—it's distracting. And both of you, please wear your seat belts."

Mike walks up to me and takes my bike and puts it into the trunk. Then I get into the passenger seat. The car smells like stale cigarette smoke, in spite of the scented pine tree hanging from the rear-view mirror. Ashes cover the dashboard and seats like grey confetti. Mike gets in and turns on the engine. A guitar screams from the speakers and I barely make out Mrs. Richardson saying "Turn that down!" as Mike squeals out of the driveway.

We ride without saying anything for a couple of minutes. Then, because I can't stand the silence, I break the ice. "Do you mind if we turn the music down? I have a bit of a headache."

He shrugs. "Suit yourself."

"So… ," I say, a few minutes of silence later. "What's new?"

"Not much," he says, leaning over to push in the cigarette lighter. "What's new with you?"

Imagine if I actually told him. That I'd been planning to kill myself by taking the pills I've been stealing from Mr. Whitlock. But then my grandma told me my long-lost father is coming back in a couple of days. Oh, and did I forget to mention my father is also a gay drag queen?

"Not much," I say. "Do you have any plans for the summer?"

"Work," he says, lighting his cigarette. The tobacco crackles. "Might go camping with a couple of buddies."

"Oh, yeah?" Trisha told me once that all of Mike's friends are losers. None of them have jobs and they sit around listening to grunge music, complaining about how they could've played the instruments better.

"Might go away for a few days to Toronto too. See a baseball game or something."

"I didn't think you liked baseball."

"I don't, but the girl I'm going with does."

He glances over at me, making sure I've heard.

"Oh," I say. So he's found someone else. Not a big deal.

What was I expecting him to do? Spend his whole life pining over me? Who do I think I am, anyway? The girl he never got over? I used to have fantasies about him, out for dinner with his wife, years from now. Maybe it's their anniversary.

"There's something I need to tell you," he'll say between the appetizer and the main course. "Something I've never told you."

And then he'll tell his wife about me. Toby—the girl who killed herself so many years ago. How I've always stayed with him. I'm like a stain. He's always wondered if he could've done something to stop me. If only he'd known. Mike's wife will be silent. Or maybe she'll say, "Oh," as she dabs her lips with her napkin. She'll know what this means, how this changes things. The living can't compete with the dead. I know this better than anyone.

"What about you?" Mike asks. "Any plans?"

"No," I say. "Nothing out of the ordinary. We can't really go anywhere on account of the cows."

"It'd be nice if your grandpa had a day off," Mike says. "That guy's basically a prisoner to those cows."

I always thought of it the other way. But Mike might have a point.

"I know it's weird between us," I say. "And I'm sorry about that. I just want us to get to a place where it's not so weird. Do you think that's possible?"

He takes a long drag of his cigarette. "Here's the thing, Toby. You were the one who said you didn't want anything anymore. And that's cool. Whatever. But you don't get to decide how *we* act after *you* make up *your* mind about something. Especially when your decision isn't something everyone agrees on. You don't get it both ways. Okay?"

"Okay," I say. Then, because I can't think of anything else to say, because I can't tell Mike that the real reason I can't be with him is because I can't have feelings for anyone, I keep my lips pressed shut the rest of the way.

CHAPTER 10

When I get back home, Grandma Kay is sitting at the kitchen table, almost in the same position as when I left this morning. Her eyes look tired and I know I'm to blame. I wish I was a better granddaughter. I wish I wasn't such a disappointment.

She looks up when I walk in. "There you are," she says. She smiles weakly. "I was just about to start dinner. In all the excitement today, I forgot to take the pork chops out of the freezer. Are you okay with tuna noodle casserole?"

"Sounds good," I say. "Do you need any help?"

"To open a couple of cans and boil some noodles? I hope to God not. Do you want peas in it?"

"Sure. If you have them."

Then Grandma Kay pats the kitchen chair next to her, so I sit down. She pinches the bridge of her nose with her fingers and squeezes her eyes shut.

"About your father... ," she says.

I wait for her to finish the sentence.

"About your father... ," she repeats. I guess that's the end of the sentence.

"What about him?" I ask.

"I got a bit wound up earlier. No surprises there. I was caught off guard by the whole thing. And I don't like surprises. You know that."

"I remember your fiftieth birthday party," I say. "You were pretty mad."

"The idea of being the centre of attention bothers me," Grandma Kay says. "Makes me feel icky. Like I owe people something when I didn't ask for it in the first place. It's hard for me to explain."

I understand.

"When I'm caught off guard," she says, "my thoughts twist around and around. Everything inside my head becomes a big black ball of words and sounds. Do you ever feel that way?"

"Sometimes," I say. She must know about the pills. They're still inside the aluminum foil, inside my sock, inside my suitcase, inside my closet. Knowing they're still there makes me feel safe, like being in a dark room and knowing there's a flashlight if you need it.

"Your father and I didn't have the best relationship," Grandma Kay says. "You might be able to guess that. We didn't see eye to eye about a number of things, especially when it came to my daughter. When he left, without any notice at all, I was furious. He didn't even have the decency...and then when I found out Heather was pregnant, well, that made the situation go from bad to worse. Arthur refused to acknowledge anything. As though Heather's pregnancy would just fly away, like some kind of bird. I found out where he was living in Toronto and went to see him. This was right before you were born. I got Frank to drive me, and you should've seen his face when he opened the door and saw me standing there. I told him to cut out this foolishness. That there was a girl back home who needed him, a girl who was in tears every night. A very…fragile girl who needed special care and attention."

Grandma Kay slowly shakes her head.

"I still remember his laugh. As though I'd just made the funniest joke. People's cruelty never ceases to surprise me. How hard some people get. Hearts like charcoal. I told myself he'd come back, one day, especially after what happened to Heather. But nothing. Only silence. And cold, cold air."

"But he's coming back now," I say. "That must mean something. It must mean he's changed."

"I don't know what it means," Grandma Kay says. "I can't stop you from meeting your father. In spite of everything. That's your right. And maybe it's wrong of me to speak of him so poorly, but I want you to be prepared. He may not be the person who you thought he'd be."

It's a little late for that, I think.

Grandma Kay gets up from the table. "You meet him and make up your own mind. And maybe you're right. Maybe he's changed. I just hope for your sake—and his—that he has. And I just wish I could believe it."

My father will be here in twenty-four hours.

CHAPTER 11

When I wake up the next morning, I lie in bed, not wanting to get up. It's the same as every morning. I feel paralyzed. But when I finally manage to pull my covers off, they don't seem as heavy as they usually do, and I don't feel as anxious when opening my bedroom door. I go into the kitchen to find Grandma Kay rooting through the cupboards.

"I was going to make a pie," she says. "I froze those peaches last summer, but I haven't made a pie in ages. Today seemed like a good day for one. It's the crust that's the trickiest. I can't find my pastry recipe, though."

I find her recipe box and start flipping through the index cards and magazine clippings, most containing recipes for things she's never made. All of Grandma Kay's good intentions in one small Tupperware container.

"You ready for today?" I ask, scanning an index card with a recipe for Cheerio Chews written in her perfect handwriting.

"I'm not sure," she says. "How about you?"

"It's one of those days where you wake up and the first thought you have is, 'How is this day going to end?'"

"That sums it up pretty good."

"I found the recipe," I say and pass her the index card.

"I don't know what I'd do without you," Grandma Kay sighs.

✳ ✳ ✳

We spend the next hour preparing the breakfast for the hired hands. The day is warming up, so we serve it on the back deck. Mike is there, of course. And, of course, we pretend not to see one another. I've made things so awkward for both of us. Another life I've managed to screw up.

Grandma Kay and I wash the dishes and dry them and set the plates back into the cupboards. We'll take them down again, in a few hours, when it comes time to serve lunch. It's the same day in and day out for Grandma Kay, and I think about what Mike said. How Grandpa Frank is a prisoner to the cows. The same is true for Grandma Kay. I don't know how she's going to manage when she gets older. Who will make the lunches for the hired hands? Who will wash the dishes and put them away and take everything out a few hours later to start all over again? But I tell myself those thoughts don't matter today, not with the day being what it is, a giant, quivering ball of expectation. I feel so many things. Fear. Hope. Dread. Excitement. I can't pin down any one emotion. I can't squeeze all of my years of longing and dreams and disappointment into a small hole.

A little later, we make lunch, wash the dishes and put everything away. Grandma Kay makes her pie. I tidy up the living room. Grandma Kay wonders if she bought enough potatoes. If she should make a turkey for dinner instead of a ham. She can't remember if Arthur likes ham.

"There's still time for me to get one," she says. "There's still time for a mind to be changed."

"I think a ham is fine," I say, at the same time thinking, *Is my father going to show up in a dress?* This question has been overtaking my thoughts since I woke up this morning. I have no sense as to what my father will look like or what he'll be wearing or what he'll say to me when he sees me for the very first time. Will he notice my green eyes? Will he see himself in me? And, most important, will I see myself in him?

The phone rings and I walk over to answer it.

"Anything yet?"

Trisha.

"No. I told you I'd call you."

"The minute he leaves, Toby, you pick up that phone. You promise?"

"I promise."

After Grandma Kay and I are done our cleaning, as the late afternoon stretches itself out and the cows are lying in the fields, chewing their cuds with no idea what's about to happen, we sit in the living room and wait. I've changed into my new top, the grey one with the hearts that I got with Trisha. I hope my father notices it. I hope he says something about the hearts. The smell of lemon furniture polish mixes with the smell of Grandma Kay's peach pie, cooling on the counter. It feels like the last moment of life as I know it. It's not that much different from when I stood in front of my mom's bedroom door.

"He must have family here," I say. I've never mentioned this before. I've never asked about siblings or uncles or cousins.

Or grandparents.

"Far as I know," Grandma Kay says. "But I suppose people move."

A few years ago, Grandma Kay and I were grocery shopping and ran into a woman in the canned goods aisle. Right away, I sensed this woman was different from the usual women Grandma Kay knew. It was the way her back stiffened. I could almost hear her bones snap.

"Hello, Joyce," Grandma Kay said. She put her hand on my shoulder.

The woman looked to be around Grandma Kay's age, but she seemed more formal. She was wearing a green and purple dress and thick, black shoes. Her coat had a fur collar, even though it was a warm day. A silver chain with a cross hung from her neck.

"Kay," the woman said. She wasn't looking at Grandma Kay. She was looking at me. The expression on her face was strange, as though I was some kind of magic trick that she was trying to figure out. I watched as the woman's eyes went from my windbreaker to my jeans to my sneakers. I wished I'd combed my hair. There was a stain on my jacket.

"Nice to see you," Grandma Kay said.

"I think spring is finally on its way."

"I certainly hope so. How's your husband? And family?"

"Fine. And yours?"

"The same."

They spoke in a guarded way. I felt a sense of danger, as

though they were two wolves circling one another. As though talking was stopping them from doing something else.

"I should be going," the woman said. "I'm hosting my women's church group tonight and need to pick up a few things. No rest for the wicked." She looked at me again.

"No rest indeed," Grandma Kay said and told me to come along. Grandma Kay didn't say my name or introduce me, and we walked so fast down the rest of the aisles, it was hard for me to keep up.

"Who was that?" I asked.

"No one of importance," Grandma Kay said.

Later, I realized who that woman must've been. My other grandmother. My father's mother. It was the way she looked at me, as though she already knew who I was. There was a whole other side to me that I knew nothing about. My father's family. Where did they live? Did they all know about me? Why hadn't they ever come to visit?

Then I slowly came to understand.

They're ashamed of me too.

∗ ∗ ∗

Just before six o'clock, there's the sound of low rumbling in the distance. Grandma Kay sits up straighter in her chair and I notice the way the sunlight catches her face and how, in spite of her wrinkles, it makes her seem young and full of hope. The rumbling grows louder until it becomes clear what the sound is.

A car. Heading our way.

Grandma Kay gets up and walks over to the front window,

pulling aside the curtain. I want to join her, but I can't. I stay glued to my seat, my heart beating faster as the rumbling gets louder and louder.

"Is it them?" I ask, just before a blue Chevette comes into view. Shirley's car, followed by a small dust storm. It slows in front of the entrance to the farm. Grandma Kay freezes in place. I watch.

The car turns into the driveway. I stand up. From this distance, I see someone sitting next to Shirley in the passenger seat.

My father, after all these years, is finally here.

CHAPTER 12

I watch, my breath stuck in my lungs, as the passenger door swings open and my father steps out of the car. First one leg, then the other. An arm, a shoulder, then his head, until he's standing, and I can take him all in for the first time in my life.

I'm relieved to see he's not wearing a dress.

He's shorter than I was expecting, with black, curly hair that spirals out from his head. He's wearing a white shirt, wrinkled from his long trip, and a pair of dark pants. He's also wearing boots. This strikes me as strange because never once did I imagine my father in a pair of boots. When he goes to pat his hair down, I see he's wearing a large gold ring on the middle finger of his right hand. This seems strange as well, but maybe men wear larger jewellery in Europe. Then again, he's a drag queen. My thoughts are racing all over the place.

After all these years. After all the television shows I'd watched, pretending he was an actor playing a father, after all the times I imagined seeing him in the most everyday places. The grocery store standing next to the cantaloupes, on a bench in the park, pumping gas next to a station wagon. Or as the guidance counsellor at school, the one who always wore cardigans, and I'd think how nice it would be to be hugged, to be taken into a man's arms and feel safe and protected.

And now, my father is here, in the flesh. Finally. And while I'm a little let down to see that he doesn't look like a movie star or someone you'd think twice about if you passed him on the street, he's still *my* father. And I'm his daughter. His blood runs through me.

He puts his hands on his hips and looks around, his head turning this way and that. It's hard to figure out the expression on his face. It's somewhere between bored and puzzled. I realize he looks nothing like the photograph my mom had, of the two of them at the carnival, but I guess that's not surprising. People change, after all.

The driver's door opens and Shirley steps out, looking frazzled.

"I am NEVER driving on the 401 again!" she yells to no one in particular. There's a pair of sunglasses perched on her head. She walks around to the front of the car, resting her hands on the hood and closing her eyes, like she's saying a prayer.

"They're here," Grandma Kay says, and I walk closer to the front window, to where she's standing. This is the first time she's seen my father in over fifteen years, so it must be overwhelming for her too.

"Who's that?" she asks, her head tilting to one side.

I stop in my tracks. "Isn't that him?"

"It's been a few years, but my eyesight isn't that bad. That's not Arthur."

I look at the man. If he's not my father, then who is he? And where is my father?

Shirley walks over to the driver's side, leans in and gives the car horn two long honks. The hens start to cluck.

"We need some help out here!" she yells.

Grandma Kay turns to me. "Oh no," she whispers. I watch fear spread across her face.

✳ ✳ ✳

Grandpa Frank goes out to the car, followed by Grandma Kay. I stand at the front door, hidden behind the gauze of the screen. I can't bring myself to step out of the house. I can't be seen. Not yet.

"What's all the fuss about?" Grandpa Frank asks.

"In the back seat," Shirley says. "Bruno, stop looking at the chickens and get over here."

Bruno?

Grandpa Frank looks at him. "You a hitchhiker or something?"

"I no understand what you ask," the man says.

"Frank, I need you to focus," Shirley says. "The back seat, please. I can't do this on my own. I don't have the strength."

Grandpa Frank opens the car door. I watch as he takes a step back and puts his hands on his hips. "For the love of Christ... ," he says, shaking his head.

"Please tell me he's not—" Grandma Kay says, coming down the front steps.

"He sure is," Shirley says. "Some homecoming."

"Oh my Lord," Grandma Kay says.

I'm trying to make sense of the scene in front of me, but it's impossible. I can't understand anything. The faces and voices are blurring together. Shirley's car. This Bruno man. Grandma Kay's voice. Grandpa Frank's disgust. What's going on?

And is my father in the back seat?

"Give me some help here," Grandpa Frank says to the man. "How he'd get this way, anyway?"

"It begin with a rye and ginger," the man says. "It end with a martini."

"It always does," Shirley says with a shake of her head. Her sunglasses slip down in front of her eyes.

Grandma Kay is standing at the base of the front steps. I can't see her face, but I can see the tightness of her neck and shoulders.

I watch as Grandpa Frank and the man pull a shape from the back seat. At first, I think it's a carpet. But then I see it's a person, wrapped in a brown cloak or blanket. I can't see the face. The person's head is slumped forward, like they have no neck bones.

Grandpa Frank and the man struggle as they slip an arm underneath either side and begin the slow walk up the gravel driveway to the front steps.

"Easy does it," Grandpa Frank says.

"Be careful," the man says.

"Watch your back, Frank," Grandma Kay says.

A white arm, thin and smooth and almost glowing, pushes out from the brown material, lifting high into the air, like it's saying hello or surrendering.

Shirley is leading the way, the world's most depressing band leader.

"A few more steps," she says. "That's right. Just a few more steps."

"How could you do this?" Grandma Kay asks when Shirley reaches her.

"I didn't *do* anything," Shirley says. "All I did was pick him up."

"You didn't have to bring him here. Like *that*. You could've let him sober up first."

"I drove with the windows open the entire way," Shirley says. "Look at my hair if you don't believe me. But nothing was going to sober him up in time."

"Don't talk to me about time. More than fifteen years have gone by and nothing has changed."

I'm frozen behind the screen door, watching as the limp parcel makes its way toward me. I understand now that the man I first thought was my father *isn't* my father. Instead, this thing, this shape heading toward me, that's my father.

As they get closer, I notice a smell. Sour milk.

"Toby, hold the door open," Grandpa Frank says.

I do as I'm told and step out, like a robot, holding the door as widely as I can.

The three of them walk past me and into the house.

CHAPTER 13

They take him to my grandparents' bedroom and lay him out on the bed. The sound of his snoring escapes past the half-closed door.

"Honestly, Kay," Shirley says. We're all sitting in the living room. "What was I supposed to do? Leave him at the airport?"

"You couldn't take him somewhere else?" Grandma Kay asks. I've never heard her so angry before. "Instead of bringing him here? Instead of letting her see him like that?"

All eyes turn to me. I see expressions of anger and confusion. Pity and shame.

"And who are you again?" Grandma Kay asks, looking at the man. Her eyes narrow as if she's trying to bring him into focus.

He sits up straighter from his place on the sofa. "I am Bruno. The manager of Arthur. He ask me to come. He no like to travel alone."

"He doesn't travel well, period," Grandpa Frank says. "The man stinks like a back alley on New Year's Eve."

"Frank… ," Grandma Kay says sternly.

"Sorry," Grandpa Frank says. "I didn't know we were trying to hide the fact that he's so sauced he can barely walk."

"How does anyone get that drunk on an airplane?" Shirley asks.

"He make friends with the stewardess," Bruno says. "And it's a long flight from Rome."

"Is that where you live?" Grandpa Frank says. "In It-lee?"

"Italy," I whisper, wishing he didn't sound so much like a farmer.

He nods. "That's where I'm from."

"Well, why didn't you try to stop him from drinking so much?" Grandma Kay asks. "You're his manager. Aren't you supposed to look after him?"

"It's best not to try and stop Arthur."

Grandma Kay lets her head fall into her hands. "I knew it would be like this. All these years later and still the same. I almost hoped...well, never mind. It doesn't matter what I hoped. It doesn't mean anything. Hope doesn't fix what's in the bedroom."

I keep staring straight ahead, beyond the glass of the living room window, past the driveway and the road, looking at the evergreens, imagining the space where I'll lie down. The grass will feel so cool against the back of my legs. So soft. Inside me, there's a noise, like a lid sliding over the opening of a well, closing out any last pieces of light.

"You should've hung up when he called," I hear Grandma Kay say. "You got some of those phone calls in the past yourself, just like I did. The middle of the night and he'd start talking garbage in that slurred voice. I hung up years ago. You should've done the same."

"I couldn't hang up," Shirley says. "Not after hearing what he had to say."

"What did he have to say?"

"He said... He just... All he said was that he really wanted to come home. That it was important to him."

"And why wasn't it important any other time?" Grandpa Frank asks.

"I think this time is different." Shirley looks quickly at Bruno. "I think he's learned a few things."

"Not from what I can see," Grandpa Frank says.

"Well, I'm sorry to say but he'll have to be your problem," Grandma Kay says. "You can bring him back when he's sobered up. When he's ready to start acting like a decent person and not a drunkard."

"He's not staying with *me*," Shirley says. "He's staying with *you*."

"*What?!?*"

"I have a one-bedroom apartment," Shirley says. "Where are they going to sleep? On the sofa?"

"Who's 'they?'" Grandma Kay asks, before looking at Bruno. "Well, we don't have the space either."

"You live on a ten-acre farm! Why wouldn't they stay here? They came to see you. And Toby, of course."

Grandma Kay shakes her head. "No, I am sorry, but that will not do. That was never discussed or agreed to, Shirley. And I find that very deceptive of you."

"I never lied."

"You didn't tell the truth either," Grandpa Frank says. "This might be the first time I've ever said this in my lifetime, but

Kay is right. If your intention was that he was going to stay here, you should've said so."

"We ask her what she want, no?" It's Bruno. He's gesturing toward me. "She is why we visit."

"What do you want to do, Toby?" Shirley asks.

"Yes, what do you want?" Grandma Kay asks.

"I want—" The words start but become trapped. "I want—"

The only thing I want are the pills. I want darkness. I want to erase. To forget.

"I want—"

"How about giving an old whore a light?"

Everyone turns. There, in the doorway of the living room, a man is standing. At first, I think he's naked, but then I see he's wearing a pair of beige underwear. There's a blond wig on his head, the hair knotted and shooting in all directions. His mouth is a gash of red lipstick. There's a cigarette dangling from his mouth.

"What in the hell?" Grandpa Frank says.

Bruno gets up from the couch and grabs the man's arm. "Arthur, go back to sleep."

"Don't you manhandle me, you meatball," he says, yanking his arm free. "I can't sleep. That bed smells like Aqua Net and failed dreams."

His voice is raspy, higher than I've heard from a man. I remember what my mom had said, that my father's voice was neither male nor female but somewhere in between. He runs a finger along the elastic band of the underwear. I see then that they're not men's underwear.

"Are you wearing my panties?" Grandma Kay asks, rising out of her chair.

"I didn't know they still make this kind," he says. "Please, no one put me near an open flame."

You went through my dresser drawers?

He saunters into the centre of the living room. I see how pale he is. There isn't a hair on his body. His belly hangs like dough.

"This is outrageous!" Grandma Kay says. "You get out of here."

"Now how do y'all like that hospitality?" he asks. "And here I thought Pa would have his squeezebox out and we'd have us a little jig round the outhouse. By the way, Shirley, you're a horrific driver. I've never heard anyone scream like that at a transport truck."

"He kept veering into my lane!"

"Does anyone have a light, or will I have to start rubbing twigs together?"

"Get him back to bed, Frank!"

His gaze lands on me. He slowly walks over. He bends down so that we're eye to eye. I'm looking into his green eyes just like I always imagined. But there are no emeralds. His eyes are the colour of puke. His hand goes to my knee. It's then that I see his fingernails are red.

"And you must be the long-lost daughter," he says, the corners of his smile like two knife points.

CHAPTER 14

They manage to get him back to bed. Bruno and Grandpa Frank lead him down the hallway while he sings "Clang! Clang! Clang! Went the trolley! Ding! Ding! Ding! Went the bell!" at the top of his lungs. Once things quiet down, we sit, silent, in our chairs and on the sofa. It seems like everyone is afraid to speak. Or they don't know what words to say, as if words could erase any of this disaster. I keep seeing him in Grandma Kay's panties, that messy blond wig, his cruel smile. It's the fingernails, though, that bother me most. They were blood red.

"I thought his drinking was under control," Shirley says to her lap. "He sounded sober when I spoke to him on the phone."

"How often is he hitting the bottle?" Grandpa Frank asks Bruno.

"He no hit," Bruno says. "He drink."

"I mean, how often does he get drunk?"

"Depend," Bruno says with a shrug. "It's not bad like before, when he performing. Things now not so busy, which is good. He had to slow down. He was nervous to come.

Maybe it's no surprise. When he's nervous, he drink. And other things."

"*Other* things?" Grandma Kay asks.

"He can't stay here," Grandpa Frank says. "Not in this condition."

"We can get a hotel," Bruno says. "You have hotel here?"

"It's Tilden," Shirley says. "Not Middle Earth."

"How long were you intending to stay?" Grandpa Frank asks.

"Two nights. We have a show in Toronto on the weekend. Then we go back."

"A long way to come for a few days," Grandpa Frank says.

"It was important to Arthur," Bruno says. I feel him glance in my direction. My eyes are back on the evergreens.

"Doesn't seem that way to me," Grandma Kay says.

"I'm sorry," Bruno says. "I was afraid of this. Maybe it's not right. He want to come. He says he want to see everybody."

I look over at him and our eyes lock for a moment. *Why couldn't you have been my father? I think. Why couldn't it have been you when you stepped out of the car? You know how to make conversation. You're not drunk or wearing my grandma's panties. I could even deal with you being gay and a drag queen, so long as you acted normal, like a father, most of the time. I could walk down the street with you and no one would think a thing. Just another father and his daughter, spending time together.*

"I suppose I should start supper," Grandma Kay says, getting up from her chair. "Do you eat ham?"

"We leave before dinner," Bruno says. "But *grazie*."

Grandma Kay places her hands on her hips. "There's too much food. It'll go to waste. You might as well stay, provided he wakes up in time. My issue isn't with you. You seem like a nice enough fellow. It's with Arthur. It's always been with Arthur."

Grandpa Frank says he needs to finish mowing the timothy grass. Shirley says she'll help Grandma Kay with dinner.

"Not that I'm much use in the kitchen."

"Have you ever peeled a potato?"

"No, but I try to dream big."

"Toby, why don't you take Bruno to look at the cows?"

"I'm sure he's seen cows before," I say. I don't want to talk or look at anyone, let alone some man I've just met. I just want to fall into a dark, deep hole and never come out. The only thing getting me through these minutes is knowing that I won't be here much longer. This sorry life. But I still need to be careful. I can't raise anyone's suspicions.

"I don't mind," Bruno says. He gives me something like a smile. I have no idea what I'm going to talk to him about, but I say, "Okay" and manage to stand up.

Grandma Kay tells Bruno to put on a pair of Grandpa Frank's rubber boots. "I don't want you to mess up those fancy boots you have on, and there's a lot of crap out there."

"There's a lot of crap in here as well," Grandpa Frank says before walking out the back door.

"Don't mind him," Grandma Kay says, handing Bruno the boots. Bruno's eyebrows shoot up and he takes the boots from her like they're a stinky garbage bag. He isn't what I'd call good-looking, but there's something about him, the shadow of stubble on his cheeks, the way his chest hair creeps past the collar of his T-shirt. Is he gay too? I can't be sure, but he doesn't seem gay. Well, not as gay as my father. I look down at the gold ring on his finger and see there's a ruby in the centre, the size of a jellybean. Is it real? He's different from what I'm used to seeing, between Grandpa Frank and Mike and the other hired hands, the boys at school with their uncombed hair and awkward bodies and defensive eyes. He's from Europe, a place I've only ever seen on a map. A world away from here.

"Have you ever been on a farm before?" I ask as we walk toward the barn.

"When I was young," Bruno says. "My *zia* had a pig farm."

"What's a *zia*?"

"Sorry, *zia* is Italian for aunt."

"What about uncle?"

"*Zio*."

"Those are definitely more fun to say than *aunt* and *uncle*."

I lead him toward the coop. "These are the chickens. I don't like them very much because they peck at me when I take their eggs."

"That's a mother for you," Bruno says.

"No," I say. "They just like to hurt people. I take a tennis racket with me to shoo them away. When I was younger, I was more afraid of them. Not so much anymore."

"How long you live here?"

"Since I was ten."

"Yes," he says with a nod, and I wonder how much he already knows about me. If he knows about my mom. He must. My father would've said something. Or else Bruno would've asked by now. It makes me feel raw and exposed, like my insides are on the outside of my body. It's not fair that a stranger can know these things about me when I don't know the first thing about him.

We walk to the barn. "The cows aren't here. They're out to pasture. Grandpa Frank will call them in soon though. You'll hear him banging his plastic bucket, although they never listen. Cows are smart. They know what stalls to go into. Then Grandpa Frank and the other hired hands will hook them up to the milking machines."

"Do they mind?"

"They don't seem to," I say. "But I've never asked them."

I show him the name plaques above the stalls. "Grandpa Frank names them all. Sometimes I do too. The name comes from where they were born. These here are the calves."

I take him to the small pen where the calves are kept. Three come walking over to us. "They think it's their feeding time, but it's not. They drink out of these hoses."

"Not from their mothers?" Bruno asks, kneeling down to pat one on the head.

"No," I say. "They're kept separate from their mothers." I realize then that I'll miss these calves once I'm gone. Not that I'll be able to miss anything when I'm dead. Which I guess is the point. "It's easier that way."

His head turns slightly. "You think?"

"That's just the way it is," I say. "How long have you been his manager?"

"Arthur? Maybe eight years."

"That's a long time. Is he an alcoholic?"

"No. Yes. He was. Then he get better. Then he get worse. Then he get better. He's better. For a while now. But this trip, it make things worse again. He's nervous."

"Is he really famous? That's what my mom told me."

"Arthur is very talented. When he was younger, he used to play the biggest concert halls. People, they loved him. Then, things changed."

"How did things change?"

"Some people, they run away from things. You can't catch them because they are fast. But then they get tired. They no can run any more. Arthur did not have self-control. He let things take over. He had a shadow over him. When I meet him, he was not good. He was like a scared child. So I take care of him. And he get better. Most times. But he still have the shadow. That's what he was running from. I no sure if I make sense. That's the best way I can speak about it."

"Do you think my grandma was right? That it was a mistake for him to come here?"

"Today, yes," he says, standing back up. "Tomorrow, that's another day."

On our way back to the house, I see Mike piling up the hay bales. He stops when he sees us. His mouth falls open quickly before he realizes and he shuts it quickly. I can only imagine what he must be thinking, seeing me with this strange, older man. Not that I mind. And not that I'll tell him anything either. I can't let him know about my father, who he is. I'm too embarrassed, and I can only imagine what Mike would say. He'd never understand. Not that I do either.

✳ ✳ ✳

When we return, the kitchen is damp with ham-scented steam. I'm suddenly starving. There's a pot on the stove, foam spilling from its edge. A can of No Name peas sits on the counter, a clear plastic bag filled with dinner rolls next to it. Grandma Kay used to make all of her own bread but hasn't for years. The kneading bothers her hands.

"Supper should be ready soon," she says, tightening the apron around her waist.

"I'll go wash up," I say and excuse myself. But instead of going to the washroom, I go to my grandparents' bedroom and gently open the door. He's still sleeping. His face is slouched to one side, his mouth open. I'm surprised by how young he looks with his own hair. It's brown and curly. I can see now the boy who posed with my mom at the carnival all those years ago. I search his face for traces of my own. Maybe it's there, in his nose and ears. But maybe it's not. I'm not convinced.

This is the man I've carried deep inside me for all these years. The man that I'd dream would rescue me from my sadness. And now, here he is, a thin line of drool sliding down his chin, a raspy snore escaping his throat.

This was the angel from the gymnasium. The one who had broken my mom's heart and stomped on all the pieces. The one who never came back.

He. Was. Magic.

There's nothing magical about the man sleeping in my grandparents' bed. Even the tiny bits floating through the air, lit up by the sun's fading beams, are nothing more than dust.

CHAPTER 15

Grandma Kay slides a large casserole dish of scalloped potatoes from the oven.

"We can discuss where you can stay," she says to Bruno. "There are some motels not far from here. Most of them are decent enough."

"We go back to Toronto and find somewhere," Bruno says. "We no stay here. Not when Arthur is like this."

"You go wake him up," Grandma Kay says. "Then we'll see what we're dealing with."

When he leaves, she turns to me. "I'm sorry about all of this, Toby."

"Why are you apologizing? You didn't do anything."

"Yes, I did," she sighs. "I opened the door. And you should always think twice before you open any door. You never know what's on the other side."

what stays shut, stays hidden

"When I saw him coming out of the car like that," she says, "more of a heap than a man, I should've told them to go back. But I didn't. And now you know. Who your father is. And in some ways, I can't help but think that's worse than *not* knowing who he is."

She sets the potatoes on the table.

"The only hope is to have no hope at all. Then you're not disappointed. That's the only way you'll make your way through life."

I realize then how much Grandma Kay and I have in common, the guilt about my mom that we carry around like a boulder. And I think about telling her. About the pills. It would be so easy to let the words slip out. And if anyone would understand, I think she would. But I can't be certain. I can't trust anyone. So I bite down on my bottom lip.

Grandpa Frank comes through the back door. "Second milking is done."

"Make sure you wash your hands," Grandma Kay says.

Shirley comes up the stairs from the basement, a jar of Grandma Kay's homemade bread-and-butter pickles in her hand, just as Bruno comes back into the kitchen.

"He is up," he says. "In the washroom. He's not happy. But that is the same like home."

A few moments later, I turn to see my father standing in the living room. No, not my father. Never my father. He won't ever be that. I'll think of him like he is—a stranger. Someone who means absolutely nothing to me.

Arthur.

His back is slightly turned to me. He's wearing regular clothing now, a pair of jeans and a T-shirt. He's staring at something I can't see. It holds his attention. And for a minute, I wonder if it could be the evergreens too. It's the way he breathes in deeply and closes his eyes. I watch as he leans over, his fingertips pressing against his temples, like a sudden head-ache has come over him. I look away before he catches me.

"What's for dinner?" he asks when he appears in the doorway.

"What does it look like?" Grandma Kay asks, passing by him with a serving spoon. "Nice to see you're dressed."

"You haven't done much with the kitchen."

"No reason to."

"It looks like the set of a seventies sitcom in here."

"Yeah, and you're the nitwit star," Shirley says. "Kay, I couldn't find the napkins."

"Paper towel is good enough."

I catch Arthur rolling his eyes at Bruno. Bruno shakes his head at him and makes a motion with his hand, as though slicing the air.

"I'd kill for a glass of wine," Arthur says.

"Well, you'll have to drive into town for that," Grandma Kay says. "I don't keep liquor in this house."

"I'd like to speak with the manager, please."

"You're looking at her." Grandma Kay sets a platter of sliced ham on the table, along with a jar of mustard, a plate of Saltine crackers, a dish of red Jell-O, and a bowl of buttered peas and cubed carrots.

"Everything smells wonderful," Shirley says before mentioning that she'll have to pass on the Jell-O. "On account of my diabetes."

Arthur arches a thin eyebrow. "You still have diabetes?"

"Of course I do. It's not a zit. It doesn't go away."

"I was always suspicious of you, Shirley. Playing your diabetic violin strings. I can't help but wonder if it was all for attention."

"Are you high?" Shirley's hands go to her hips. "What an ignorant thing to say. And if anyone around here knows about the need for attention..."

Grandma Kay tells everyone to take a seat. I end up sitting across from Arthur, but I refuse to look at him. I can't believe he's acting like such a jerk.

"Toby, pass the ham," Grandma Kay says. "Does anyone want barbeque sauce? I have some in the fridge."

The bowls and plates are handed around. Bruno asks what the brown things are in the ham.

"Cloves," Grandma Kay says. "You've never had a ham with cloves before?"

"He's Italian," Arthur says. "They don't do ham. They do prosciutto."

"What's that?" Grandpa Frank asks. "Pasta of some kind?"

"It's raw pig. It tastes like sweat socks."

"Eye-talians must have strong stomachs," Grandma Kay says under her breath.

I keep my attention on my plate. The appetite I had before is gone. I don't know how I'll get anything past my lips, but I need to. I have to eat something. If I don't, there will be questions.

"You're not having much to eat," Grandma Kay says, and I look up, assuming she's speaking to me. But she's not. She's speaking to Arthur.

"I'm not that hungry," he says.

"You need to eat something," she says.

"Especially after all that drinking," Shirley says.

"If I eat, I get fat. And if I get fat, I won't be able to fit into my dresses. I'm already a size twelve."

The table jumps.

"Ow!" Arthur says, bending over to rub his shin. "Which one of you assholes did that?"

"No swearing at the dinner table," Grandma Kay says, pointing her fork at him.

"No swearing *or* drinking," Arthur says. "This is the worst dinner party of my life. Next you're going to tell me there's no cocaine."

"Arthur… ," Bruno says.

"Oh, shut up," Arthur says. "You should've heard him on the plane here. 'Arthur don't do this.' 'Arthur don't do that.' I'm not a fucking puppet. You can't pull my strings and make me perform for you. I've spent my whole life performing for others, for complete strangers. You'd think I wouldn't have to deal with this. In fucking Tilden, of all places."

"That's enough," Grandma Kay says. "No one needs to hear language like that at the dinner table."

Arthur turns to Shirley, his eyes like slits. "Shirley, you've got too much foundation on. Honestly, you're orange."

"I'm not wearing any foundation."

"Well then, you're eating too many carrots. You're a diabetic rabbit, dear Shirley."

"You're a complete jerk."

"Oh, I'm only kidding. Just having a laugh. You still have a sense of humour, don't you? Diabetes hasn't robbed you of that, I hope."

"Please be quiet for two seconds," Grandma Kay says. "It's the least you can do."

"Keep quiet?" Arthur says, rising out of his chair. "I've been quiet for years. Have you heard one peep from me in all that time? Have you heard the slightest thing from me?"

"No, we haven't," Shirley says. "And that's the goddamn problem."

"Please… ," Grandma Kay says.

I slice through the pink circle of ham on my plate.

"So here I am and what do I hear?" He starts walking around the kitchen. "Arthur, shut up. Arthur, be quiet. Do you have any idea how insulting that is? Now that I'm finally here?"

"You're not here," Shirley says. "You're anywhere *but* here."

"Well then, where am I?" He throws his hands up into the air. "If I'm not here, then where could I be?"

"How about up your own arse," Grandpa Frank says around a mouthful of potatoes.

Arthur throws his head back and laughs. I see dark pockets where he's missing teeth. I don't like the sound of his laugh. It's not laughter at all, but the opposite of laughter.

"Good one, Frankie. You always did have a ripe sense of humour. Of course, you needed one, being married to Kay."

"Arthur!" Shirley slams her hand down on the table.

I can't believe what he just said. I've never heard anyone talk about Grandma Kay like that before. He's more than just a drunk. He's a cruel drunk.

"You've got a lot of nerve, saying something like that,"

Grandpa Frank says. "We didn't have to open our door to you."

Arthur's head tilts. "Then why did you?"

"Because we thought it might do some good," Grandma Kay says. "And it could've. If only you hadn't wrecked it. Showing up here like we're all supposed to bow down to you or something. Like you're walking on water. In ladies' high heels."

"Don't you trivialize my art."

"Is that what you call it?" Grandpa Frank chuckles. "Dressing up in ladies' clothes? An art? I had no idea."

"You don't know me."

"Oh, I have a very good idea," Grandpa Frank says. "And if it were up to me, you wouldn't have a place setting at this table. I don't sit with…"

"With what?" Arthur crosses his arms. "Say it, Frank."

Grandpa Frank scoops more potatoes into his mouth, pretending not to hear.

"Then I'll say it," Arthur says. "Frank doesn't sit with faggots."

Shirley gasps. The word hangs in the air, heavy and full. I can practically see it settle in the centre of the table, next to the bowl of red Jell-O. I grip the sides of my chair to stop myself from running away. I need to escape from this table, these people.

"Look at you all, sitting here," Arthur says. "Acting high and mighty when I'm the only one who's been honest. I left here because I couldn't stand the hypocrisy. I couldn't stand the suffocation, the sameness. The dead dreams. Your beige lives. What did you expect me to do? Buy into the lie you all told yourselves?"

"Who are you calling a liar?" Grandpa Frank says.

"*You're* the liar," Shirley says. "You're a frigging drag queen. You spend your life wearing makeup and prancing around in dresses, pretending to be someone else. That tells you a lot."

"I am *not* a drag queen!" Arthur yells. "I am a female impersonator. One of the most famous female impersonators in the world."

"I'm sure the competition is real stiff," Shirley says.

"At least I had talent. At least I made something of myself."

"I'll give you that," Shirley says. "You certainly made something. A fucking mess."

There's a sound, something torn and jagged. When we turn to look, it's coming from Grandma Kay. She's sitting there, her shoulders sloping downwards, her face all crumpled. She looks so pathetic. I should go over to her, tell her it's all right. But I stay frozen in my seat. So long as I stay sitting, I'm safe, I tell myself. Invisible. I'm not part of this scene.

Grandma Kay's eyes are tightly closed, disappearing into her face. A shiny, thin stream slides out her nose and stops at her top lip.

"What you did to Heather," she says. "I can never forgive you."

It's the first time anyone's mentioned my mom since Arthur arrived. She's here too. Like the awful word Arthur said, heavy as a water balloon.

"We will go," Bruno says.

Arthur pulls a package of cigarettes from his shirt and lights one. He blows the smoke out in a thin, flat line. "I'm not re-sponsible for what Heather did," he says. "Don't you try to pin that on me."

"You're a vicious, horrible man," Shirley says.

"Tell me something I don't know," Arthur says.

"Finish the cigarette," Bruno says. "Then we go."

"Where are you going to go?" Shirley asks. "And with who? The only way I'm taking him anywhere is if I'm drag-ging him from the back bumper."

"But then you'll mess my hair," Arthur says.

"The Eye-talian fellow is right," Grandpa Frank says. "You're not welcome here."

It-talian, I say inside. *It-taly.*

"I'm devastated, Frank. Really I am."

"Arthur, be quiet," Bruno says sternly. "For once."

Arthur stubs out his cigarette on a plate. "Sorry about this, kid," he says to me. "As usual, the past got in the way."

I almost look up at him, but I don't want to give him the satisfaction. I keep my eyes down.

✳ ✳ ✳

They leave. I refuse to watch the car pull out of the driveway and back the way it came, a reverse of what had taken place just a few hours earlier. When there was hope. Instead, I get up from the table, walk out the back door and look at the shapes of the evergreens, swaying in a soft evening breeze.

He didn't notice my new top.

Tomorrow night, I'll take all the pills. They won't get down my throat fast enough.

I stay there, watching the trees, until I hear my grandmother calling my name and I go back inside.

CHAPTER 16

Grandma Kay comes to my room later, after we've washed and dried the dishes and put everything back into the cupboard. We worked in silence. It was easier that way, not to mess things up even more with words. It was just, "Pass me the tea towel," and the clatter of dishes being put away. The leftovers were wrapped, some in tinfoil pie plates with a double layer of plastic wrap and aluminum foil and placed in the deep freezer in the basement. Grandma Kay stuck a piece of masking tape across each and wrote out what was inside.

ham potatoes peas

I'm not surprised by her knock. I've been expecting it. I know that Grandma Kay wants to speak to me, that she won't be able to get through the evening without saying something about what happened.

"Come in," I say.

Grandma Kay slowly enters and sits down at the foot of my bed, her hands on her knees. She looks straight ahead at my closet door, where the pills are, inside their hiding spot, and I think again that she knows.

"I had some idea of how this might go," she says. "But in

my wildest dreams, I didn't think it would go as badly as that. Arthur brings back so many painful memories. I shouldn't have set myself up like that. I don't have the patience. I don't have that kind of goodwill. It's long gone."

She takes a deep breath. "I can only imagine what it was like for you, hearing all those things come out of his mouth. I don't know what Heather saw in him. But she was so young then. A girl's heart can be a dangerous place. Maybe she wanted an escape. Maybe she wanted someone like her. I don't know. Your mom, as you know, wasn't well. She always had problems with her mind. Heather heard voices. Voices that told her to do things. There were times when I was sure that I'd lost her to her imagined world, but I always managed to bring her back. Eventually. Arthur made her feel less like a weirdo. That's what she told me once."

"Why didn't he ever come back?" I ask.

"That depends on who you ask," Grandma Kay says. "If you ask Arthur, he'd say he wasn't welcome. That's not true. He was welcome to come back any time so long as he understood that meant behaving like a normal person. No alcohol or drugs. And no carrying on with the other thing. You know what I mean. But if you ask *me*, the reason he didn't come back was because he was scared. Sometimes, it's easier for people to pretend they've done nothing wrong, like putting on a blindfold, than to admit the truth. Arthur had a lot of people to reconcile with. Me, your mom, Shirley. You, most of all. But it was too much for him. Arthur had a good voice. I'll say that much. But with talent comes weakness."

"He won't come back."

I mean this as a question, but the tail end of my words falls flat. Instead, it's a sentence. A fact.

"I don't think so," Grandma Kay says. "But you never know. Maybe we'll all try again one day. How do you feel? About everything? Now that you've met him?"

"I don't know," I say. "In some ways, he's just a stranger, someone from my mom's past. It's not like he means anything to me. Not now. He's no one special."

I can tell Grandma Kay is trying to figure out if she really believes what I'm saying. I lock eyes with her and don't look away. I know this is important. I know she'll think about this moment later, once all the pills are gone, and she'll ask herself, "Did Toby really mean that?" I need her to believe that I'm being honest.

"Maybe he'll call sometime," Grandma Kay says. "Christmas. Or your birthday."

"I know I'll see him again," I say, almost wishing it were true. "Some day."

"When the time is right."

* * *

Trisha calls later, wanting to know all the details.

"What did he look like? What were his first words to you? Was he wearing makeup? I'm dying here, Toby. You were supposed to call, remember?"

"Sorry," I say. I didn't forget to call. I just didn't want to talk about anything. "I got distracted. It's been a busy day."

"Duh. No shit."

I don't even know what I'm going to tell her, but I have to make something up.

"He's...different than what I thought he'd be," I say, trying to make my voice sound lively. I have a job to do—tell a lie, make Trisha believe it so she doesn't suspect anything, and then get off the phone. "More animated. Kind of like a comedian only not as funny."

"Okaaay... ," Trisha says. "A non-funny comedian. Not exactly a promising start. Was he really gay?"

"What do you mean by that?"

"I mean, did he wiggle his hips a lot? Or did he kind of gallop?"

"He's not a horse, Trisha."

"You know what I mean. God, it's like pulling teeth with you. Let me put this another way. Was he Rock Hudson gay or Liberace gay?"

"I don't know. Somewhere in between, I guess. Who's Rock Hudson? We didn't really talk that much, with everyone else around. Shirley was here. And his manager."

"Oh my God! He has a manager? Was he wearing sunglasses?"

"The manager or my father?"

"Either."

"I don't think so. I can't remember. Everything happened so fast."

"What does he look like?"

"Kind of average, I guess. Curly hair. Not tall, but not short."

"Toby, you're making this very difficult for me."

"I'm sorry, Trisha. It's just a lot for me to take in. It...it hasn't been easy." I want to confide in Trisha, tell her how horrible everything was. The sight of him in that brown blanket, his white arm, how he came into the living room almost naked in that tangled wig. The cruel words he said, like grenades exploding in the kitchen. But I can't say anything. I'm too ashamed and I can't deal with more questions.

"Of course," Trisha says. "Look, I shouldn't be grilling you like this. This is your father. Your gay drag queen father. Who you've never met before. And here I am, asking if he wore sunglasses. I'm an insensitive asshole."

"You're just curious."

"Hold on a minute. My bitch mom is calling me... *What?!?*" I have to hold the phone away from my ear.

"I'm on the phone with her now! Yes, I'll ask! Stop bugging me! God!"

Trisha sighs. "She wants me to remind you to pick a date for the cabin this summer."

Suddenly, I have an idea. The cabin would be a better place to take the pills, away from here. I don't want Grandma Kay or Grandpa Frank to find me. I couldn't do that to them. Not after what happened to me. The cabin is perfect. I'll find a spot in the woods. No one will ever find me.

"Sure," I say. "We can figure something out. Maybe mid-July? By the way, is there anyone at the cabin right now?"

"You mean like renters? No, it's empty. Who'd pay to stay at that dump? I hate it. Nothing but bugs and the sound of raccoons having sex. Sometimes Mike goes up there. God knows what he does. Sacrifices animals and compulsively masturbates, no doubt. So when are you seeing your dad… I mean, your father, again? And, more important, when can I meet him?"

"Soon enough," I say. "I promise. I just have to take care of a few details first. Thanks for caring about this, Trisha."

"Uh, that's a weird thing to say. Of course I'm going to care. I'm your best friend, remember?"

She must be so tired of me and all my problems. She'll be so relieved when it's over.

"How could I forget?" I say. Then I tell Trisha goodbye for the last time and hang up the phone.

CHAPTER 17

The time has come. And Mike will be the one to help.

He has his car, and I know I can trust him. He won't make this complicated, like Trisha. He won't ask a lot of questions. He'll do what I want him to do because it'll make him feel important. And that I still have feelings for him.

Which I do, but I also don't. I can't figure it out.

I feel bad about manipulating Mike like this. But I can't let my conscience take over. I need to be determined. I have a job to do and it needs to get done as quickly as possible. There's no time for second-guessing.

This morning, while I help Grandma Kay prepare breakfast, I watch Mike from the kitchen window as he's moving bales of hay. When it's time to eat, I help bring out the BLTs, juice and coffee. Mike grabs a sandwich from the platter, turns his baseball hat around and burps into his fist. I notice there's a piece of hay stuck to his shirt. I start having second thoughts about asking him, but when no one is looking, I pass him a note. He thinks it's a napkin and starts wiping his mouth with it before I tell him to stop.

"Read it when you're alone," I whisper.

So of course he opens it up and starts reading it at the table. I'm ready to smack him in the head. At least he holds the paper under the table so no one else can read it. The note tells him to meet me by the hay bales in a half-hour.

"TELL NO ONE," I wrote in capital letters with three lines under each word.

After he folds the note back up, Mike looks around casually and slips it into his front pocket. When he reaches for his glass of juice, he gives me a quick wink. I know what he's thinking, and I don't blame him. But I can't let that bother me. Or what his new girlfriend might think, whoever she is. Besides, it isn't like that at all, and little does he know what I really have in mind.

* * *

He's standing next to the hay bales when I get there.

"Hey Tobe-ster," he says coolly.

"Hi," I say. I look down at my feet, at the crushed-up pieces of hay scattered across the barn floor. Anywhere but his face.

"What's up?" He takes a flattened package of cigarettes from his back pocket. If Grandpa Frank catches him smoking around the hay, he'll hit the roof.

"I need your help," I say.

"Oh?" He strikes a match and lights his cigarette.

"You can't say a word of this to anyone. Please. Not to Trisha. Or my grandparents. Not your parents."

"I don't tell my parents shit about me, let alone someone else."

"I need you to take me somewhere. In your car."

"Anyplace special?"

"Your family's cabin."

"Why do you want to go there?"

"I need to get away for a few days. There's been a lot going on."

"I saw that. Who were those guys?"

I'm not about to tell Mike about Arthur and Bruno. I can only imagine his reaction.

"Some distant relatives. Anyway, I need to get away. Be by myself for a day or so to figure things out. I can't ever find time here. I have a problem that I need to think through. I just need some time alone. Even one night."

"Okaaay," he says. "When do you want to go?"

"Tonight," I say, and I can tell he's surprised. "I know it's last minute, but it has to be tonight. It has to."

"You can't wait a couple of days?"

"No!" I say, too loudly. I try to calm down. "I can't take another minute here. I'll leave a note for my grandparents so they won't worry. I just... I just need to get out of here. Can you help, Mike?"

"I'll think about it," he says.

"Please," I say, grabbing his arm. It's the first time we've touched since we broke up. "Can you drive me there tonight or not?"

"Okay, Toby," he says. "I'll help you."

✳ ✳ ✳

My grade nine English teacher, Mr. Duzzy (everyone called him Mr. Dizzy), told us once that the destination in life isn't what's important. It's the journey. Most of the time, he said, you think it's the place you're going to that's the best part.

"But you don't think about the days leading up to your trip or the airplane or the car or however else you're getting there," Mr. Duzzy said. "You only think about the place. But it's not just about the place. It's about *getting* to the place."

Me and my grandparents have never gone anywhere for vacation, on account of the cows. But one time, we went to Niagara Falls for Grandma Kay's birthday. I think I was around eleven. It was the year after my mom died. I was looking forward to the trip because my class had recently talked about the Falls and I thought there was nothing more exciting than going to a place that you'd ever only known as a photo in a book. We went on the *Maid of the Mist*. We visited some of the wax museums, even the scary ones, which Grandma Kay said would only give me nightmares, but I reminded her there was nothing scary about neon-orange blood. We ate fudge and I bought a snow globe that I kept on my dresser until black fluff started to form in the water and I had to throw it out.

It was only when we got back from Niagara Falls that I realized how disappointed I was. Not by Niagara Falls, but because I didn't have the getting-to-Niagara Falls in my head anymore. It was like opening a present before Christmas and rewrapping it and trying to tell yourself you don't know what it is. But you can't. Because you know. And a wrapped present is always better than an unwrapped present.

Sometimes, when the shadows in my mind go from grey to black, I think of my mom in the same way. That because she's dead she's a better mom than she'd be in real life. I know that's a horrible thing to think, but what would we be doing now if she were still alive? She'd go to work. I'd go to school. We'd eat dinner at the end of the day. Watch TV. Sometimes the voices would take over inside her head and she'd have to go lie down in her bedroom while I waited to get her back. It wouldn't be like commercials, where you see moms and daughters laughing and hugging and acting like best friends. It wouldn't be like we'd be different from any other mother and daughter. I wouldn't know the flip side. What life would be like without one of us there at the dinner table. That, without having it taken away, we never really know what we have, or *who* we have, sitting across from us, quietly chewing their french fries.

So, I've come to understand, in some terrible way, that I'm better off that my mom isn't here. I love my mom more dead than if she were still alive.

I think people would love me more if they lost me too.

CHAPTER 18

It seems like 1 a.m. will never come. That's the time I'm going to meet Mike by the row of evergreens on the far side of the farm. He's supposed to pull over to the side of the road and wait with his headlights on.

I'm lying in bed, fully dressed. Grandma Kay and Grandpa Frank went to bed a couple of hours ago. I listened as they passed by my door, the floorboards snapping under their feet, Grandpa Frank farting as they made their way down the hall.

"That wasn't necessary," Grandma Kay said.

It was all so familiar, but it felt like the first time I was hearing their routines. The bathroom faucet turning on. The click of the light switches. The whining bed springs beneath their bodies. Then, a silence so loud I could almost feel it inside the house.

Grandma Kay gets up shortly before midnight, just like I knew she would. She always does. I hear their bedroom door open, then the *whish-whish* of her slippers on the floor (she's never barefoot, and thinks her feet look like blue cheese), and, as I listen to her, I feel something grab my heart. A tenderness, like what you'd feel when someone you cared for didn't realize you were watching them. The toilet creaks as Grandma Kay settles down on it, and I imagine her, her nightgown with the periwinkle flowers on it, her pillow-flattened hair, her face frowning into the dark. She has no idea what's in store for her. And thinking that almost makes me change my mind. What if I cause Grandma Kay to have a heart attack? And what about Grandpa Frank? I can see him sitting in his tractor, in the middle of the timothy fields, and thinking about me. How could I do that to them? What kind of person am I?

And what will Arthur say when he finds out? Will I finally have his attention, after all these years? He'll understand how much he hurt me. The damage he's caused. But it'll be too late. Time has run out. For everyone. There are no second chances.

The toilet flushes. The seat bangs down on its base, making me jump. Then Grandma Kay shuffles back down the hallway and I think I hear a soft sigh and I wonder about all the things that might have caused that sigh and how I'll never know any of my grandmother's secrets.

It will hurt at first. I know that. But, in time, they'll understand they're better off without me. I did what was best, what was needed. For everyone.

Grandma Kay closes her bedroom door. The house is silent again except for the ticking of the living room clock.

"Goodbye, Grandma Kay," I whisper.

❊ ❊ ❊

At 12:30 a.m., I consider getting out of bed, wondering why I'm waiting to head out. What does it matter? But I tell myself that if I get out of bed too soon, my plans will fall through. Everything will be ruined. This is the way my mind works sometimes.

So I patiently wait until the glowing red numbers of my clock turn to 12:55. I pull the covers back, aware of every little noise I make, as though all of my movements, even my breathing, are being played over a sound system. I swing my feet around and step out of bed, wincing with every creak I make. I arrange both of my pillows into a long shape and pull the covers over, just like they do in the movies. Then I grab my shoes and hoodie and slowly inch my way down the hall.

I tiptoe through the kitchen and to the stairs that will take me down to the basement. I'll sneak out the window. In the laundry room, hidden under the stairs, beneath Grandma Kay's jarred pickles and beets, there's a knapsack with food and a suitcase. The pills are inside the suitcase. I don't need food or clothing, since I'll be taking the pills as soon as Mike leaves, but it would look suspicious if I didn't bring anything. I grab the suitcase and knapsack and awkwardly make my way over to the window, thankful that Grandpa Frank took off the storm windows last month. I open the latch, prop the window open with my head and unhook the screen before sliding it over. Then I push my knapsack through the window, followed by my suitcase and, once that's done, I pull myself out and let the window gently fall back into place.

Now, I'm standing, surrounded by the night. Crickets are singing, and the moon overhead looks like a fingernail clipping. Stars are everywhere. The cows are here too, although I can't see them. But I can feel them, giving me courage.

When I first came to the farm, I was afraid of the country, especially at night. The silence bothered me. Not that I wanted to be around other people, but it was comforting to know that they were there, in the apartment next door or walking their dog along the sidewalk. I know I was supposed to be happier in the country. I've read books where girls skipped around fields, making friends with rosebushes and hollyhocks. But not me. Hollyhocks were only good for one-sided conversations. After a while, though, I got used to things. I even came to like the country a little more. But I still liked the city better, with all its noise. The strangers around me.

Standing here, alone, in the darkness, brings back some of that fear. I imagine coyotes lurking behind tree trunks. A man with an axe slowly approaches me from behind. I hold my knapsack tighter against my chest and listen. But there's no time for fear. Mike will be here any minute—if he isn't already—and I need to get to the evergreens.

Something nudges my leg and I almost scream. I look down and see that it's Ladybug, our collie.

"What are you doing out here?" I whisper, crouching down to pet her. "You're supposed to be sleeping."

She rubs the side of her snout against my pant leg and I almost start crying because she's just an old dog and one day she'll die, even though she doesn't know that.

"I have to get going, Ladybug," I say and give her a quick kiss on the top of her head. "I've got things to do. Be a good girl."

I walk away, knowing that she's staring after me. But I try

not to dwell on this. I can't. So I make my way through the fields, my sneakers soaking up the dew, the cans inside my knapsack thumping against my back. Why wasn't I smart enough to bring packages of soup, instead?

In the distance, I see a pair of headlights, two giant owl eyes.

"Please be Mike," I whisper and head toward them.

CHAPTER 19

The week before she died, my mom and I went to a family reunion with Grandpa Frank and Grandma Kay. I didn't want to go and told my mom that.

"Toby, please don't start with me," she said in a tired voice. "This is something I promised your grandma. She wants us to go. As to how I feel, I'll keep my mouth shut."

I watched her get ready. A few times, I heard her mumble it was all "crap," and it seemed like she was nervous about something. It took my mom a long time to pick out her clothes and she put on mascara and blush, which she only did for special occasions.

"The sooner this is over, the better," she said.

She'd been acting strange the past few days. Not strange enough to make me worry, but I could tell when something was off. My mom's eyes would look at me, but I knew she wasn't seeing me. It was like my mom was doing everything she was supposed to do, but she didn't understand why she was doing it in the first place.

We picked up Grandma Kay and Grandpa Frank at the farm. Grandpa Frank had on a thick, brown tie and Grandma

Kay was in a pleated dress with daisies. Her fingernails were pink. It was the first time I'd ever seen a colour on my grandma's nails and I couldn't stop staring at them. Grandpa Frank told us he'd drive up north to the reunion because he didn't trust anyone behind the wheel except himself.

"Suits me fine," Grandma Kay said. "I'd sooner be skinned alive than drive on the highway."

"You make it sound like going off to war," my mom said.

"That's what it feels like when she's behind the goddamned wheel," Grandpa Frank said.

"Watch your language," Grandma Kay said. "There's a child in the car."

I had heard the word *goddamned* before. Worse words too.

Grandpa Frank apologized. "Goldern, I meant to say."

"Goshdarn," Grandma Kay said, and my mom pinched my leg, to show that we were in on a joke. That my grandparents were funny in a way they didn't understand.

The reunion was held in a hall in an arena. I remember the smell of the arena, like damp straw and old wood. My mom's smile was fake as we made our way through the people. Other kids were there, running around what I guessed would be the rink in the wintertime. Grandma Kay told me to go and play with them.

"These are your kin, after all," she said, like I should be proud, and nudged me with the back of her hand.

But I didn't move from my mom's side. I wasn't comfortable around other kids. They made me nervous. They still do. It's like they don't care what they look like or what they say, and I can't get out of my head to be like that. I don't know if that makes sense. It's like I feel both too old and too young.

"Go on," my mom said. "I'll be right here."

I saw the look on her face. She wanted me to go and I didn't want to upset her. I knew that being around other people could make her nervous.

Be a good daughter, Toby, I told myself. *Don't make your mom mad. You know what will happen if you do.*

So I walked to the centre of the rink and stood there, trying to look friendly, whatever friendly was supposed to look like. My stomach felt like a stormy sea. Eventually, a boy came up to me. I didn't hear his name. He seemed stupid in the way most boys were stupid. He had a twisted front tooth and eyebrows that were very close to one another.

"Who are you?" he asked. He was panting, like he'd just run from somewhere.

"Toby," I said.

"I'm related to you," he said. "We're probably cousins." He looked over his shoulder. "I dare you to do something."

"What?" I hoped it wasn't something like showing him my underpants. I'd seen stuff like that at recess.

"Go up to your mom and say, 'Mom! Mom!' and then when she says 'What?' you say, 'Oh, I forgot,' and walk away."

I waited for the second part, but nothing came. He was stupider than I thought. But it gave me a reason to go back to my mom, so I said, "Okay."

He started to jump up and down as I walked away. "Make it seem like an emergency. Like you're on fire or something. That'll make it funnier."

I gave him a thumbs-up and walked back to the hall to find my mom.

It was hard making my way through the crowd. By that time, the hall was full of people. The sound was a thousand buzzing bees; voices were bouncing off the walls and ceiling, like the hard rubber balls that were banned from school because a kid got hit in the face and came back to school with an eye like a purple doughnut.

I couldn't find my mom. All I could see were strangers.

"Are you lost?" I heard a voice say, but I didn't stop. I knew better than to talk to strangers, even if those strangers were related to me. All I wanted was to find my mom. If I didn't keep moving, I'd lose her. I was sure of that.

By the time I found Grandma Kay, hot tears were falling down my face. My nose was running too. I could taste it in my mouth. The salt. I worried it would leave a mark on my dress.

"What's the matter, Toby?" Grandma Kay asked. "What happened to you?"

But I couldn't speak. I couldn't say anything except for "Mommy!" I could hear my own voice, so high and breathless, like the boy's voice had been, only different.

We found my mom. She was only a few feet away, sitting at a table with a couple of women, eating a brownie. I could smell the chocolate on her as I buried my face into her shoulder, her hair stiff from hairspray.

"Toby, calm down," she kept saying. And I knew I needed to; I didn't want to make my mom upset. But I couldn't calm down. I couldn't get over the fear that I wouldn't find her. Of her not being here. Of leaving me alone, in this arena, with these boys and their twisted teeth and stupid dares. Of leaving me with all these strangers.

My mom excused herself from the other women and led me out to the parking lot.

"What is the matter with you?" she asked.

"I couldn't find you," I cried. "I thought you left me."

She crouched down so that she was looking into my eyes. "Why would you think that? I'd never leave you, Toby. Never."

And I believed her.

CHAPTER 20

oly shit, Tobe-ster. I didn't think you'd actually go through
with it."

"Don't joke with me," I say. "This isn't the time."

"I'm not joking. You're the one who's running away in the
middle of the night. When was the last time you did something this crazy?"

I try to think of something. Taking Mr. Whitlock's pills?
Not that I can tell Mike that. "I can't remember," I say. "You
didn't say anything to Trisha, did you?"

"She knows nothing. She's probably snoring away right
now, sucking up her bedroom curtains into those huge,
double-car-garage nostrils."

"Her nostrils aren't that big."

In the silence that follows, I have a few minutes to catch
up with my thoughts. I can't believe it. My plan has become
reality. I'm here, in Mike's car, on the highway, heading for
the Richardsons' cabin, in the middle of the night. Have my
grandparents discovered that I'm missing yet? Have the po-
lice been alerted? I keep checking the passenger-side mirror
for flashing red and blue lights. What would I do? Tell Mike

to pull over or tell him to press down on the gas pedal? Can I get arrested for running away? Could Mike for helping me? I shouldn't have brought him into this. I shouldn't have involved anyone else.

But it's nice having him here, next to me. He's leaning back in the seat, his cigarette dangling from his lips, his thumbs loosely hooked onto the steering wheel. It's hard not to notice how tight his jeans are across his thighs. My eyes travel up to his crotch, but I quickly look away before he catches me. Trisha told me last week she caught him blow-drying his pubes.

"I'm scarred for the rest of my life," she whined. "He was using a brush and everything. Oh, God. I think it was *my* brush."

I wanted more details. Why was he blow-drying his pubes? Did he have a date that night? With his baseball-loving girlfriend? Whoever she is.

"Who knows and who cares?" Trisha said. "I'm trying to forget it. You, on the other hand, seem a little *too* interested. Please, Toby. I know you haven't had a boyfriend yet, but let's not start looking through the trash can."

Oh, Trisha. If you only knew, I thought.

Mike says we're almost there. I inhale, choking on the smoke filling up the car's interior. The smell reminds me of my mom. Once, she made me a pair of tiny cups from the foil sleeve inside her cigarette pack.

"This is how ladies drink," she said, giggling as she poured a small amount of apple juice into each one. We tapped our glasses together and my mom told me to keep my pinkie raised.

I loved those cups, and remembering this makes me sad. So many memories of my mom aren't happy ones. When was the last time I felt truly happy? Maybe a couple of years ago. I was out walking in the fields. It was around the same time of the year, June. The fields were green velvet. In between the blades of grass, dewy spiderwebs dangled like rhinestone necklaces. The day made me happy, happier than I'd let myself feel for a long time. Generally, I talk myself out of happiness before I feel it. But this day was different. I let the happiness melt over me. It poured over my head and ran down my arms and legs. I let the grass and air and the cloudless sky above me take over. Summer was coming. And I was looking forward to returning to the house, to being with Grandma Kay and Grandpa Frank. I knew there would be a roast in the oven, surrounded by carrots and potatoes, and that by the time the roast was done the carrots would be sweet and mushy. And, for the first time, I knew that I loved my grandparents. Not in the way that I had loved my mom. But enough. Enough to make things worthwhile. But now, that memory—and that happiness—seems like it happened to someone else. A complete stranger.

* * *

It's darker up north than I thought it would be. Not that we're that far north. Or east or west for that matter. The Richardsons' cabin is only forty-five minutes away, but it's the way that the night seems to be swallowing the car. It just keeps rolling on and on, a bottomless sea, tipped on its side. Maybe, for the first time, I understand that I'll be in that darkness too.

The thought comforts me. No more Toby. No more dead mom. No more absent father. No more hurt. I can't imagine myself stopping, fading to cool like an unplugged iron. I can't imagine having no thoughts.

"Almost there," Mike says. "Miller's Lane should be coming up on the right. Past the gas station."

Before long, the gas station comes into view, even though the lights are off and it's closed. Seeing the unlit sign makes me realize how isolated we are.

I want to ask him about his new girlfriend, but I can't. Not that I care, anyway.

Mike slows down the car and turns onto a gravel road, the windshield turning a deeper shade of black. I imagine the car's tail lights behind us, evil, red eyes. But then I start to see the signs with family names on them. The Zantigs. The Donaldsons. The Fishers. It dawns on me that there are other people around. Strangers, but people just the same. Then I start to get nervous for Mike. He has to drive back himself. What if something happens to him? What if he falls asleep and crosses into the path of an oncoming truck? What if he goes to light a cigarette and loses control of the wheel? I'll never forgive myself.

Not that I'd know. Not that I'd know anything.

"I don't think you should go back tonight," I say. "It'd be better if you went back in the morning."

He gives me a look and I realize how my words sound. What he thinks I must mean.

"I don't mean it like that," I say. "I know you have a girlfriend. And I'd never…" My words trail off as I try to find the right ones.

"I can't stay," he says. "I mean, I can. For, you know, a while. But not overnight. I have to be at the farm first thing in the morning."

"Right," I say. "Is there a coffee maker at the cabin?"

"Beats me," he says. "I don't drink coffee, anyway. Only beer. I've got some in the trunk. We'll have a couple before I head back. Besides, it's already two o'clock. We won't have much time, anyway."

Much time for *what*?

It gets quieter. The dings of the gravel against the car seem to soften. I imagine deer cocking their heads outside.

I want Mike to stay. I want to be with him. I don't care about his girlfriend. I don't have time for guilty feelings. All I know is that I don't want him to go.

I need to feel close to someone. To break down the brick walls surrounding me. Even if it's only for one night.

"Maybe one beer," I say and reach over to place my hand on his. He looks over at me again, a half-smile on his face. I want to feel what I've been searching for for so long. A connection. To feel whole again, instead of in pieces. I want to feel loved, even if it's only for a few moments. I'll take whatever I can get. If that means sex—and if that's what Mike wants—I'll do it. There's nothing left for me to lose, anyway.

"There," Mike says and points.

A sign with a painted arrow pops up in the headlights. He turns, and the road gets narrower. The car dips and rises. We seem so close to sliding over the edge. I ask him to be careful and squeeze his hand.

"I could do this blindfolded," he says, but he sounds nervous.

I see the Richardsons' sign. Mike turns right and then the cabin appears in the beam of the headlights. He stops the car. We get out. The air is cold and there are no sounds except for our feet on the gravel. Even though I can't see the trees, I can feel them around us, leaning in.

"We're here," Mike says.

✳ ✳ ✳

The cabin isn't as nice as I remember it. Not that I'm expecting a palace. The Richardsons aren't rich, after all. But I was expecting something a little more picturesque. A stone fireplace and a fur rug. A glass-eyed moose head staring back from the wall. There's none of that. The cabin smells like a book left out in the rain. Wood panelling covers the walls. There are two tiny bedrooms. An even tinier kitchen. It's cold too. Colder, it seems, than the outside.

Why did I imagine something different? I'm disappointed, but it will have to do.

"We can light a fire," Mike whispers, and even though I'm tempted to ask him why he's whispering, I know why. It feels like something we should be doing.

After he gets the fire going in the wood stove, he goes to get his beer and my luggage from the trunk. I'm sitting on the couch, covered in a thin blanket that smells like mothballs. There's no electricity, but Mike found a kerosene lamp. It's sitting in the corner, a small, glowing sun.

Mike comes back and hands me a beer. "Open it carefully. It's been bouncing around."

I do as he tells me. The can hisses as I crack open the tab. Mike's beer fizzes out and he makes a loud slurping noise as he sucks back the foam.

"This is my dad's beer," he says. "Tastes like piss, but it's beer."

I agree about the piss part. It doesn't help that the beer is lukewarm.

He sits down beside me on the couch. The weight of his body causes mine to tilt toward him.

"Mission accomplished," he says. "We're like Bonnie and Clyde."

I don't know who they are but don't bother asking. I'm still surprised that we pulled it off, that we're sitting here, side by side, in the middle of the night, in this cabin. But my plan has only just begun.

The label on the bottle in Mr. Whitlock's drawer read *Zopiclone*, which seems like a nice name. Something you'd call a dinosaur. The instructions were to take one tablet at bedtime as needed for sleep. I'm assuming twelve pills are enough to do the trick, but I can't say for sure and it's not like you can look these sorts of things up at the library. And it's not like I could ask Mr. Whitlock.

"So, what will you be doing up here?" Mike asks.

"Thinking," I say. "Getting my life on track."

He takes a long gulp of beer. "You must need to think

through a lot to want to come up here. Most people do their thinking at school. Or in a park."

"Trisha said you come up here by yourself sometimes. Do you come to draw?"

His head snaps toward me. "How do you know I draw?" he asks before turning away. "I don't like talking about it."

"It's nothing to be embarrassed about. Does it help you think?"

"Maybe," he says, looking down into the open hole of his beer can. "Drawing makes my mind go blank. It's the only time I can shut off my thoughts."

"Do you have bad thoughts sometimes?"

"Are you my shrink now?"

"No. I don't mean to pry. I have no business asking. Not anymore. Now that we're not...you know."

I take another sip of beer. "What's her name?"

"Who?"

"The girl you're dating."

He rubs his hand against his mouth, like he's trying to brush something away. "Yeah, about that. Truth is, there is no girl. I sort of made that up."

"Why would you lie?"

"I don't know. Maybe because you ditched me for no good reason. Maybe I wanted to hurt you a little. The way you... Never mind."

"The way I hurt you?" I ask.

"I'm not talking about it, so you can ditch the questions, Toby. I'm fine. No big deal." He clears his throat. "Should get going. Sun's going to come up soon." But he doesn't move. "When do you want me to come back?"

He can't leave. It's too soon.

"Tomorrow," I say, trying to make my voice sound calm. "After your shift at the farm."

"You sure you're going to be all right? I still think this is kind of weird. Then again, you're a female, and experience has taught me that girls do a lot of fucked-up things."

"I'll be fine," I say.

"Okay, then," he says. He gets up and slowly walks toward the door. I follow him. He's leaving, but he can't. Not yet. Not until I try, one last time, to feel something. To be reminded what it's like to be loved. To hear someone breathing and to hear their heart, thumping, like a spoon against a bucket. And now that I know he doesn't have a girlfriend, it opens the door wider. It's now or never.

"Mike?" I ask.

He turns around. I know what I have to do to get him to stay. So before he can say anything, I start kissing him.

CHAPTER 21

His mouth tastes like an ashtray. And beer. It's a familiar taste. Mine probably isn't much better, but he doesn't seem to notice or care. He slides his tongue into my mouth, a thick, blind worm. It makes me feel powerless, as though Mike is eating me, taking me over.

I remind myself to not overthink the moment, and how can I do that if I'm thinking about Mike's tongue? His hand goes to my breast, kneading it and bringing his fingertips to a point, like he's trying to draw something out. I'm glad I'm wearing a bra; otherwise it would hurt. His other hand is on my lower back, pressing me into him. Not too firmly, but enough.

We stumble backwards and fall onto the couch. I'm sitting on his lap, my legs on either side of his. We're still kissing but we're taking breaks and Mike keeps sniffing my neck. It's a bit weird. I'm not wearing any perfume. Maybe he's drinking me in. That's a phrase Trisha read in one of her mom's dirty paperbacks. Mrs. Richardson used to keep them under her bed. Trisha had all the sex-scene page numbers memorized and would read the passages to me.

"His tongue darted inside her," she read once.

"Inside her what?" I asked. All I could picture was a tongue popping up and down like a mole head in the Whac-A-Mole game at the fair.

"Her vagina, stupid," Trisha said. "Whenever they say, 'inside her,' they're talking about her vagina."

"He's sticking his tongue *there*?" I found this really disturbing.

"Of course," Trisha said. "That's what adults do."

I'm nervous that Mike is going to ask if he can dart his tongue inside of me, like some kind of soft jackhammer. I can't imagine letting someone's face get that close to me. Especially down there.

His hands are reaching up the back of my shirt now. He's making little grunting sounds, like he's trying to push something out. It's hard for me to see his face, but I want to. I want to see his expression.

"We should stop," he says into my neck. I can feel the vibrations of his voice under my skin.

"We can if you want," I say. "Do you want to stop?"

"Uh-uh."

"Okay. Do you have something?"

I always wanted to ask my mom why she was so reckless the night she got pregnant. Why didn't she take precautions? Why did she give in without thinking of the consequences? But now, as I wait for Mike to answer my question, I begin to understand her a little more. My father was leaving. My mom was in love. And love can make you believe any lie. Or bend the lie enough so that it becomes the truth. Or what you want the truth to be.

Will I still have sex with Mike if he has no protection? Does it even matter?

He opens his wallet and brings out a foil square. He stands up and I can see the curve sticking out under his pants. He turns his back. I hear the zip of his jeans and then watch as he fumbles with something, muttering under his breath. He inhales deeply, exhales, and turns around. I really don't want to see it. I'm too nervous. The erect penises I've seen in pictures always seem so serious and unfriendly.

But when Mike turns around, it doesn't look serious at all. It looks green.

"I got the condom on St. Patrick's Day," he says.

"Oh," I say. My first—and only—penis is going to be green. I'm trying not to laugh. It wouldn't be a nice thing to do. Mike's penis points to the right, as though it's more interested in something happening in the corner. Out of his pants, it doesn't look as big.

Mike takes a step toward me, his arms at his sides, hands turned up and slightly open. The green penis dips and bobs like it's tied to an invisible string that someone keeps pulling. Everything seems so stupid. His hands go to my shoulders, his lips back on mine; his kisses are more tender, closed, but still urgent. I feel his penis on my thigh. Then his hands are on my buttons and he's trying to get them undone. He slips my shirt over my shoulders and it makes a soft whisper as it falls to the floor, an angel surrendering. Mike's kisses are becoming more urgent. Harder. He's a train picking up speed.

We're at the foot of the bed now. I can feel the mattress against my calves and for a moment, I think about the grass beneath the evergreens, how I wanted to feel the grass against my legs as I died. Maybe it would've been better to stick to my original plan. But it's too late now.

Mike's working my bra clasp. The sound of our kissing starts to bother me. Like a suction cup pulled off a bathroom wall over and over. I can't do this. I can't allow anyone inside of me, even if it's my last opportunity. I'm afraid that if I let Mike inside, he'll know. About my secret. My shame. My darkness. What I plan to do.

"Stop," I say. I'm afraid he won't hear me. Or pretend not to. But he pulls his face away. He's so close, his face is a blur. I can only focus on his nose.

"What's wrong?" he asks.

"I can't do this," I say. "I'm sorry. The time isn't right."

"You sure?" He sounds so disappointed I almost change my mind.

"Yes. I'm sorry."

He sits down on the bed, his green penis still bobbing. "I had a feeling this was too good to be true. You really know how to play games with a guy, Toby."

"What are you talking about?" I ask, even though I already know.

"First you make me think you like me, then you tell me we need to break up for no reason. Then you pretend I'm some kind of mutant that you can't stand the sight of. Then you ask me to drive you to my parents' cabin, so you can think.

Then you start kissing me. And now you're closing up shop. Again. I can't figure you out."

"I can't figure myself out," I say, and then I start to do the worst thing I could possibly do. I start to cry.

"Hey," Mike says, putting his arm around me. "What's going on?"

How can I begin to tell Mike everything when I can't even find the words myself? "It's nothing," I say, wiping my eyes and trying to regain my composure. "There's just been a lot going on lately."

"Does this have something to do with the visitors you had the other day?"

"That was my father," I say. "It was the first time I met him. It turns out he's a drunk asshole who doesn't give a crap about me."

"Who was that other guy?"

"His manager."

"No shit? What does your dad do? Is he a boxer or something?"

"God, no." I can't tell Mike. He wouldn't understand. "Other stuff."

"I'm sorry your dad is an asshole," Mike says. "Most dads are."

"Do you really believe that?" I ask.

"I don't know. I'm just trying to make you feel better."

"I know." I look down at his green penis, which looks more like a gherkin pickle now. It seems so sad. "And I'm sorry about everything. The way I've been acting. It's nothing to do with you. It's all me. As usual."

"It's fine," he says, even though I know he's lying.

"Can I ask you one more favour?"

"Sure."

"Can we just lie here, together, for a little while? Could you put your arms around me and just say nothing?"

So we do.

*　*　*

It's nice having him here, next to me, listening to his breathing, the thump of his heart. This will be my last memory of him and his last memory of me. I hope he holds it close in the years ahead.

"I still can't believe you ever liked me," I say.

"Why would you say that?"

"I don't think of myself as very likeable."

"That's stupid. Of course you are."

"Just know that I liked you. I still like you, very much."

"I like you too."

I don't want him to go, but I'm nervous he'll get caught. So I tell him he should head out.

"Yeah," he says. "I should hit the road."

"Make sure you're on time for work," I say. "Make sure Grandpa Frank sees you there right away."

He sits up. "Why?"

"I don't want you to get into trouble."

"I don't give a shit about that." He pulls his T-shirt over his head and I see how skinny he is. He's nothing more than a little boy. Who smokes and drives a rust-stained car and draws dirty pictures of big-boobed women in superhero costumes. My heart cracks.

I need Mike to be seen because I don't want anyone thinking he had something to do with my death. I know what it looks like. A teenaged boy and girl. A middle of the night drive to a cabin. One comes back, the other doesn't. But there's a letter in my pocket, explaining everything. There's no chance of Mike getting blamed.

He'll wonder if he could've stopped me. He'll search for clues. Something he could've said. But there's nothing. I wrote that in my letter. There's nothing anyone could've done to stop me. I place my hands on either side of his face. "I want you to know I had the best time tonight."

"Really?" His mouth falls open in a surprised way.

"It was nice," I say and lean forward to kiss him on the lips. It feels different than it did before, when we were making out. More real. The backs of my legs tingle.

"I'll come back tomorrow," he says. "After work. Will that give you enough time?"

"I think so."

"What happens here? With us?" His finger moves from his chest to mine.

I suddenly feel stupid. "I guess we can see about that."

"Okay," he says, and his mouth is somewhere between a frown and a smile. It's not the answer he's looking for. I wish I could tell him something different, but that would be cruel. And a lie.

"Drive safe," I say.

I watch from the window as he backs up his car. Maybe I

should go out and guide him, but I decide he's all right. He's a good driver. Mike will find his way. I have a very firm belief in that.

After the sound of Mike's car has faded, I turn around to face the cabin. Now, it's only me.

The time has come.

CHAPTER 22

The day my mom died, I told myself I was looking for a girl pirate costume. That's why I went to Greer's. But it wasn't true. Not the real truth. I'd gone to the variety store because I didn't want to go home. I didn't want to see my mom. I loved my mom, but I was tired of worrying about her. I was ten, and most kids my age had parents who did the worrying, not the other way around. I wanted a mom who was like other moms. One who didn't wear gloves or hear voices. One who had a baby *after* she was married. A mom who had a husband.

I was tired. Tired of my mom. Tired of myself. Tired of our life.

But there's something I never told anyone. I went to Greer's that day to look at the coloured hairspray and plastic witch noses because, deep down, a part of me knew my mom wasn't alive. It was a feeling. It's hard to put into words. I walked around Greer's and tried on some masks, lining up the eyeholes so I could see my reflection in the mirror, breathing in the plastic, chemical-y smell. And I thought how easy it was, to be someone else. It wasn't a lot of work at all. All you had to do was think of yourself in another way. There are different people inside all of us, and sometimes, the pieces get larger and take over.

I don't think that's such a bad thing.

"Those masks aren't for trying on," the woman behind the counter said. "That's how germs get spread, you know."

I yanked off the Frankenstein mask I was wearing and put it back on its hook. I bought a pair of red wax lips because I felt guilty for trying on the mask. And I liked to wear them and pose in front of my bedroom mirror, pretending I was a movie star. Someone beautiful. Glamorous. Someone not me.

I took the small paper bag from the cashier. Then I headed home.

* * *

I've decided to die in the Richardsons' small rowing boat. It reminds me of a poem I read once called "The Lady of Shalott" about a woman who is forbidden to look at the real world, only the reflection in her mirror. But one day, a hot prince comes by and she turns to look at him and then her mirror cracks and she gets into a rowboat and dies.

I've looked too long at the real world too.

I'll row to the centre of the lake in the early morning mist, swallow my twelve pills and then die in my cradle, rocked by the water, the rising sun's light spreading across my lifeless body.

That seems like the best way to die.

In History class, we learned how the Egyptians left things behind in the tombs of loved ones who had died. Trinkets and statues and gold coins to take with them to Egyptian heaven (or whatever it's called). I like this idea, so I brought the things that mean the most to me. My mom's old key ring. The stuffed parrot I made in Home Ec class. The photo of my mom and father at the fair. It seems so stupid when I lay it out on the table. Maybe that's what everyone's life comes down to. Pieces of plastic, paper, fake fur.

I get up from the table and gather everything. Looking at these things makes me sad. I go outside. The sun has just begun to crack over the horizon, but night is still hanging on. Things are in the in-between stage. The birds have begun to chirp. The raccoons are making their way home after a night of scavenging.

I walk down from the back deck. The Richardsons' cabin sits on top of a slope that leads to a lake. There's a path that zigzags down and I'm careful not to trip. I don't want to commit suicide by breaking my leg and starving to death. I'm nervous about the unseen things around me. But now that I've reached this final hour, there's no reason to be afraid. A shield surrounds me. Danger no longer matters. The animals sense that. They know to keep their distance.

I hear something a few yards away. A soft licking sound. It reminds me of the sound of me and Mike kissing. I know where the sound is coming from, in this night/not-night world. I can smell it, waiting for me.

The lake.

* * *

I knew something wasn't right the minute I opened the door to the apartment. There was a stillness, a quiet cloud, hanging in the air.

"I'm home," I said and turned to shut the door, sliding the chain link across the lock, like I always did.

"Mom?"

There was no answer.

From where I stood, I could see my mom's bedroom door. It was shut.

what stays shut, stays hidden

Just like it had been that morning. There was a blanket on the couch and cushions on the floor, which meant that my mom had come out of her room at some point, because they weren't there when I left for school.

I put my knapsack on the floor and told myself that my mom was probably sleeping. I'd knock on the door to wake her up. But not yet. I wasn't ready. I went to the fridge and poured myself a glass of apple juice. Then I sat down at the kitchen table. There were bills and magazines and other pieces of paper lying around. I picked up an envelope addressed to "Ms. Heather Goodman." A telephone bill. I sighed as I looked at the numbers, the same way my mom did whenever she looked at a bill. I took another sip of juice and felt very grown up.

The bedroom door stayed shut.

I opened a few more bills, even though none of them made much sense. I looked through a Sears catalogue that my mom must've picked up from work. Everyone inside was smiling, even the old people who needed special toilets and adult diapers. One of the photos was of a young girl, around my age, leaning against her mom's shoulder. The girl was looking at her mom and the mom was looking at a picture in her lap. They were laughing.

After a while, I got up from the table and rinsed my glass in the sink. Then I dried it and put it back in the cupboard. I never used to be able to reach the shelf, but I had no problems doing it since I'd started fifth grade.

"You're getting so tall," my mom had said. She sounded surprised.

I understand why people might think I would've gone to the bedroom by that point. But I didn't. Instead, I sat down on the sofa, turned on the TV and watched a bit of *Scooby-Doo*. The door was behind me and I didn't turn to look at it once, even though I felt it, like a shadow on my neck. It was only when the credits started to roll that I knew I needed to get up.

I had to go to the door.

"Mom?"

I knocked and waited. There was nothing. I knocked again. Silence. I tried to open the door, but it was locked. I went to the bathroom and found a bobby pin. I stuck it into the small hole of my mom's doorknob. As I fiddled with it, I was hoping my mom would call out, "What are you doing, Toby?" or "Stay out of here!" But there was nothing, and that made me stick the bobby pin in harder, in and out, in and out, until I heard a clicking sound and I knew the door was unlocked.

I took a deep breath. It was hard to explain, but I knew life was going to be different as soon as I opened that door. I waited a few seconds, my hand on the doorknob, counting to ten.

I understood that as soon as I finished counting, one of us would still be here. And one of us wouldn't.

So I counted very slowly.

CHAPTER 23

I make my way down to the lake. There are all kinds of rocks and stones I have to navigate around, and my ankles flop this way and that. At one point, I almost fall, but I grab a low-hanging tree branch and steady myself. Soon, the sound of water gets closer and the sky starts turning purple, then dark pink.

Across the lake, there are trees and other people, still sleeping at this hour, or maybe awake. But I don't see any lights. The lake is a black mirror of everything around it. I see the boat, a flash of silver poking out from under a tied tarp. It's upside-down.

It's going to be a beautiful day. I look up at the leaves and think of the lace tablecloth that Grandma Kay used to put out for Christmas dinner. It's been packed away for years. Grandma Kay never uses any of her nice belongings. Her china has been sitting in the cabinet for as long as I can re-member. She didn't even bring it out for dinner the other night. Not that the company deserved it. The way Arthur spoke to Grandma Kay was terrible. To show up, after all these years, and use those words?

More than anything, I'm hurt. He barely said two words to me, his own daughter. He didn't ask what my favourite colour was or what I was taking in school. He didn't say anything about my hair or my eyes. He didn't apologize for never contacting me. For not coming back.

He didn't say sorry for pretending I didn't exist.

And now that I know that, now that I'm left with the cold fact of him, I understand that it would've been better if he'd stayed away.

Because now I can't dream about him.

I untie the tarp and pull it off the boat. I flip the boat over, half-expecting an animal to come racing out. Nothing does. But it's filthy and wet and smells rotten. This isn't what I wanted at all. This doesn't fit into my plans, this crappy, stinky boat. I don't want to die in filth. I look around to see if there's another boat, but there isn't. I almost start to cry, but I manage to stop myself.

"Don't lose sight of the big picture, Toby," I tell myself. "Keep focused on what you need to do."

But why, even at the end of my life, can't I have just one thing that I want? Why am I always denied every time I reach for something?

I walk back up to the Richardsons' cabin. I think about going into the woods, but I don't want animals to find my body. I don't want to be torn apart by bears. Then I think I'll do it inside the cabin. But what if my body starts to smell? What if they can't ever get the smell of me out of the air? So I'll have to do it outside. On the back deck, on one of the lawn chairs. It's not what I wanted at all, but it will have to do.

Besides, I'm used to settling for less.

I get back up to the deck, sit down in one of the chairs, which is damp with dew that soaks into my jeans, making me even more annoyed, and take the pills out of my pocket.

They're very small and it's hard to believe that something that size, even twelve of them, could do the trick. I put the first pill in my mouth and realize I didn't bring anything to drink. I can't believe I'm so stupid. I go into the cabin and grab what's left of my beer and bring it back outside. I take a sip and swallow my pill. The beer tastes even more disgusting now, but I know the combination of alcohol and pills will help speed things up. I put another pill in my mouth and take another sip of beer. The pill goes down but I almost gag. I take a third pill. I don't feel anything, but I know these things take time. Death won't come that quickly. But just how long, I wonder, as I slip the fourth pill past my lips? The beer isn't getting any easier to drink. What if I pass out before I finish taking all the pills?

Pill five.

* * *

The first thing I noticed was my reflection in my mom's dresser mirror. I'd been growing my hair, but I hadn't paid too much attention and I was surprised to see it that long. It curved into a pair of S's at my shoulders, like the hard ribbon candies Grandma Kay puts out at Christmas. I saw my mom's perfume bottles and makeup and her necklaces hanging from the corner of her mirror. And then I saw my mom's pink bathrobe on the floor and the chair she never sat in because it was always piled with clothes. I saw my mom's fuzzy pink slippers, sticking over the edge of the bed. I saw my mom's ankles and a part of her leg. I saw my mom's hair. It was brown, like mine.

I heard the ticking of the Big Ben wind-up clock next to my mom's bed.

I stepped into the room, reminding myself not to be afraid. It was only my mom in the bed, not a stranger. I walked to the other side of the bed and looked down at my mom's face. Her mouth was open, and her lips looked like she'd rubbed blue eyeshadow on them. I held my hand in front of my mom's mouth, waiting for a faint breeze, but there was nothing. My mom looked like a painting, someone from another time. You'd look and wonder, who is this person and what was she like?

My mom didn't have her gloves on. Her hands were scratched and red. Her fingertips were purple.

I went to my mom's dresser and found the picture that she'd shown me, of her and my father at the parking lot carnival. It felt like the most important thing in the world. Without this picture, I wasn't real.

I went to the living room and called Grandma Kay.

"You need to come over," I said. "My mom won't wake up."

I heard Grandma Kay scream and even then, I didn't cry. Grandma Kay said she'd call an ambulance.

"Stay there, Toby," she said. "I'm on my way. Don't panic."

But I wasn't panicked. I wasn't anything.

I went back to the bedroom and lay down on the opposite side of the bed. I saw the empty pill bottles on the night table. There were three of them. I reached over and picked one up. A red-and-blue pill fell onto my sweater. I picked it up and held it in front of me. Did my mom take all of these pills? She was only supposed to have two a day. I heard Mr. Whitlock tell her that. I put the pill back into the bottle.

After a while, I heard sirens. I kissed my mom on the cheek because that was what she did every night before I went to sleep.

"I love you, Mommy," I said. I knew this would be the last time I'd be alone with her. Then I got up and walked to the door of the apartment. I slid the chain link off the lock and opened the door all the way.

what stays shut

Then I sat on the couch and waited for help.

* * *

I won't miss the cows, not all their pooping and peeing and watery, marble eyes. I don't think they'll miss me either, even though Grandpa Frank says they know who I am.

"Cows recognize voices," he told me.

Maybe that's true. But it doesn't mean they liked me.

Pill six.

Everyone will be better off without me. I've never been more certain of anything.

Pill seven.

Pill eight.

I'm getting sleepy now. I'll have to take the rest of the pills before I pass out.

Pill nine.

Pill ten.

They are taking effect now. My blood is poison.

Pill eleven.

They abandoned me. I couldn't keep anyone. I wasn't enough. I've never been enough.

My mom meant to take all of her pills. She couldn't wait to get away from me, from our life together.

I need to lie down. The sun starts to spin. Somewhere, a bird screams.

No one ever wanted me.

Pill—

CHAPTER 24

CHAPTER 25

Toby!"

I'm behind a mask.

"Toby!"

A stone.

"Answer me!"

I'm nothing and no one. Darkness wraps me, a black blanket.

"Tob-eee!"

Call all you want. I'm already gone.

CHAPTER 26

Scratches.
Burning.
Fire.

CHAPTER 27

O pen your eyes!"
There's nothing worth looking at.
"Stay with me, Toby."

CHAPTER 28

Hands pressing into me. Taking pieces of me. I don't need anything.

"Hang in there."

My stomach. My ribs. Give them to someone who can use them.

But not my heart.

It doesn't work.

CHAPTER 29

Something bright. My eyes crack open.

A small star.

I made it.

Heaven.

"Can you tell my mom I'm here?" I ask the light.

CHAPTER 30

I didn't die. I can't even kill myself. That's how much of a failure I am.

From my hospital bed, I watch the cars roll in and out of the parking lot on the other side of the window. I'm in a room with two other women. There are four beds, but one is empty. Waiting for another nutcase to take a bunch of pills at her best friend's family cabin. One of the women is named Meg. She looks around fifty. The other woman is younger than Meg, but older than me. I heard she has a couple of kids at home. She doesn't speak to anyone, so I don't know her name.

Meg hasn't slept for two weeks, even though she's convinced she sleeps all the time. The nurses keep telling Meg she hasn't slept, but she says they're full of it.

"That's what they do, Tina," she tells me. She never gets my name right. "Tell you things that aren't true. Try to make you feel crazier. That way you can't ever leave. Make sure they know that you can't be fooled." She raises her finger in the air. Her eyes look like she squeezed lemon juice into them.

"Beat them at their own game."

Then she goes to the nurses' station to ask for a cup of coffee, which they tell her she can't have.

There's only one hospital in Tilden, but I'm not in the regular part. I'm in the section where the doors are kept locked. There are no mirrors, only rectangles of flat, silver plastic screwed into the walls. The windows are double-paned, so no one can throw something through them. The furniture is made heavy. Too hard to lift.

There are no electrical cords.

We can't be trusted. We're like alarm clocks and the nurses have to keep an eye on us because you never know when the alarm will go off.

I just want to die. I keep imagining the bed swallowing me up, like it's a mouth. And when the nurses come to give me my medication, they'll be so shocked to see I'm gone, all the pills meant for me will drop to the floor and roll away.

✳ ✳ ✳

It's hard to keep track of time, but I'm told I've been here for two days.

"Are you up to seeing visitors?" the psychiatrist asks me. Her name is Dr. Singh. She's Indian. It must be hard for her, living in a place like Tilden. There aren't many non-white people. I think about what Shirley said, about the three Chinese people living in Tilden. Was I really over there just last week? Everything feels upside-down.

"Not really," I say to Dr. Singh. I feel stupid and ashamed. How can I look at Grandma Kay? Or Grandpa Frank? How will I ever be able to face anyone ever again? I need to stay here, hidden away. I want everyone to forget about me.

"Are you sure, Toby? It might do you some good. And

your grandparents are worried about you. No one is angry. But they want to understand. Do *you* understand? Why you did what you did? What drove you to think that was your only option?"

I try to find some words, but none come. When I was a kid, I remember running through the laundry that Grandma Kay hung on the line. Sheets and blankets and towels. And sometimes, the wind would pick up and the laundry would swoop and cover me. Like the bedsheets were trying to stop me from seeing where I was going. And I'd start to panic because there were all these sheets in my face and I couldn't find my way out.

That's what it feels like inside of me. But I can't tell Dr. Singh that because it makes no sense.

"No," I say.

"That's okay," Dr. Singh says. "You don't need to understand. Not yet, anyway."

I notice her eyes for the first time. They're brown and soft and sad. Her bangs hang like upside-down question marks. I wonder how many patients she has. Broken people like me. It must be so hard, day after day. So depressing. I wonder if she has kids, what she tells them about her day. I want to make it easier for her.

"You can tell my grandparents they can visit me," I say.

Dr. Singh smiles and nods. "Okay, Toby."

* * *

One time, my mom went away. For about two weeks. I stayed with Grandma Kay on the farm.

"Your mom is getting some good care," Grandma Kay said. "She just needs a little rest."

I remember wanting to ask, "From me?" But I already knew the answer, even though I knew Grandma Kay would say "no."

I found out later that my mom was in the hospital. She was there because the voices in her head got too loud. Now that I think about it, she must've been in the same hospital as I am now. Maybe in the same room. The same bed, even. She must've looked out the same window, watching the cars coming in and out. Cars driven by people with normal lives in a world that doesn't include my mom and me and Meg and everyone else inside this place.

Knowing that I'm here, in the same place as my mom, makes me feel closer to her. I look down at my hand, the wristband with my name typed on it. But I don't see Toby Goodman. I see another name. Heather Goodman.

Then I realize it's finally happened, what I've known all along.

I've become my mom. We're the same person.

* * *

Mike was the one who found me on the deck. Only I'd fallen out of the chair. I was lying on my stomach, the chair on top of me. I don't even want to think about what I must've looked like. He put me in his car and drove me to the hospital.

This is what Grandma Kay is telling me. I'm watching her, her red eyes, her hair that looks like she hasn't combed it for days, her hands that flip-flop in her lap like fishes out of water. And even though she's telling me this, I can't really *understand* it. It's like she's speaking another language, just sounds, not words.

Grandpa Frank is standing a few feet away from the foot of the bed. He looks tired, as well. His ball cap is off and he's rubbing the brim, over and over. He's barely said anything, and I know he's angry with me. For getting in the way of what needs to be done on the farm. For being such a problem. I've only been able to look at him once.

"Mike called when he got you here," she says. "I remember screaming into the phone. My worst fears came true. I was always afraid, Toby, that you might do something like Heather did. That fear would keep me up at night. I ran out to the barn, to get Frank." She glances over at him, but his eyes stay on his ball cap. "He didn't know what was going on. Not at first. Said I wasn't making any sense. But he figured it out, eventually, and we tore away in the truck. I've never seen that man drive so fast."

"I'm sorry I put you through that," I say, quietly.

"I'm just glad Mike got to you in time," she says. "If he hadn't. Oh, if he hadn't…" She fumbles to undo the clasp on her purse. For a second, I think she's going to pull out a letter from Arthur. But, no. That wasn't her. That was my mom. And that was years ago. Inside Tops. Instead, Grandma Kay pulls out a crumpled tissue.

"I've cried many tears these past few days," she says. "I thought I'd drown in them. Or that I'd run out. But there's no end, I guess. I'm more water than blood."

I can't keep apologizing, but I don't know what else to say.

"I'm sorry."

The words sound so helpless, a featherless baby bird that's fallen out of the nest.

"I have so many questions," Grandma Kay says. "But there will be time to answer them. We'll have time for all of that later on. Right now, the important thing is that you get better, Toby. That's why you're here. I know it's not the nicest place." She glances over at Meg, who's sitting in the chair next to her bed, counting something on her fingers. "But they'll help you here. More than I ever could."

She reaches out and grabs my hand. "Oh, Toby. If only I had known. I *should've* known. That was my job. It was all right in front of me. But my eyes were closed. I'll never forgive myself. Never."

"It wasn't you," I say. "You aren't to blame."

But I know she's not listening. Her tears are louder than any words I can say.

CHAPTER 31

Before they leave, Grandma Kay tells me that other people want to visit me.

"Who?" I ask, afraid that it might be Mike. Or Mr. Whitlock. I can't even think about seeing either of them again. They must be so angry at me.

"Shirley wants to stop by," Grandma Kay says with a roll of her eyes. "She's pretty shaken up. She said it would make her feel better to see you. I told her it wasn't about her feeling better. It was about *you* feeling better. But, given everything, I understood what she meant. Are you okay with that?"

"I suppose," I say, hoping Shirley doesn't bring up Arthur. I don't want to talk about him ever again. He's where he should be—out of my life.

"I'll let her know she can come by," Grandma Kay says. She looks over at Grandpa Frank, who's been standing in the same place the whole time. "Anything you want to say?"

"Nope," Grandpa Frank replies, and I feel my face burn red. Knowing he's so angry with me hurts most of all.

"Well, then," Grandma Kay says, clearly not impressed. "We'll be back tomorrow. Is there anything you want from home? Not that I can bring just anything. There are...rules, I guess. Although most of them sound stupid to me. But it's not my place to question what the nurses tell me."

"No, I'm fine," I say.

A few minutes after they leave, Meg walks over to me.

"Those your parents, Tracy?" she asks.

"Grandparents," I say.

"They seem young."

"I guess they are," I say. "For grandparents, anyway. My mom had me young."

"Where's she at?"

"She died."

"Oh. That's too bad. And your dad?"

I don't even know where to start, so I say what's easiest. And, in some ways, what's most true. "I don't have a father."

"Wow, you really have it rough." She shakes her head. "Say, do you have a quarter? I could really use a coffee."

"No, Meg," I say. "I don't have any money. And you shouldn't have any more coffee. You need to sleep."

"I sleep just fine," she says.

* * *

The next morning, Shirley's head pops through the door-frame. Her hair is still dark red. Not that I was expecting anything else.

"Hi, sweetie," she says.

I feel so exposed in this place. Vulnerable. Anyone, at any time, can come walking through the door.

"I brought you a doughnut," she says, shaking a small paper

bag. "I know hospital food is terrible. I wasn't sure what kind to get so I got one with sprinkles. That seemed right."

I tried to kill myself and Shirley thinks sprinkles are going to fix me.

She nods at the nameless woman; she looks at Shirley, but doesn't nod back.

"What's up with that one?" Shirley asks in a hoarse whisper, as if the woman isn't ten feet away from us.

"I don't know," I say. "She doesn't speak."

"Oh. Well, I suppose it's none of my business."

She sits down on the bed. "How are you doing?"

"I don't know," I say, surprised by my honesty.

Shirley looks down at the doughnut bag. "I came here thinking of all the things I'd say to you. Like we were in a movie and I'd say all the right lines to make everything better. But all those lines have flown out of the window. The last time I was here, it was to visit your mom. You were staying with your grandparents. Do you remember?"

I nod, wanting to ask Shirley if this was the same room, the same bed. I look down at my ID bracelet, but it says Toby Goodman now. Did I imagine my mom's name before?

"And I thought about what your mom would want me to say to you," Shirley says. "So, this morning, after my breakfast, I closed my eyes and tried to connect with her."

I lean forward. "And? Did anything happen?"

Shirley nods. "I think so. I saw an image of an old woman, laughing. At first, I didn't recognize her. I thought, is that Heather? Then I realized who she was."

"Who?" I ask.

"She was you, Toby."

I never thought of myself growing old. I never thought it was an option. But after hearing Shirley's words, I try to imagine myself with grey hair. Glasses. Laughing, like she said. Maybe holding a grandchild in my lap.

Is that kind of future even possible for someone like me?

* * *

Trisha comes after lunch. The first thing I notice is her hair. She hasn't straightened it. It looks like there's a giant orange Brillo pad circling her head. I think about faking amnesia. It'd be easier than having to deal with the truth. I saw a movie once where a woman lost her memory on her honeymoon and then fell in love with someone else. But she ended up marrying her husband. Looking at Trisha, I think, *If I don't recognize her, then she'll have to forgive me. You can't be mad at someone for something they don't remember doing.*

"Hi," Trisha says. Her voice is so quiet I can barely hear it. She holds her hand up, fingers slightly open, like she's a priest giving a blessing. Or someone meeting an alien for the first time.

"Hi," I say.

"Your grandma said it was okay if I came. Is that all right?"

"I guess so."

She slowly walks into the room, glancing around her. I've never seen her like this. Scared, nervous and quiet. Three adjectives I'd never use to describe Trisha Richardson. I start feeling even more uncomfortable. She pulls up a chair next to the bed but doesn't look at me. Instead, she stares at the patient ID bracelet on my wrist.

"There are so many things I don't understand," she says, softly. "I don't know why you did it. Or *tried* to do it, I mean. Or why you did it at my parents' cabin. Or that you asked my brother."

"Trisha, I have to tell you some—"

"I know about the two of you. He told me. And yes, I'm so angry at you for lying to me. But I'm angrier about other things. More important things." She looks up at me and I see tears in her eyes. "Why didn't you ask me to take you to the cabin?"

"What?"

"Why did you ask my stupid brother? Even if you were dating or whatever it was. It should've been me who took you there in the middle of the night. That's what best friends do."

"Trisha, you would've asked too many questions. You don't even have your licence. It's not that I didn't want to ask you. But it was easier with Mike, that's all. It's nothing personal."

My words are tumbling out. I'm shocked that this would be the thing that's bothering her. I never expected it.

She looks down again and wipes her eyes. "I should've been there. If I was there, I would've known. I would've seen something in your eyes. I know you so well. I would've stopped you, Toby."

"But I didn't want to be stopped."

She jerks her head up. "What you want isn't always what's right. Don't you realize what would've happened if Mike hadn't gone back? Don't you understand what would've happened, what it would've meant, for all of us left behind?"

"I wasn't thinking about that," I say. "It's hard to explain."

"Well, you better try to fucking explain," Trisha says, her

voice rising. "You better try really, really hard to explain it. Because I can't believe you would do something like that. Don't you understand?"

She drops her head again. "It should've been me." Her voice sounds like it's in a thousand pieces. "It should've been me who rescued you."

* * *

We sit in silence for a while. I'm numb from Trisha's words. I knew she'd be angry about Mike, but I had no idea that she'd be angrier about something else. Another betrayal from me. Just when I think I can't screw up anyone's life more, I always find another way. That's one of my talents.

I can't take looking at her sad, silent face any more. "How's Mike?"

"Fucked up, but okay, I guess," she says, her voice coming back to normal. As if anything can go back to normal after everything that's happened. After everything I've done. "All things considered. He's been grounded for the rest of the month. And he can't drive anywhere. Unless it's for work. Which means he's been riding around on his ten-speed, looking like a loser eight-year-old. Which he is."

"Why is he grounded?"

"He took you to the cabin."

"Only because I asked him to."

"So, if you asked him to glue his eyelids shut and he did it, he wouldn't be to blame? By the way, never ask my brother to glue his eyelids."

"Is he mad?"

"I don't think 'mad' is the right word. But he's something at you." Trisha leans in. "Is this because of your mom? Because of what she did?"

"I don't know," I say.

"There's something I always wanted to ask you. Did your mom mean to kill herself? Or was it an accident? Like, did she take more pills than she was supposed to?"

I realize this is the first time Trisha and I have actually spoken about my mom's suicide.

"I'm pretty sure she meant to take them."

"But why would she do that?"

"I don't know," I say. "It's not like I can ask her."

Trisha closes her eyes and takes a deep breath. "No, you can't."

She reaches into her knapsack. "Before I forget." She pulls out something wrapped in paper towel.

"What is it?" I ask.

She hands it to me. "Open this when I leave."

"Okay."

"Can we talk when you get out of here?" she asks, glancing over at Meg. "We'll find someplace quiet. Just the two of us."

"Sure," I say, even though that's the last thing I want to do. I just want to disappear. From everyone.

She leans in and gives me a kiss on the cheek. "Get better soon, Toby," she says. "I'll be waiting."

Once she leaves, I take what she gave me and carefully roll away the paper towel.

It's an egg. With a note.

Break in case of emergency, it reads in Trisha's handwriting.

* * *

After dinner, which isn't that horrible, I decide to go to the common seating area. I need a change of scenery. They have a TV on the wall, usually showing game shows or dramas about hospitals. Which is pretty ironic, considering everything. The TV is behind a thick sheet of plastic. I guess so we're not tempted to stick our head through the TV. Or throw it at someone.

There's only one other person watching television, an older man whose name I think is Charles. I try not to talk to people. It complicates things.

Wheel of Fortune is on.

"Do you mind if I change the channel?" I ask Charles. He doesn't respond. I don't think he's even watching the TV. So I grab the remote and flip through, trying to find something worth watching. I need to take my mind off my mind, if that makes sense. I can't tell if being in the hospital is making things worse or better. I'm here for two more days. Then I'm going back home. I need to report back to the psychiatrist. They need to know that I won't harm myself again. I'll tell them what they want to hear. That's what Meg told me.

"Play them at their game," she said. "That's the only way to survive. It's the only way any of us survive, if it's in here or out there." Her finger jabbed toward the window. "Remember that, Trudy."

I finally settle on a National Geographic show about lizards. I look over at Charles to see if he approves, but he doesn't seem to register anything. It's like he's watching a show on the other side of the television.

Just as a frilled-neck lizard comes racing across the screen, I hear a voice behind me.

"I don't understand why you nurses insist on wearing such pedestrian clothing. It's criminal. Where are the white shoes with the crepe soles? Where are the white caps perched elegantly atop shellacked beehives? Where are the white pantyhose, darling?"

That voice. I know it. I slowly turn around and see a woman with thick blond hair talking to one of the nurses at the station. She's wearing a blue dress so tight it looks like the buttons might pop at any second. Her lips are the colour of cinnamon hearts. Her eyelashes look like tarantula legs.

Oh my God, I think, as I turn around and slide down the sofa.

It's him.

Arthur.

CHAPTER 32

I don't know what to do. If I try to slither off the couch and crawl back to my room, I'm going to be spotted. But if I stay here, he'll eventually see me too. There are only a couple of metres and two pillars separating us. My eyes dart from one side of the room to the other as I try to figure out an escape plan.

Why is he still here? He was supposed to go back to Europe.

"Personally, I think the glamour of nursing has fallen by the wayside," I hear him say. "It used to be a respectable position. Now you're all rolling into work wearing burlap sacks."

"Who are you here to see again?" He's speaking with Nancy, one of my favourite nurses. She's younger than the others and has perfect white teeth.

"Miss Toby Goodman."

"Are you her grandmother?"

"You bite your tongue before I snip it off. I am her father."

There's a moment of silence. I look over at Charles just as he turns his head toward the voices.

"You're her *father*?" Nancy asks.

"That's right. Why do you look so shocked? Surely I can't

be the only father who's shown up in full face before. Especially in a place like this. It goes with the territory, if you don't mind me saying so."

"And your name is?"

"Arthur Turner. But my friends call me Anne T. Christ."

"I hate to think what your enemies call you," Nancy says. "Is Toby expecting you?"

"Yes. For the past fifteen years."

"Well, I'll speak to her. Please wait here. Don't go anywhere, Mr… . Christ."

I slowly twist around. My eyes hover over the edge of the sofa. Nancy walks toward my room. Arthur is still standing next to the station. I can't believe he showed up like this. What's his goal—to humiliate me even more? Why is he even still here, in Tilden? His head turns this way and that, like he's taking in every last detail. I see that his nails are still blood red.

"Do you have a quarter?"

It's Meg. I didn't see her come up behind him. My stomach churns. Now everyone is going to know.

"What for?" he asks, one eyebrow shooting up his forehead. "Is there a pinball machine around here I don't know about?"

"It's for a coffee."

"Where on earth are you buying coffee for a quarter in this day and age? It must not be very good."

"It's not bad," Meg says with a shrug. "It comes from a machine."

"You poor dear," he says. "Nothing worth eating or drinking ever came from a machine. My God, look at those bags under your eyes. Have you ever tried cucumber slices? Or cold tea bags?"

Meg squints at him. "There's something funny about you. Are you a man?"

"What day of the week is it?"

"Thursday."

"Then, no. I'm only a man on Tuesdays and Sundays."

"You a new patient?"

"No, but I'm open to auditioning."

"Toby?"

I turn to see Nancy standing in front of me. "Do you know this person?" she whispers. "Is he really your father?"

I don't know what to say. He's factually my father, but emotionally, he's nothing but a stranger. I glance back over at him, but he doesn't seem to hear our conversation. He's looking at Meg like she's some kind of abstract painting.

"I don't know who he is," I whisper back. "I don't want to see him."

I start to cry. I can't take any more of this. Why won't he go away? Why won't he leave me alone?

Nancy's hand goes to my arm. "Don't worry. I'll take care of it."

I watch as she walks back to him. "I'm sorry, but Toby isn't available."

"Well, I'll wait until she is."

"That's not an option. You'll have to leave now."

"But does she know I'm here?"

"Yes, I told her. But she doesn't want to see you, Mr. Christ."

He looks from Nancy to Meg and seems to deflate, like he's a balloon with a slow leak.

"Well, then," he says. "I hope she's doing well. And tell her... Tell her I hope she gets better."

"I'll let her know," Nancy says.

"I've been to this hospital before, many years ago," he says. "Visiting an old friend. And I can't say I'm glad to be back. You really do need to redecorate."

"About that quarter... ," Meg says.

"Don't even try, Meg," Nancy says.

"I couldn't help you out anyway, darling," he says. "Turns out I don't have anything of value to anyone."

He turns, a swish of blond hair, and walks out, the click of his heels bouncing off the walls.

"Good riddance," I whisper.

* * *

Nancy comes to me later and sits down on my bed. I've been hiding out in my room since Arthur left. I keep thinking he's going to show up again dressed like Pamela Anderson or someone even more embarrassing.

"I know you said you didn't know that person," she says. "But something tells me otherwise. Do you want to talk about it?"

"Not really," I say.

"Okay," she says. "No pressure. Do you want a cookie or a juice or anything?"

I shake my head. "I'm fine. But thanks."

She gets up to go. "Just let me know if you need anything."

"What he said is true," I say before I can stop the words. "He's my father."

Nancy slowly turns around. She tilts her head and smiles. "I thought that part might be true."

"What gave it away? His dress or the blond wig?"

"Well, I suppose he doesn't look like most fathers," she says. "At least, not many of the ones you see at the grocery store or the ballpark."

"I wish he *did* look like them," I say. "At least I'd feel more normal. I wouldn't feel like such a freak."

Nancy sits back down on the bed. "I can understand how you might feel that way. It's not easy when parents don't fit neatly into their packages. You had a double serving, from what I understand. Between your mom and your dad, that is."

"That's one way of putting it," I say.

"I'm guessing your father and you aren't close?"

"We aren't anything. He showed up for the first time just a couple of days ago, drunk, expecting everything to be okay. He didn't apologize or offer any explanation for treating me like I didn't exist. He should've just stayed away."

Nancy sighs. "My mom left my family when I was a little kid. She came back, eventually. But it took her a long time. A couple of years, at least."

"Why did she leave?"

"I don't think she really loved my dad. So that was part of it. But there were three kids too. So I never understood why she left *us* and not just him. It felt like she didn't care about me, that she didn't love me. Which is a pretty heavy thing for a kid to deal with. But I'm not telling you anything new."

I don't say anything and only nod.

"Sometimes, parents don't do the things they're supposed to do," Nancy says. "They act more like the kid than the parent. And you know what that makes the kid?"

"The parent?"

"Bingo. It's not fair, but you can't stop people from doing, or *not* doing, what they're supposed to do. You can only figure out how to move around them. It's like the more you learn to twist and bend, the less chance you have of breaking. I'm not sure if that makes sense."

"It does," I say.

"Good," Nancy says, getting up off the bed. "At least I've accomplished one thing today."

"Two things," I say. "You also asked if it was okay for him to see me. I bet most nurses would've just sent him to my room. I appreciate that."

"Oh, you don't need to thank me," Nancy says with a smile. "That was just common sense. Anyone in heels that high can only mean trouble."

CHAPTER 33

I never told anyone I was the one who found my mom. People knew, though. When Grandma Kay came running through the apartment door and saw me sitting on the living room couch, she knew. The paramedics who came with their stretcher, they knew too. But no one ever talked about it. No one ever talked about my mom's death or that she killed herself. Whenever Grandma Kay spoke about it, she called it a "terrible accident," like the pills fell into my mom's mouth. But that's not the way it happened. Pills don't fall into someone's mouth. You need to put them there. You need to be deliberate. So my mom's death was no accident. She made sure of that.

She meant to take every last pill.

When you don't talk about something, it means it's a secret. Or it's something that no one wants to talk about. So while *I* would've talked about finding my mom, and a lot of times, I wanted to talk about it—her fuzzy pink slippers, the colour of her blue lips, her stone face—it was clear no one else wanted to talk about it. This made me feel like I was alone in an arena, surrounded by people I was supposed to know, but everyone was a stranger.

What bothers me most is that my mom *knew* I would find her. She knew I'd be coming home from school that day. She knew I'd open her bedroom door and find her there.

Why would you do something like that to someone you love?

Unless.

Unless.

Unless you don't care.

Unless you don't love the person.

Or unless love isn't enough to keep you alive.

∗ ∗ ∗

I'm going home tomorrow. I don't know how I feel about it. In some ways, I'll be grateful to get back to my own room, my own bed. In other ways, I feel safe here. Like I'm in a hammock above a raging sea. And, so long as I'm here, I know the hammock will keep me dry and safe and will never tip over.

Dr. Singh has prescribed some medication for me to take. I don't know if this is to stop me from trying something again or not. I don't like the idea of taking the pills, but I've promised I will.

"You're not alone, Toby," she told me the other day. "You are surrounded by people who care for you and want the best for you. You need to remember that."

I said, "I will," but her words felt like nothing to me. They were dandelion fluff in the breeze. I watched them sail past.

What I wanted to say to Dr. Singh is that nothing has changed. I took the sleeping pills, I was rescued, I've been in this hospital for five days, but nothing has changed. My mom still killed herself. My father is still a jerk. My grand-parents still don't know who I am. I'm still a loser freak. But I didn't say that because I remembered what Meg told me, about playing the game. And I've decided that being home is the better place to be. For now. At least there aren't doc-tors and nurses. At least there are no Megs, walking around at all times of the day.

"How are you feeling, Toby?" Dr. Singh asked me.

Her eyes were like glue on me.

"I feel good," I said, making sure I held her stare. "I don't know why I did what I did before. But I know I won't do it again."

"I'm glad," she said, sitting back in her chair and writing something down in her notebook. I stared above her head at a tiny nail hole in the wall, imagining that it was getting bigger and bigger until it was big enough that I could crawl through it and the hole would close back up and I'd be there forever, inside the wall, safe and alone.

✳ ✳ ✳

"Do you have coffee on the farm?"

Meg looks at me with the saddest eyes, even sadder than the cows' eyes.

"Yes, we have coffee," I say. "Grandma Kay makes a pot every morning and one at lunch for the hired hands."

Even saying "hired hands" makes me feel sick inside. Going home means seeing Mike. I feel awful for what I did to him. I can't imagine how angry he'll be at me. Not only that, he was the one who found me, and there's a part of me that's curious about that. I found my mom. He found me. It's a weird connection that we have.

"Two pots of coffee a day," Meg says, closing her eyes. "Sounds like heaven."

"Listen, Meg," I say, leaning over and placing my hand over hers. "You need to get some sleep. I know you think you're sleeping, but you're not. You roam around these halls twenty-four hours a day."

"What are you talking about?" She looks so genuinely confused, my heart breaks. How can someone be so blind to their actions? To the person that they are?

"Just promise me you'll try to sleep," I say. "Even if you think you've just woken up."

"Even if I've just woken up?" Meg repeats. Her voice is soft and uncertain, a little kid learning words for the first time.

"That's right," I say. "Just try to sleep and tell yourself that when you wake up, you can have the biggest, hottest cup of coffee you can imagine as a reward."

"I'll miss you, Tracy," she says.

"I'll miss you too," I say.

✳ ✳ ✳

Nancy comes by my room after breakfast has been cleared.

"All set?" she asks.

"I guess so," I say.

"You're going to be fine, Toby. I hope you know that."

"I do," I say. "Can I ask you something?"

"Sure."

"When your mom came back, did she say anything to you? I mean, did she apologize for going away in the first place?"

Nancy frowns. "Hmm. I was pretty young, so I don't remember her saying anything at the time. I think she more or less showed up one day, and the next thing I knew, she was back in the kitchen, making dinners, telling us to clean our rooms. Like the two years she was gone hadn't happened. Sometimes, I wondered if it really *had* happened. That I didn't dream it. She died a couple of years ago from cancer. I visited her in the hospital right before she passed away. She took my hand and said, 'I'm sorry for all that.' And I knew by the look in her eyes what she meant by 'all that.' Sometimes, that's all you get. And you need to decide, is that enough? And even if it doesn't feel like enough, it's all you're ever going to get. So you need to make it enough. For your own sake, not theirs. Because you're the one that has to keep on living. Once again, I'm pretty sure I'm not making any sense."

"You are," I say.

But what I really want to say is, "At least you got an apology."

* * *

I know I'll do it again. I don't know how I'll do it. Or when. Not pills this time, because we all know how that went. Maybe poison, although I imagine myself rolling around on the ground in agony. Or foaming at the mouth. I wouldn't want that. A gun would be too violent. Plus, I don't know how to work one. Maybe slitting my wrists. I've heard it doesn't hurt if you're in a warm bath when you do it. But there'd be so much blood. I'd make a mess of the bathroom and I wouldn't want Grandma Kay to have to clean it all up.

On the far side of the farm, trains pass by a couple of times a day. Not trains with people. Cargo trains. They'll let out long whistles as they barrel along on the tracks. They travel so fast, there's no way they'd be able to stop for anything in their path.

A train is on a mission. A train won't be stopped.

CHAPTER 34

Things look a lot different when you've been away for a few days. From my view in the back seat of my grandparents' car, I notice things I hadn't before. The purple thistle in the fields, the dip and rise of the telephone wires as they fly past the window, the blue sky that doesn't have a single cloud in it.

You'd think I'd see beauty in all of this. And I do see it. See it, but not *feel* it. And I think, in many ways, that's the story of my life. I stopped feeling anything the day I stepped into my mom's bedroom.

open the door

That's why I'm always nervous opening doors. Because I'm never sure what will be on the other side. But I know that, whatever it is, it'll be bad. Whatever is waiting for me will try to drown me. That's why I have to take matters into my own hands.

Beat them at their game.

I wonder what Meg is doing right now, if she ever got that cup of coffee.

"I'm making a turkey," Grandma Kay says. "With mashed potatoes and gravy. Corn too. But not the frozen kind. I know you're like your grandpa and prefer the canned stuff. Although God knows why. Looks like old teeth to me."

"Tastes sweeter," Grandpa Frank says. This is the most he's spoken since they picked me up. Grandpa Frank has never been much of a talker, but I can't deal with his silence. Or, rather, the anger behind his silence. My stomach turns into knots just thinking about it.

"Good with me," I say, trying to sound cheerful. I know it's important. I'm supposed to reassure them. They have nothing to worry about. I'm on the mend. I've put a Band-Aid on the hole in my heart. Everything is going to be okay.

I also know I'll be under their watch. Grandma Kay and Grandpa Frank won't let me out of their sight. And while a part of me is angry about this, I also know I only have myself to blame. Like everything else in my life.

"Shirley said she might come by," Grandma Kay says. "I don't know if she'll be there for dinner or dessert afterwards. Of course, I don't know if she can eat dessert on account of her diabetes. Remind me to check for sugarless Jell-O in the cupboard."

I watch as we pass some horses in the field. I'd like to come back as a horse. Maybe a bird. Something that can run or fly away. Something that can escape.

"Do you know where he is?" I ask. "Arthur?"

I don't want to know, but he was at the hospital just two days ago. Which means he's likely still in Tilden. I cross my fingers before they can answer.

"Please say he's gone," I say inside my head. "Tell me he's away."

"He's gone back, as far as I know," Grandma Kay says. "Haven't heard from him since they left that night. Where was he performing?" She turns to Grandpa Frank.

Grandpa Frank shrugs. "I try not to listen to much of what he says."

They don't know, then. That he came to see me at the hospital. I try to figure out what this means. Was his visit a secret? Does Shirley know? And where's Bruno?

And why did my father think dressing up like a woman was appropriate? I have to smile when I remember his exchange with Meg. I can't imagine what was running through her head. She must've been so confused.

I won't say anything about his visit, then. I'm not going to open that can of worms. He knows I don't want to see him. Nancy told him that. He got the message loud and clear. I'm rid of him. For good.

We pull into our driveway and I feel my heart jump, expecting to see Mike's car. But it's not there. I'm relieved and disappointed at the same time. What will I do when I see him again? What can I possibly say?

Ladybug comes wandering over to the car as soon as I get out. She's still half-blind but she knows it's me. I can tell by the way her tail is wagging. I kneel down to rub her head, trying not to think about fleas.

"I came back," I whisper to her. "For a little while, anyway."

* * *

There's a big bouquet of flowers sitting on the kitchen table. Daisies and tulips, roses and tiger lilies.

"Those came yesterday," Grandma Kay says. "They're for you. From the Whitlocks. There's a card."

I don't want to open the card. He must know that I stole the pills from him. I feel ashamed that I've done something so horrible when he's always been so nice to me.

"I was afraid they might wilt before you got home," Grandma Kay says. "But they've held up. It was kind of the Whitlocks to do something like that."

"I suppose," I say, opening the card.

Dear Toby, it reads. *Hope is the only thing stronger than fear. You're in our thoughts and hearts. The Whitlocks.*

Does he know about the pills? Would he say if he did? Maybe he'll never notice them missing. Or, if he does, it might be a few years away and he'll never make the connection. I'll keep this a secret. I'll wrap it up and tuck it deep inside with all my other secrets.

I go to my room. I need to lie down, to be by myself. It feels like I haven't had a moment of privacy, even though the last time I was alone wasn't that long ago.

At the cabin.

But even then, I wasn't alone. Because I had all my pills. And my stuffed parrot. And the photo of my parents. I suddenly realize I don't have that photo. What happened to it? Where did it go?

Not that it matters anymore. It's just a photo.

I stare up at my Raggedy Ann light shade, trying to figure out a plan, how long I'll wait before I do it, how long I think I can last. The idea is a box of chocolates in my mind, filled with creamy centres. Pink and white and beige. I can't decide on one, but just knowing that they're there, that the options are waiting for me, is enough. All I need to do is decide when I'm going to take a bite.

In the distance, I hear the train whistle.

* * *

I must have fallen asleep because the next thing I know, there's a knock on my door and it takes me a while to place myself, to remember that I'm back home, in my bed, in my room.

"Toby?" Grandma Kay calls. "Can you come out to the living room for a minute? Your grandpa and me want to talk with you."

"Okay," I say, not looking forward to this. They're going to ask me where I got the pills. I just know it. And what will I say?

I found them. In a garbage can.

And why were you looking through a garbage can, Toby?

Because I dropped something or saw some money. And I saw the bottle of pills and took it.

So you swallowed a bunch of pills from the garbage?

Well, doesn't that sound like a good way to kill yourself?

School. I'll say I got the pills from school. Some kid. I'll refuse to name him. A drug dealer. He has connections. If anything ever got out...

They're both in the living room when I get there. Grandpa Frank doesn't look at me, and I wonder if he'll ever look at me again. I take a seat on the couch.

"We need to do something we haven't done very well around here," Grandma Kay says. "And that's talk. A lot of words are said, but that's not talking. We're going to have to do a better job of talking about our emotions and how we're feeling. Frank, you start."

He looks at her. "Why me? I don't have much to say."

"Yes, you do," Grandma Kay says. "You're just not thinking about it the right way. Start by telling Toby how you feel. About her."

"He doesn't have to do that," I say. This is so awkward. Why do I have to listen to Grandpa Frank tell me how stupid I am? I already know that.

"Yes, he does," Grandma Kay says. "Your grandfather has to learn how to use his words, just like the rest of us."

Grandpa Frank sighs and takes off his baseball hat. I'm surprised by how thin his hair is getting. He seems old and young at the same time. He clears his throat and I brace myself. *Let's just get this over with*, I think.

"I guess you could say I never had a family of my own," he says, his eyes looking down. "I took care of Kay and your mother when she was little. But when you came along, it was the first time I ever knew a child from the time they were a baby. And even though I wasn't your grandfather by blood, it never seemed that way. Not to me. You made me feel like I was someone else. More than just a farmer banging on his bucket. We need other people around to remind us of all the different pieces our life makes up. That we're not only one thing and one thing only."

His voice begins to crack. "I just want you to know that I care very much about you, even though I don't say it. I'm sorry that you felt doing what you did was the only option, but it's not. If something happened to you, a very big piece of me would go away. And I'd like to keep all the pieces of my life with me for as long as I can."

He gets up from his chair and places his hat back on his head. "I hope that's enough talking for today, Kay."

"It's more than enough," Grandma Kay says quietly.

"Then I best get back to work."

He leaves us, and I sit there, his words rolling around and around in my head.

CHAPTER 35

I think we need the china for tonight," Grandma Kay says.
"Why?" I ask. "It's just the three of us."
"Exactly," she says.

She asks me to give her a hand taking it out from the china cabinet.

"Help me wash it, will you? There's a layer of dust on everything. And a couple of dead bugs. Not cockroaches. Just mummified fruit flies."

We carefully remove the china from the cabinet, the dinner plates and salad plates, the oval platter, the gravy boat, the teacups and saucers that seem so ridiculously delicate. All the pieces have the same design—turquoise fern leaves with pink hollyhocks, the edges lined with gold. On the back, there's a stamp that reads *Paragon* and *By Appointment to Her Majesty the Queen*. Did Queen Elizabeth really appoint these? And what does that mean, exactly? I try to imagine Grandma Kay drinking from one of these teacups, her thick fingers curled around the handle, but it's impossible.

"I know I'm more of a paper plate kind of gal," she says, as though reading my mind. "I got everything from my first marriage. You do things like that when you get married. First time around, anyway. I had a hope chest where I stored things. China. Linens. Tea towels. Everything I'd need for my new life. As though I'd get married and the next morning, everything would be different. All problems solved."

"What was he like?" I ask. I've never asked about her first husband before, but it seems like the right time.

"Jack? Oh, he was good-looking," Grandma Kay sighs. "He had a thick head of brown hair and eyes that would make the North Pole melt. I was head over heels. But he was trouble. A ladies' man, you might say. He tore through my heart like a tornado and left me to pick up all the pieces."

"Why did he leave you and my mom?"

"Some men don't do well with responsibility. I suppose that comes as no surprise to you. They put on an act and make you think they've got it all together, but that's an illusion in order for them to get what they want. And once they get it..."

She runs her palm along the surface of the plate.

"People will break your heart in all kinds of ways. But you have to learn how to go on, Toby. You grab hold of whatever pieces are left and hold on for dear life. Hold on so you don't drown."

"Did you ever hear from him?" I ask. "After he left? I mean, for good?"

She shakes her head. "He walked away one day, saying he was going to sell some horses out west. And he never came back. I never heard anything from him again."

"Did you think he died?"

"Yes. For a while. That would've been easier, I think. Better than waiting. When you're waiting, someone else has the upper hand. I waited for him to come back. I waited for him to call. To write. Anything. But there was silence. And that meant I was never free of him."

She sets the plate down on the table. "Between you and me, I'm still not free. That's the damndest part of it all. It's the ones who don't want anything to do with you that keep you trapped. Oh well. Life goes on. Best get through it the only way you know how."

"I'm trapped too," I want to say. But instead, I say, "I think this pattern is beautiful," and hold up a plate.

"My mother helped me pick it out. We ordered it through Eaton's. A waste of money when you think about how often I've used it. But maybe there's a second chance, Toby. Maybe it's all how you look at things. You can make something special out of every day. There's no reason we can't bring out the china on any old day for the three of us."

I suppose she's right, but hearing her say that makes me feel weird. And I know she's only saying it to make me feel better. There's nothing special about my days.

We wash and dry the china and Grandma Kay lays her white lace tablecloth across the table. I think about the leaves at the cabin.

"It smells like mothballs," she says.

"It looks like melting snow," I say.

"You have a peculiar way of looking at things, Toby Goodman," she says. "Don't ever change that."

❋ ❋ ❋

After the table is set, Grandma Kay tells me it's our time to talk.

"Have a seat at the table," she says. "Do you want a cup of tea or anything?"

I shake my head. "I'm fine," I say, my nerves already jumping. I can't take these conversations. I can't handle people saying they care about me or that they're afraid to lose me. And I know they're only saying it because Dr. Singh has told them to. I know they don't really mean it, not deep down.

"Toby, we never talk much about your mom," Grandma Kay says. "And that's wrong. It's not that I didn't want to talk about Heather. I loved her. I still love her. Desperately. But sometimes, talking about people who aren't around makes it worse. And I never knew what to say about her. Wait." She holds up her hand. "That's not what I meant. What I mean to say, in my complicated way, is that I never knew how to *start* talking about her. With you. I didn't know how you felt. I didn't know if you wanted to talk about her, or if you just wanted to keep her up here." She taps her finger against the side of her head. "But my mistake was not asking you."

"That's okay," I say. "I understand."

"Maybe you do, but that doesn't make what I did right." She inhales deeply and then exhales, her breath spreading across my face. "Your mom's death hurt me so much, Toby. It was like my body was made of glass, and when she died everything inside me shattered. Every time I moved, every time I breathed, I felt something sharp. When someone does what your mom did, it makes you wonder about all the things you could've done. If there was one word, or one sentence, that could've stopped her. Made her change her mind. I have those thoughts a lot, even now."

She stops to brush the tears away from her eyes.

"I'm sorry about what happened with you when you were

little. How you were the one who had to call for help. It's not something that any child should have to go through. You should grow up feeling safe and protected and loved. You shouldn't come home and find your mom...like that. No child should have to experience that."

She reaches across and grabs my hand. I can feel my bones crunch.

"But you can't go down the same path, Toby. If you ever did that, if you ever left me, I don't know what I'd do. I couldn't go through it again. It would kill me too. You have to understand that. It would kill me."

She drops her head down and starts to sob. I know I should reach out to her, comfort her, tell her it's okay. But my arms stay frozen at my sides. Instead, I only watch and hope that she stops crying soon. I want her to stop so we can go back to pretending that everything is all right.

CHAPTER 36

Trisha calls later that afternoon. I've been thinking about what she said at the hospital, about how she wanted to be the one to rescue me. And it's been bothering me. Why does she always feel the need to rescue me? Is that all I am to her? A cat in a tree? I'm getting tired of always feeling this way. Especially when she has the only thing I've ever wanted: a normal life. Her normal family with her normal house and her normal friends. I can only imagine what she said to Angela and Claire about my suicide attempt. They must know. The entire school must know.

She tried to kill herself, just like her mother.

You know what they say about the fruit not falling far from the tree.

And she did it at your cabin? That's so selfish.

What a loser.

How will I ever step foot inside that school again? Not that it really matters. I'll be gone soon enough.

"I'm going to the mall tonight to have my right ear pierced a second time," Trisha says. "Do you want to come? Remember last time how I passed out? I might need someone to catch me."

I tell her about the dinner. The turkey. The good china.

"Wow, your grandparents are really going all out for you," she says. "Might be a good time to ask for a car."

I remind her I can't drive. "Not that they'd let me go anywhere. I have a feeling they'll be breathing down my neck for the next while."

"You can't really blame them."

I feel a flash of anger. "What do you mean by that?"

"I just mean...well, never mind. Anyway, if you can't go to the mall, that's fine. We can go another time. If you change your mind, let me know. Or if you want to join us later."

"Who's us?"

"Angela and Claire. They're coming too."

"Why would you invite me if you're already going with them?"

"I don't know. I just thought you'd like to get out. What does it matter?"

My face gets hot. "It matters because they don't like me."

"Let's not go down this road again," she sighs. "I've told you a million times—"

"I don't care if you've told me once or a million times. I know the truth. I'm not your charity case, Trisha."

"What the hell are you talking about?"

I start to shake. I tell myself to calm down, but I can't. My heart starts thumping like rabbits' feet. "Your poor, suicidal friend. The girl who tried to kill herself and failed. I can already hear them talking behind my back."

"Oh my God, Toby. What is wrong with you?! Angela and Claire would never—"

"They would and you know it, Trisha. I see the way they look at me. How *you* look at me."

"And how the fuck do I look at you?"

"Like I'm a loser."

"Okay, I don't know what's going on here, but I'm going to hang up. You're completely pissing me off. Are you on some kind of medication?"

"Wouldn't you like to know," I say. "Then you could tell your friends all about it."

"I'm hanging up, Toby. You're being a real asshole."

"Sorry if being honest makes me an asshole."

"Being honest doesn't make you an asshole. Being an asshole makes you an asshole. Goodbye, Toby."

The line goes dead. I stand there, staring at the telephone in my hand. I've never spoken to Trisha like that before. I don't know what came over me. But I'm glad I've done it. I needed to break off ties with her. It's easier this way. For both of us. I need to be alone. I can't figure things out with all these other people around. I can't focus on my plans.

But my hand won't stop shaking as I put the receiver back.

* * *

I don't have much of an appetite for dinner, thanks to my fight with Trisha, but given all the work that Grandma Kay has done, I can't not eat. Everything is laid out so nicely on the table. She's even brought out her cloth napkins instead of the usual paper towels.

"You opening a restaurant or something?" Grandpa Frank asks when he comes into the kitchen.

"Yes," Grandma Kay says. "It's part of my plan to become

a millionaire so I don't have to deal with those damn cows anymore."

"You don't deal with them much now," he says. "Last I saw."

"Oh, I deal with them enough," she says. "Our entire lives are built around those animals. You can't blame me for wanting something a bit fancy every now and then."

"What do you need something fancy for?" Grandpa Frank asks, pulling off his boots. "Besides, I took you out for dinner on our anniversary."

"You're right," Grandma Kay says. "How could I forget about that romantic night over a quarter-chicken dinner at Swiss Chalet?"

She tells him to hurry and wash up. "The food is getting cold."

By the time we sit down, my appetite is back. I realize how long it's been since I've had roast turkey, let alone a home-cooked meal. The gravy is thick with specs of pepper. There are soft white dinner rolls in a wicker basket. A bowl of red Jell-O with tangerine pieces suspended throughout. There's corn and mashed potatoes and dressing and a small jar of gherkin pickles. I can't help but think of Mike.

"What army were you planning to feed?" Grandpa Frank asks as he piles a small mountain of mashed potatoes onto his plate.

"Whatever doesn't get eaten will find its way into the lunches for the help," Grandma Kay says. "And frozen dinners."

"For the next year?" Grandpa Frank asks, but he says it with a smile. He's enjoying this dinner too, and I'm so relieved he's not angry with me. I'm still thinking about what he said earlier, but I don't know what to think. His words just keep rolling around inside my head, like marbles.

I wasn't expecting this, but the food actually tastes better eating off of Grandma Kay's china. It's hard to explain. Maybe it's just that everything seems so fancy; even the Jell-O looks like it could be a giant jewel. I pour gravy on top of my mashed potato mountain. It runs down the sides like brown lava. It makes me realize how much food I've eaten in my lifetime, but how I don't really *taste* it. I think this is true for other parts of my life.

I eat and eat until my stomach is a balloon.

I insist on cleaning up. Given all the work Grandma Kay's gone to—and everything I've put her through over the past couple of days—it's the least I can do. I need to do something that helps.

Grandma Kay and Grandpa Frank go to the living room to watch the news. I scrape the plates, wash the china, put the leftovers in Tupperware containers and foil pie plates, shake out the tablecloth. I need order. I need to feel things are back to normal just for one second.

Just as I'm wiping down the kitchen counter, Grandma Kay calls out, "Here's Shirley!"

I roll my eyes. I don't know why Shirley can't stay away. I don't need company. I don't need to make small talk. I don't need to be around people who don't really matter to me.

Then I hear Grandma Kay say, "Oh no!"

Followed by Grandpa Frank saying, "What in the hell?"

Followed by Grandma Kay saying, "Over my dead body."

I hurry out to see what the matter is and then I see what they see. It's not just Shirley getting out of the car. It's him. Arthur. Wearing a cowboy hat. Bruno's with them too, and steps out from the back seat. There's a wrapped box in his hands. Who's that for? Me?

"No, no, no," Grandma Kay says. "Frank, get them out of here. We can't have this nonsense again."

I feel something rise up inside of me, a slow simmering of my blood. I can't believe the nerve of him, showing up here again. After everything. What gives him the right?

We go to the front porch.

"Shirley, what the hell is going on with you?" Grandma Kay asks.

"I can explain," Shirley says.

"I highly doubt that," Grandpa Frank says.

"Well, howdy pardner," Arthur says, doing this kind of theatrical bow. He's wearing jeans and a pair of cowboy boots. There's a red handkerchief tied around his neck. Why is he dressed like this?

"Mighty fine day out here, isn't it?" he says. "Yep, mighty fine."

Who is he now? I wonder. *The Lone Ranger?*

"In case there were any doubts," Grandma Kay says, "you are not welcome here."

My father takes off his hat and presses it against his chest. "I just want to talk to Toby," he says in his normal voice. "Five minutes. That's not too much to ask, is it?"

"What do you want to talk to her about?" Grandma Kay asks.

"I just want to know she's okay."

Something snaps inside of me, an elastic band that's been

pulled and pulled and pulled and it finally breaks. I march down the front steps toward him.

"You don't get to know if I'm okay!" I yell. "You had *fifteen years* to find out if I was okay and never once did you think to ask or reach out or even send me a card on my birthday! Do you know what that was like? Do you know what it's like when your grade three class is making Father's Day cards and you're the only one who can't? Because you don't have a father? Do you know what it's like to wait, year after year, for some sign that you cared about me? That you even *thought* about me?"

I'm crying now but I don't care. Even if I wanted to, I couldn't stop. The train is coming down the tracks, hard and fast. Everyone looks like they're on the other side of a rainy windshield. I hear Grandpa Frank call my name, but I also hear Grandma Kay say, "No, let her speak, Frank."

"Do you know what it's like to have your mother die on you and watch as your whole world falls apart? What did I do that was so wrong? What did I do to deserve parents who didn't love me?"

I feel a pair of arms around me, but I don't know who they belong to. I shake them off.

"So, no, Arthur! You don't get to come back here and ask if I'm okay! You had plenty of time to ask that question! But it's too late. Do you understand that? IT'S TOO LATE AND I NEVER, EVER WANT TO SEE OR HEAR FROM YOU AGAIN! I WANT TO FORGET I EVER HAD A FATHER IN THE FIRST PLACE! I'M BETTER OFF WITHOUT YOU!"

I turn and stumble back inside the house, ignoring the voices calling my name.

* * *

There's a knock on my bedroom door a while later. I can tell that it's Grandma Kay.

"Can I come in?" she asks.

"Yes," I say, sitting up and trying to wipe away whatever tears are still hanging on to my cheeks.

The door slowly opens, and she steps in. "Everything okay?"

"I guess," I say. "I just don't know why he keeps coming here when I don't want to see him. Doesn't he have a family of his own that he can visit while he's here?"

Grandma Kay sits down on the bed. "They don't think too much of him. He doesn't speak to them and hasn't since he left. I think that was one of the main reasons he ran away in the first place. His mother was religious and didn't approve of his lifestyle."

I want to ask if she means him being gay or him being a drag queen, but I guess they're more or less the same thing.

"That's too bad," I say.

"You'd think he'd be better with you," Grandma Kay says, "on account of what happened to him. But people repeat the things they learn, for better or worse."

"Is he still out there?"

She shakes her head. "No, they left. But he wrote this out and asked me to give it to you. I was going to read it before you because I was nervous about what he might say. Then I thought, what's he going to say? It can't get any worse. Besides, you know more about him now. What he's like. And you're older, Toby. Only a few years from being an adult. I sometimes forget that. Or maybe it's just easier on my heart to forget it."

She passes me a folded-up piece of paper. "You don't have to read it if you don't want to. I wouldn't blame you if you tore it up. But that's your decision. And given everything, I don't think there's a right or wrong decision. It's whatever you decide is best for you."

"Thanks," I say, taking the letter from her.

"I'll leave you alone." Grandma Kay gets up from my bed. "Anything you need or want?"

"No," I say.

"And you're ready for school tomorrow?"

School. How am I going to go back there, even if there are just a couple of weeks left? What if I see Trisha? Or Claire or Angela?

"I guess," I say.

"It'll be good for you to get back to your regular routines," Grandma Kay says. "Besides, summer starts soon enough."

She leaves, and I lie back on the bed. I hold the letter up and can see Arthur's handwriting on the other side. I'm really like my mom now, I think. We both got letters from the man who let us down. I consider not reading it, but curiosity gets the better of me. I unfold the paper.

Dear Toby,
You're angry at me and I understand. I haven't been a very good father figure. Or a very good person, for that matter. I'm sorry for what happened and what you did. I only hope I wasn't the

reason for it, but I wouldn't be surprised if I was. I have made a real mess of things, haven't I? I'm going back to Europe in a couple of days and I'm hoping you'll give me another chance to talk to you. That's all I want to do. This will likely be the only time I'll be back in Tilden, or Canada, for that matter, so it could be the last time we see one another. I'm hoping you'll agree. Even if it's just fifteen minutes. And I promise I won't be drunk or dressed up or anything. I'll look like the one thing you've deserved for all these years—a normal dad.

Please call me at Shirley's if you're open to it.
Yours,
Arthur

I sigh and fold the letter back up. I think about what Grandma Kay said about his family, about how they've dis-owned him.

I think: What if this really *is* the last time I see him in person?

I think: Maybe fifteen minutes wouldn't be so bad.

I think: But he doesn't deserve any of my time.

I think: I won't do it. I won't talk to him.

I think: Maybe I'll regret it if I don't.

I think: Maybe I'll regret it if I do.

I think: I already know the answer.

So I pick up the phone and dial Shirley's number.

CHAPTER 37

Shirley picks up on the first ring, as though the phone is sitting in her lap and she's been waiting.

"It's Toby," I say.

"Hi, sweetie," she says, like we haven't seen each other in twenty years. "I'm so glad you called. How are you feeling?"

"A little better," I say. "I've calmed down."

"I'm sorry we showed up like that. It wasn't fair to you. Arthur convinced me otherwise. I should've known. Sometimes, it's easier to give in than to listen to him natter on and on and on. He's driving me crazy."

"He's still staying with you?"

"God, yes. I'm pulling my hair out. You can't believe how much time that man spends in the bathroom. It's obscene."

"What does he do in there?"

"Who knows? He says he's tending to a garden. I have no idea what that even means. Bruno has the patience of a saint."

"He's there too?"

"Yes, but I don't mind him. He's shown me how to make good tomato sauce. Did you know you're not supposed to put oil in the water when you boil pasta? All these years, I've been doing it wrong. Anyway, I'm assuming it's not me you called to speak with. You got Arthur's letter?"

"Yes. Is he there?"

"He's in the bathtub. He takes a bath every night. My water bill is going to be through the roof. Hold on, I'll bring the phone to him."

"Don't," I say, but she must not hear me. The idea of talking to him while he's naked in a bathtub is too disturbing. I consider hanging up. Then I hear her knocking on the bathroom door.

"Hey, Blanche DuBois," she says.

Who's that? I wonder.

"There's someone on the phone for you."

"I'll be out in a minute," I hear him say.

"Hold on, sweetie," Shirley says to me. "His Royal Highness is emerging from the sea."

I wait for a few minutes, still thinking about hanging up. This is so stupid. I don't want to talk to him. I don't want anything to do with him. But I stay on the phone for whatever reason.

"Is this Toby?" he asks when he picks up. He sounds breathless.

"Yes."

"I'm so glad you called. I was afraid you wouldn't. Not after that scene on the porch earlier. You certainly have a set of pipes, darling. No doubt you get that from me. Never mind, though. No harm done, and it was well deserved. I shouldn't have shown up unannounced like that. But I had no other choice, you see."

"You *did* have another choice," I say. "To *not* come."

"My dear, I'm afraid that wasn't a choice at all. How are you feeling?"

"Fine."

"You've been through quite the ordeal."

"What do you want to talk about?"

"This is hard to do over the phone. Especially when I'm standing here naked and dripping water on Shirley's synthetic rug."

"I didn't need to know that."

"Can we arrange to get together?"

"I don't think so."

"You're sure of that, Toby? I promise I won't drink. And I'll wear pants."

"I'm not sure."

"Just a few minutes to talk. I can tell you some things about your mom. Things you might not know. We were friends back in the day, you know. I knew her when she was your age. Hard to believe, isn't it? Look, darling. You're obviously open to talking to me or else you wouldn't have called in the first place. How about we go for dinner tomorrow? Is that restaurant still downtown? What was it called? They served these speciality hot dogs."

My mouth falls open. That was the place my mom took me. The day she told me about my father. "You mean Tops?"

"That's the one. Heather loved that place. I don't know why. But she had simple tastes, I guess."

And then I realize, for the first time, how much he *did* know my mom.

"Tops closed," I say, hoping my voice doesn't crack. "A long time ago. But there are other places we could go."

"Fantastic. I'll ask Shirley if I can borrow her Chevette. Not that I trust that piece of shit to go anywhere. The car, I mean. Not Shirley. Well, maybe Shirley too. I'll pick you up right after school, Toby. Okay?"

"All right," I say.

"I'll even pay," he says. "See you tomorrow."

I hang up the phone and look at my reflection in the mirror.

"I'm going to be alone with my father tomorrow," I tell the girl in the mirror.

Neither of us knows what to think.

✳ ✳ ✳

The next morning, I wake up early. I want to spend some time picking out my clothes, even though I've never really cared before. But it's my first day back at school. I know that eyes will be on me. Trisha's eyes. People will be judging me, and even though I'm used to that, it never stops bothering me. It never goes away.

Plus, Arthur is picking me up after school. I'm afraid that someone I know will see us together. Questions will be asked. Eyebrows raised. How am I ever going to explain this to anyone?

But I also wake up early because I want to see Mike.

I haven't seen him since I came back. I mean, I've seen his car parked in its usual spot next to Grandpa Frank's truck. But I haven't seen *him*. Not since that night at the cabin. And

I'm hungry to see him again. I know that's a weird way to describe it, but it's how I feel. It's like there's something inside me that will only feel full once I see him again. I just don't want him to see *me*. I can't even imagine it. I know it'll have to happen. Eventually. It's not like we can keep avoiding each other (although we did a pretty good job of it before). At some point, our paths will cross.

So I'm up early to see him come to work. I move my desk chair next to the window and open my curtains just enough so that I can see out without anyone seeing me. The morning light is just starting to fill the sky. It's going to be a nice day. I think about my plans. The train. Or another way. And it's still there, the desire to end it all, but maybe I'll wait a little longer. There's this morning with Mike. And then there's tonight with Arthur. I'll do it later, I decide. After things settle down a bit. Once everyone forgets and we go back to normal.

I'd like to keep all the pieces of my life with me for as long as I can.

Grandpa Frank's words come back to me. But what if that's all life is, I want to ask him. Pieces. And what if those pieces aren't enough? Or what if they never fit back together and all you're left with is a life made up of weirdly shaped holes?

I hear something and wait, my breath trapped in my lungs. Then I see Mike's car approaching our driveway. I move my face over slightly, so more of it is hidden behind the curtain.

The car pulls into the driveway. There's no music blasting from the speakers like usual. It's dead quiet, except for the sound of the tires on the gravel and then Mike's keys jangling as he pulls them from the ignition. He steps out of the car and I move behind the curtain a little further. Does he look any different? More tired, maybe. But he always looks tired in the morning. His hair is uncombed. He's wearing a Nirvana T-shirt and a pair of jeans that look like they haven't been washed in years.

I think about his penis, the green condom. And it feels weird to think that I saw him like that, exposed. I've seen parts of him that he keeps hidden from the rest of the world.

He looks around nervously, then ducks back into the car. He brings something out. It looks like a rolled-up tube. Then, after a quick glance around, he starts walking up the path to the front door. Why is he coming to the house? Has he seen me? He's only a few feet away. I hear the rusty creak of the screen door as it opens and then slaps shut. What's he doing?

Then I see him walk away, the rolled-up tube now gone. He pulls a package of cigarettes from his back pocket, lights one and then walks toward the barn, a cloud of smoke trailing him.

Grandma Kay is up by this time, getting breakfast ready.

"You're up early," she says when I come out of my room. "Ready for your first day back?"

"I guess so," I say. I don't want her to know what I'm doing, so while her back is turned, I quickly go over to the front door and open it. The tube rolls out to my feet. It's tied with red ribbon and there's a tag on it. I pick it up. The tag reads: *To Toby.*

I take the tube and go back to my room and shut the door. I undo the ribbon, which takes forever because it's tied so tight, and unroll the tube. It's a picture. Or, rather, a drawing. One of Mike's superheroes. A woman in a cape and a pair of thigh-high boots. Her fist is punching the air and she's flying through the sky, over the treetops and office towers.

Then I notice her face.

It's me.

Mike has drawn me as a superhero.

My body explodes in pinpricks. How could anyone see me this way? Doesn't he understand what I did to him? How I used him? How could he possibly not hate me?

Something drops onto the paper. A tear. I can't look at this anymore. But I do. I keep staring and staring until my tears start to blur the girl and the buildings and I roll it back up, tie the ribbon around it and put it safely in my drawer.

CHAPTER 38

No one says anything to me on the school bus. Not like anyone ever does. It's just a typical ride in, with me trying to ignore the sounds of everyone else and pretending to read the book I'm supposed to finish for English.

The morning passes pretty uneventfully. I don't catch anyone looking at me and I think I might make it through the day okay. Then lunch hour comes.

I know I won't be eating in the cafeteria on account of Trisha and her friends. But I forgot to pack a drink, so I get into line. While I'm waiting, I look over and see Trisha, Angela and Claire in line for the hot table. I immediately put my head down. If I leave, I'll have to pass by them. If I stay, there's a good chance they'll see me anyway. I can't figure out what to do. After a few seconds, I casually look up. Trisha is staring directly at me. It's hard to read the expression on her face. It's like she can't decide if she feels angry or sorry for me. Just as it looks like the corners of Trisha's mouth are about to turn upwards, as if to smile, Claire looks over and her mouth falls open to make this perfect lip-sticked "O" and she nudges Angela, who, of course, turns to look as well. Then Angela says something to Claire who says something to Trisha and Trisha shrugs and turns her back to me.

It doesn't make a difference if I stay or if I leave now. I've been spotted. So rather than continue waiting to humiliate myself even more, I quickly leave. I think I hear one of them say something as I pass by, but I can't be sure. I can't be sure of anything anymore. Other than the fact that I'm a freak.

I find a spot on the bleachers outside and eat my lunch, trying not to think of Trisha's face. How she brought me that egg. How she's been there for me all this time. How glad she must be to finally be free of me. To have her normal life back.

I can't blame her for smiling.

* * *

I make it through the rest of the day Trisha-, Angela- and Claire-free. When the final bell rings, I make a pit stop in the bathroom. I secretly hope Arthur forgets to pick me up. But I also secretly hope he doesn't. It's complicated. Nothing I ever feel seems simple.

I wait until it feels like most of the school is cleared out. Then I go out the side entrance and scan the parking lot for Shirley's blue Chevette. At first I don't see it, and I consider that maybe he really *has* forgotten and how that wouldn't be a surprise, given everything and what I know about him. But then I hear a car horn honking and someone yell, "Yoo-hoo, darling! Over here! Your chariot awaits!"

A few heads turn, and I look in the same direction. Sure enough, there he is, standing next to Shirley's car. He's waving a white handkerchief in the air. I say a prayer of thanks that he's not wearing a wig or a dress or makeup. At least, not from what I can see at this distance. I hurry over before he creates more of a scene.

"Did you have a nice day at school?" he asks when I get closer. "Learn anything new?"

"Nothing I didn't already know," I say.

"Spoken like a true smart-ass," he says. He's wearing a pair of grey jogging pants that look two sizes too big and a T-shirt that reads *Las Vegas is for lovers*, only the *o* in lovers is a pair of dice. He catches me looking him over and wags his finger at me.

"Don't you give me a hard time. I made Shirley take me to the Goodwill and this was the most decent outfit I could find. Needless to say, you won't be seeing me walk any runways in this."

"Why didn't you wear your own clothes?" I ask.

"Because everything I own is sequinned or bedazzled or has feathers. And I promised you I'd behave like a normal dad today." He twirls around. "How's this for Tilden-dad realness?"

"But you were dressed like a cowboy the other day."

His nose crinkles. "That was a bit too butch, don't you think? I mean, even for Tilden. I was overcompensating. Which is the story of my life."

He opens Shirley's passenger door. "I'm warning you, it smells like cheap cosmetics and a perfume called 'Needy' in here. She doesn't even have a CD player. I feel like I'm driving a car from a *Flintstones* episode."

"Have you been drinking?" I ask before getting inside. "You're not supposed to drive drunk."

"I'm as dry as a bone," he says, going around the back of the car toward the driver's side. "Unfortunately for you. I'm much more entertaining when I've had a martini. Or two. If you fall asleep during dinner, I won't blame you. Have you thought of a place we can go?"

"No," I say. "There aren't many choices in Tilden."

"You got that right, dumpling."

I keep forgetting that he's from here. He probably knows Tilden just as well as I do. Maybe even better, since he left when he was older than me. But only by a couple of years.

"If memory serves me correctly, there's a Chinese restaurant off Highway 7," he says. "Right before Tilden spills away like sludge in the rear-view mirror. I remember going there as a kid. They brought the food out in these silver pedestals with lids, like little spaceships. I was mesmerized. It made the chop suey seem like something far more exotic than celery pieces and bean sprouts. Do you know the place I mean?"

"I'm not sure," I say, clicking my seatbelt into place. "I think so. We don't go out to eat very often. On account of the cows."

"I can only imagine. Well, let's try it. Worst case, there's always McDonald's."

We pull out of the parking lot and turn onto the street. I make sure my seatbelt is locked. I feel like I'm about to go on a roller-coaster ride.

"Where's Bruno?" I ask.

"With Shirley. She's got him doing some colour therapy

bullshit. I'm going to come back and his hair will be green. Mark my words."

"You don't really like Shirley."

"It's not that I don't like her," he says with a pout. "We tolerate one another. She and I have a long, complicated history. And sometimes, when you know someone for that long, you can't move beyond who they used to be. You can't see them in the present day. Everything you were mad about when you were sixteen, you're still mad about. Well, I can't say I blame her. She has her reasons, I suppose. Although she's no blessed angel herself."

There's a moment of silence.

"So," he says. "Burgers or pizza?"

"I thought we were going for Chinese food."

"We are. Burgers or pizza?"

"I'm confused."

"I'm trying to get to know you. Baths or showers?"

"I don't know."

"You don't know if you prefer baths or showers?"

"I've never thought about it. I have a hard time describing myself."

"Well, just pick one."

"Showers."

"Chocolate or potato chips?"

"Chips."

"See, I can already tell so many things about you. And a word of advice: never eat chips in the shower. I'm speaking from experience."

We come to a red light. I realize he's trying, and while it

might be fifteen years too late, at least he seems interested in me, instead of prancing around drunk and half-naked. He looks over at me.

"You look so much like her," he says. "It's like she's sitting across from me. She was around your age when I met her, you know. The same straw splat of freckles, the same mouth, like a heart on a Valentine's Day card."

"Can you tell me a story about my mom?" I feel embarrassed to ask the question, but I can't help it.

"Okay," he says.

CHAPTER 39

When my mom turned sixteen, Arthur told her she needed to get her driver's licence. But she didn't want to learn how to drive.

"It's the only way you'll escape Tilden," he said. "Unless you want to try hitchhiking. And we've all seen those movies about teenage hitchhikers. You'll either end up a prostitute or locked in a box under some farmer's bed."

So he said he'd teach her how to drive.

"I don't know why she was so nervous," he tells me. "Kay drove. Not *well*, mind you. But she still drove."

He borrowed someone's car one night and told my mom he was taking her driving.

"We'll go to the cemetery," he said. "You can't kill anyone there."

My mom was nervous, but she agreed. It was dark. She suggested visiting the cemetery during the daytime.

"There's absolutely no point visiting cemeteries during the day," he said. "You can't see any spooks then."

"Don't say that, Arthur," she said. "You're going to give me nightmares. I'm serious."

They drove past the wrought iron gates and found a place to park. He got out of the car and told my mom to take a seat behind the wheel. After giving her a brief overview of the mechanics, he told her to put the car in drive and slowly make her way around the winding roads. They were crawling at a snail's pace, the headlights flickering off the ivory tombstones.

"What's that?" he kept asking, and my mom told him to stop it.

"It's not funny, Arthur! I'm nervous enough as it is."

Then he began playing with the headlights, turning them on and off, and that got my mom yelling at him to PLEASE STOP or else she'd get out.

"I don't care," he said. "Remember, I'm the one with the car."

They rounded a short bend and then, someone appeared in the headlights. A person, running toward them. My mom hit the brakes and started screaming, covering her ears.

"Why did she cover her ears?" I ask.

He says he doesn't know. "She always did when she was scared."

He told my mom to back up the car and get the hell out of there. My mom did, but she hit something.

"I just ran over someone!" she screamed.

"Meanwhile," he tells me, "this man is getting closer and closer. I was beside myself, so I screamed at your mother to get the hell out of the way. She started to crawl into the back seat and I shifted into the driver's seat and tore out of there. I can still see her ass in the rear-view mirror as she struggled over the seat." He laughs.

"I'm telling you," my mom said as they sat eating Buster Bars in the Dairy Queen parking lot afterwards, "it was a pirate running toward us. He was wearing a hat."

"There are no pirates in Tilden," he said. "Dead or otherwise."

"He had a hook for a hand!"

"Oh, for God's sake, Heather. I know you hear voices, but the last thing you need is to start seeing pirates. It was a jogger. He had a headband on."

"What I saw was real," my mom said. "It doesn't matter if you or anyone else believes me."

I have to steady myself and grab the door handle tightly. The pirate. It was what my mom had wanted me to be that Halloween. Does he know this? It's impossible. My mom said she wasn't in contact with him. It's so weird, hearing him talk about it, as if I'd been there that night, running through the tombstones. I can't get the picture out of my head.

"That wasn't bad for a first effort," he said to my mom. "Pirates or no pirates."

"I'll never learn to drive," she said quietly.

"Sure, you will. It's not that hard."

"I won't drive, and I won't leave Tilden and I'll be stuck here forever."

"Don't say that. You'll get out. You just need to have a plan."

"I wouldn't even know where to start."

"What do you dream about?" he asked.

"Being happy," my mom said.

CHAPTER 40

He says maybe it wasn't the best story to tell.

"I mean, I started with the cemetery and her pirate hallucination, thinking it would be funny," he said. "Show off your mother's wackier side. But it didn't end that way, did it?"

We pull into the parking lot of the Chinese restaurant and he turns the car off.

"Of course, most stories don't have happy endings. Not the interesting ones, anyway."

He told me something I never knew about my mom. It's like she's a book and I've only read some pages, but there are pages and pages that I can't read. I need someone to read them to me. And only then will I have her full story.

"I can tell you more," he says to me. "But first, chicken balls."

＊ ＊ ＊

There are only a few tables with people in the restaurant, which makes sense, given that it's a Monday. I don't imagine many people go out for dinner on Monday. And even fewer go out with their long-lost drag queen father.

"Your best table, please," he says to the hostess. "This is a special occasion."

"Someone's birthday?" she asks with a smile, looking at me.

Before I can say no, he says, "Yes. A day of beginnings."

She takes us to a table in the corner, next to some windows that overlook the parking lot.

"Well, it's not the Taj Mahal," he says. "But it'll have to do."

There are placemats on the table with the Chinese zodiac printed on them and we read to see what animals we are.

"I was born in fifty-nine," he says, using his finger to trace along the words. "That means I'm a pig." He looks up at me and scrunches his nose. "I don't like the sound of that. It says pig people are caring, unique, self-sacrificing and creative. It also says we're insecure, cunning and pessimistic. I guess that sounds about right. What type of animal are you, Toby?"

"You don't know?" I ask.

"Well, let's see. You were born in...what year?"

"You don't know the year your own child was born?" I'm trying not to raise my voice, given how quiet the restaurant is. But my anger makes it hard. How can he not even know the year?

"I was never good at math," he says quickly. "You're fifteen now, right?"

I stare blankly at him and say nothing.

"Fifteen. That's right. Yes, fifteen years old. It's 1992, which means that you were born in..." He stops to tap on his fingers. "1977!" He says it like he's on a game show and just answered the million-dollar question.

"When's my birthday?" I ask.

He looks around. "When was the last time they redecorated in here?"

"When's my birthday?"

He sighs. "I'm not good with dates. Honestly, I never remember Bruno's birthday, and half the time I forget my own. I'm terrible with numbers. They're like another language to me. Do you like fried rice?"

"When's my birthday?" I ask again. "Go on. Take your best guess."

"April?"

"April what?"

"April...eleventh?"

"Wrong," I say, just as the waiter shows up. He places a couple of menus in front of us and fills our water glasses. He's wearing a black bow tie and a burgundy vest. He smiles widely.

"We'll need a couple of minutes," my father says. "Toby, do you want a drink?"

I shake my head, keeping my eyes on the menu. I'm regretting this: How can he not know my birthday?

"Water is fine for now," he says. "Can I smoke in here?"

"Sorry, non-smoking only," the waiter says.

He leaves, and my father opens his menu. "I wonder if we should get the Dinner for Three. Strange, isn't it? Why would they do a Dinner for Three? Such an odd number. Who gets the Dinner for Three? Triplets? Couples with a third wheel?"

"Maybe a daughter out with both of her parents," I say.

"Touché," he says.

"March twenty-first," I say.

He places his menu down. "I should know your birthday. There are a lot of things I should know about you. But I don't. That's what I'm trying to do now."

"By asking me if I prefer chips over chocolate?"

"That was just a little ice-breaker. I know it's more than that. But I don't know how to start with you. This whole thing makes me nervous. I'm trying to be playful. Winning you over with my humour and charming personality." He holds his hands up on either side of his face and wiggles his fingers.

I look back down at the menu.

"God," he says. "I wish I could smoke in here. What are they going to do if I light one up? Arrest me?"

"Don't even think about it," I say.

The waiter comes back, and my father orders the Dinner for Three.

"You can take home the leftovers."

The waiter collects our menus and walks away. We sit at the table in silence. It's so awkward and I just want to go home and jump into my bed and pull the blanket over me and forget about everything.

"How about this," he says. "How about you ask *me* a question? Then, I'll ask *you* something. Sound good?"

I shrug. "I guess so."

He gives his shoulders a little shake, closes his eyes and inhales sharply. "All right, Toby. Fire away."

"Why didn't you ever come back?'

He cracks open one eye. "I see we're starting with the heavy stuff."

"It's the only question I have for you."

"The only one?"

"The only one that matters."

"Lord, I could use a drink. Uh, okay. Why didn't I come back? Let me try to put this into words. I was…afraid."

I cross my arms. "Of what?"

"Heather. Kay. You. I was afraid that everyone would be angry at me. And if I stayed away, they wouldn't be angry. They'd just…forget about me. I'd fade away, like a shadow on the sidewalk after the sun goes down."

"But weren't you curious about me? Who I was? What I was like?"

"Sometimes, yes. But mostly, no."

My face must show the hurt I'm feeling, because his hand reaches across the table. His fingers stop, though, just shy of my arm.

"I don't mean that like it sounds. But if I thought about you, it hurt me. To know what I'd done. Or *hadn't* done, as the case is. Toby, I'm not normal." His fingers make air quotes around the word. "I suppose that doesn't come as any surprise. My mind works in funny ways. You'd think that someone like me, an entertainer, someone who will step out in front of an audience and perform for hours, would have all the confidence in the world. But it's not that way at all. It's the opposite. I want people to like me, but I never believe they will. Maybe that's why I act the way that I do. I pretend I don't like people so they don't not like me first."

I try to make sure my face remains blank, but inside of me, it feels like there's a thunderstorm. Clouds and lightning. Rain so heavy, it's like a wall. I feel exactly the same way as him but have never been able to put it into words like that. I think of my fight with Trisha, how I tried to push her away when all she wanted to do was help. And what do I really know about Angela and Claire? When have I ever heard them say anything mean to me? I imagine so much of my life and make everything seem true. But it's not true. It's only the way I want to see things. I want people to stay away so I don't get hurt when they leave me.

"Look, I'm not saying that's a right response," he says. "But it's an honest one."

The waiter comes to the table and sets a small plate with three egg rolls between us. They're golden brown with little dots, like blisters.

"Everything okay here?" he asks.

"Yes, just fine, thanks," Arthur says.

The waiter leaves and Arthur passes me the plate with the egg rolls. I take one with my fingers but it's burning hot and I drop it onto my plate.

"Careful," he says.

I cut into it and steam rolls up.

"I didn't come back because I was afraid no one wanted me back," he says.

"I don't understand how you could think that," I say as I squeeze some plum sauce from a plastic packet. "But if that's what you say."

"I'm not father material, Toby. I'm a child. I'm a raging

homosexual who dresses up in women's clothing. I'm hardly someone you'd want to bring to parent-teacher night."

"But you never asked me," I say, looking up at him. "You weren't here. And I think having a raging homosexual father in women's clothing is better than what I had."

"And what did you have?" he asks.

"Nothing," I say.

CHAPTER 41

I tell him I lied. Why he left isn't the only question I have. There are more. Lots more. I don't even give him the chance to ask his question to me.

"Did you love my mom?"

He looks up from his chop suey. "Very much. Don't ever doubt that, Toby. I know I'm not exactly someone who inspires trust, but I did love Heather."

"But how can you love a woman if…" It's hard for me to say the word.

"If I'm gay? Being gay doesn't stop you from loving people of the opposite sex."

"Fine, but there's me, remember? The two of you were… romantic."

He sighs. "I don't know if *romantic* is the word I'd use. We loved one another. Just not in that way."

"My mom said she loved you," I say. "In that way."

I watch as his eyes start to glisten. He sets down his fork and rubs the bridge of his nose. He doesn't say anything for a few moments and I'm thinking I should say something, but I don't know what else to say, so I just wait.

Eventually he clears his throat and sits up straighter in his chair. "Your mom wanted me to be someone I couldn't be. I couldn't be her boyfriend. Or her husband."

"So why didn't you just tell her that? Instead of running away? Maybe it would've made it easier for her."

"Maybe it would've. But I felt like a pretzel inside. Living here made me feel like a freak. Your mom was the only one who made me feel normal. She loved what I did, my impressions. She was the only one, you know? The only one in this entire stinking town who celebrated me. Everyone else was trying too hard to make me feel ashamed of who I was. Especially my own family."

He looks so sad, and my heart cracks the tiniest bit.

"Your mom needed someone to see her not as crazy Heather, but as who she actually was. A teenaged girl who only wanted to fall in love. Problem was, she fell in love with the wrong person. And while I loved your mom, Toby, I didn't love her in that way. Not in the way that she loved me."

I know I already heard my mom's side of the story, but I need to hear it from him. "How did it happen? The night I was…made."

He sighs. "The night before I left, we met in the playground at an elementary school. I had told Heather I was leaving. I remember her crying, saying that I was the only one who could keep the voices inside her head away. 'What will I do without you?' she asked. I felt so guilty, but I knew I couldn't stay. Toby, if you learn one thing from me, it's this: living your life to make other people happy will only make you miserable. I had to go. I had to leave or else I'd die inside. I hugged her, and she hugged me, crying against my shoulder, and I remember how smooth her hair felt against the palm of my hand and how all the stars in the sky seemed to come out that night, just to say farewell. I'll spare you the details, but one thing led to another. That was the night you were conceived."

"How can you be sure?" I ask.

"Because it was the only time. You were conceived that night, on the playground, under those stars, by two people who loved one another. But two people who were barely older than you are now."

I never really thought of that before, that my parents were more or less the same age as me. And what do I know about life? Or about love? What do I know about anything? They weren't all that different, even though it's hard thinking of your parents as the same age as you, imagining them passing you in the hallway at school, or sitting in front of you in class, what you'd think about them, the kind of people they were.

"We loved one another," Arthur says. "In a broken kind of way, but it was still love."

∗ ∗ ∗

He asks if we can stop off at the mall.

"I haven't been there in ages," he says. "Your mom and I would hang out in the food court, eating french fries smothered in gravy from a place called Handy's. Is it still there?"

"I don't think so." What if someone I know sees us? What will strangers think? Even in his jogging pants and Las Vegas T-shirt, he looks like a misfit. He's going to attract attention to himself. I'm beginning to understand that he can't help it. It's just the way he is. Maybe that's true for everyone like him, for everyone who's different in some way.

I don't want to go.

"Is the record store still there?" he asks as we get back into the Chevette. "And the Laura Secord? What about the movie theatre? Let's see a movie tonight, Toby. What do you think? We'll get popcorn and Milk Duds."

"I'm not really hungry," I say, nodding at the containers of leftovers. Dinner for Three ended up looking like Dinner for Six.

"That's fine," he says. "We can skip the movies. But let's go to the mall. Just a quick walk around. For old times' sake. I'm a nostalgic boob at the best of times."

Hearing him say "boob" makes my face feel hot. I haven't asked him anything about why he dresses up in women's clothing or what kinds of songs he performs or anything about his profession at all. I don't want to know. My mind can only take so much information; it feels like my skull is going to bust, given everything that's happened in the past week.

I could say I've got homework or that Grandma Kay will start to worry, but if I say either of those things, I'm afraid I won't sound convincing. So I say, "Maybe just a quick walk," and I cross my fingers that no one will be there. It's a Monday night, I remind myself.

What's the worst that could happen?

CHAPTER 42

ook at these tragic clothes," he whispers to me loudly. "Have you ever seen so much polyblend in your life?"

We're in one of the women's clothing stores in the mall. At first, I didn't want to go in because I was afraid he might want to try something on. But he said we could look for something for me.

"You'd do well with some colour," he says. "Purple, or maybe a nice chartreuse."

I don't even know what colour chartreuse is, but I don't bother asking. I just want to get out of here. The saleswoman comes over to us.

"Can I help you folks find anything?" she asks.

"My dear, what we're looking for can't be found in a store like *this*," Arthur says. The smile disappears from her face. She looks at him, then back at me. Then back at him.

"I'm sorry," she says.

"Don't be," he says. "You're the one who has to work here." He's dangling a pink blouse between two fingers.

"Can we get out of here, please?" I whisper to him. "You said we'd only go for a short walk around."

"I got distracted," he says as we leave. "Shopping has that effect on me."

He asks if we can go to Sears.

"I used to love that store. It was the closest I ever got to big-city life. I'd spend hours poring over the catalogue. It was the entire world to me."

"I need to go home," I say. "Grandma Kay will start to worry."

"Oh, Kay will be fine. We'll pick her up something. A pair of glamorous earrings."

"She'd never wear them," I say.

"I know," he sighs. "Depressing, isn't it?"

Sears isn't busy. We walk past the men's department.

"I have no interest in any of this," he says, with a flick of his hand. "Just look at all those browns and blues and beiges. It's enough to make me want to kill myself from boredom."

He stops, realizing what he's said. He looks at me. "Sorry, darling."

I don't say anything. My suicide, or my *attempted* suicide, is only one more thing people won't want to talk about, just like my mom's death.

"Now *this* is more like it," he says as we approach the makeup department. "Follow me. I'm going to show you a few tricks."

I don't want to, but I'm realizing how demanding Arthur is, and how the only way to deal with him is to give in when he wants something. I think I'm starting to understand Shirley a lot better. And Bruno.

"Can you believe this pedestrian garbage?" he asks, looking at the displays of lipstick, foundation and blush. "Never mind. I can make a silk purse out of a sow's ear. Not that your face is a sow's ear. Or a purse for that matter."

"Why are you talking about my face?"

"I'm going to give you a makeover."

"Here?" I ask, looking around. "Right now?"

"Can you think of a better time? Take a seat on this stool. Don't worry, I'll be gentle with you. I'll do my best to not have you walking out of here looking like a Parisian whore. Not that there's anything wrong with that."

"This isn't a good idea."

"Nonsense. Have a seat."

I sit down, against my better judgment. "Please hurry up."

"You can never hurry up beauty," he says, taking some sample bottles from the counter. "The Sistine Chapel wasn't painted in a day. Close your eyes."

I close them and feel him move closer. I press my hands together to stop them from shaking. I don't know why I'm so nervous. He starts by smoothing foundation over my face. It feels like a cool kiss.

"First rule of makeup is blending," he says. "That rule seems to have eluded poor Shirley. Have you noticed her face? It looks like a paint-by-numbers of a sunset. You've got a couple of pimples that we'll cover up. I don't miss my teenage years, I'll tell you that much. Lord, I was a pizza face at your age! The blind students used to read my face."

"You're making that up," I say, trying not to laugh.

"I swear on Helen Keller's grave, it's the absolute truth."

If I open my eyes, I'll see his face inches from my own.

He's that close. I'm breathing his air, pulling it down into my lungs, holding it for a few moments before letting it go.

I hope he notices he's breathing my breath too.

"How much longer are you staying in Tilden?" I ask as he dusts eyeshadow across my lids. I want to know the answer to this and I don't want to know.

"A couple more days," he says. "Then it's back to Toronto to the airport and then back to Rome."

"I thought you had a show in Toronto."

"I cancelled it. There were more…pressing…issues."

"I'm sorry about that."

"Don't be sorry. You have no reason to apologize. Besides, cancelling shows only strengthens my reputation as a temperamental diva. Drives fans crazy. It ups my street value."

I don't think I'd want to see him perform, all dressed up. It would be too weird. But I'm curious too. To see what he can do. To see what my mom saw in him.

He. Was. Magic.

The thing about magic is that it's never real. It's always an illusion. You're tricked into believing something that isn't true.

"Can I ask you something?"

"Sure," he says.

"Is Bruno more than your manager?"

I don't know why I feel the need to ask him, but again, I'm curious.

"Well, that's a complicated question," he says. "Open your mouth for me, will you? I'm coming in with the lipstick. If I say yes, it means putting my relationship with Bruno into a box. And I've never been a fan of boxes. I spent too much of my early years inside one. But if I say no, then I'm not being honest. Because he *is* more than my manager. He means the world to me. I'd be lost without him. He saved me at a time in my life when things were very dark. I think of him as my lighthouse. I don't know if I've answered your question."

"You have," I say. "Sort of. Have you always been…you know… ?"

"A raging homosexual? Yes, darling. There was no way this fruity-tooty was fooling anyone. Not with these cheekbones. I've always known exactly who I am, for better or worse. Which may seem like a strange thing for an impersonator to say. But maybe not. Maybe it's only when you know yourself really, really well that you have the freedom to be someone completely different."

I feel his fingers working on my cheeks now, rubbing the makeup in. Blending.

"I don't imagine a gay father was ever something that fit into your idea of who your father might be," he says.

"It's a bit strange," I say. "But maybe not that strange. You can get used to pretty much anything."

"Open your eyes."

I do and he's right there, staring back at me. And it happens. I see myself reflected in his green eyes, the same eyes my mom saw. The same eyes I always imagined.

"Look at you," my father says softly. "You're gorgeous."

No one has ever said those words to me before. They sound so strange. I can't imagine I look anything close to that word. He hands me a mirror and I hold it in front of my face.

I can't help but gasp. These red lips, these long lashes. Where did these cheekbones come from?

"It's not me," I say.

"It is," he says. "A piece of you, anyway. She's been waiting to show herself for a long time. She just needed a little help."

I keep turning the mirror this way and that, trying to take in all the angles of my face. It's shocking to see myself like this. All grown up. But childlike too. It's like I'm a little girl pretending to be someone older. Someone more confident, but it's just a mask.

And just as I'm about to hand the mirror back to him, I catch the reflection of Mrs. Richardson staring at me from the other side of the cosmetics counter.

CHAPTER 43

"Toby?"

You'd think I was a ghost, the way Mrs. Richardson says my name. Maybe, to her, I am. Or it could be all this makeup on my face.

I need to get out of here. My eyes move left to right, trying to figure out the best escape route. I can't talk to Mrs. Richardson, after everything that I did, at their cabin. I can't even—

"Oh, do you two know one another?"

Arthur. Oh, God. Please shut up. I squeeze my eyes shut, telling myself this is a bad dream and that I'll wake up any minute.

"Yes," I hear Mrs. Richardson say, but her voice sounds like she's hesitating. "We've known Toby since she was a girl. My daughter Trisha and Toby have been best friends since grade school."

Her voice is getting closer. She's walking over.

Please don't. Please don't. Please don't. Please—

"Isn't that remarkable?" he says. "I always say, you never know who you'll meet at the Sears cosmetics counter on a Monday night. Who's going to show up next? Julia Roberts?"

"Stranger things have happened," she says. My eyes are still closed. I can't bear to look at her. "How are you doing, Toby?"

She's right there, beside me. I feel her hand on my shoulder like a fifty-pound weight.

"I'm fine," I say, slowly opening one eye. I see she's wearing a blue top. Her hair is pulled back into a ponytail.

"I spoke to your grandmother. I've been worried sick about you. We've all been worried."

"I'm okay now." I try to smile.

"I hope so. I really do." She turns to Arthur. "Do you work here?"

"Me? At the Sears cosmetics counter?" He lets out a loud laugh. "I've been desperate at times, but never *that* desperate."

I can tell Mrs. Richardson is confused. I don't blame her, I suppose. Here's a girl who tried to kill herself, at their cabin, who is now sitting on a stool in a full face of makeup, next to a man with a high-pitched voice wearing a Las Vegas T-shirt. I can only imagine what's going through her head.

"Is everything all right, Toby?" she asks.

I nod. "Everything is fine."

"I'm Betty Richardson," she says, extending her hand toward him.

He's going to say he's my father. And that's the last thing I want him to say. I look over at him and try to send him a telepathic message.

Don't say anything. Don't say anything. Don't say anything.

"Well, pleased to meet you, Betty Richardson," he says. "My, isn't that an exotic name? I'm Arthur Turner. Toby's…"

don't say don't say don't say

He glances at me then and smiles softly.

"I'm an old acquaintance of Toby's. From many years gone by. We're just getting to know one another again."

"Oh?" Mrs. Richardson looks from him to me. I have to get rid of her before this gets any worse.

"Arthur is visiting from out of town," I say. "He offered to do my makeup for me. We were just about to head home."

"Well, you do look stunning," Mrs. Richardson says. "I hardly recognized you when I first saw you. All grown up. Not the girl who used to play Barbies with Trisha in the basement. Don't let me keep you."

"Thanks," I say, stepping down from the stool. "It was nice seeing you."

"You, too, Toby," she says, and the look in her eyes makes me want to cry.

"It was nice meeting you, Mr. Turner."

"Oh, please. Call me Liza."

She raises her eyebrow.

"I want to talk to you sometime, Toby, in private," she says. "After things settle out a bit. I just want to know you're doing okay."

"I am, Mrs. Richardson," I say. "Don't worry about me at all."

"Easier said than done." She gives me a quick hug before walking away.

"Nice meeting you, Bettina," Arthur calls out.

Mrs. Richardson turns around, pauses, her forehead a wave of lines, and turns back around, leaving my father and me alone again. What is she going to tell Trisha?

"That woman screams vanilla," he says. "Speaking of vanilla, how about we get an ice cream?"

* * *

We sit on a picnic bench outside the Dairy Queen on Colborne Street. The neon OPEN sign in the window flickers like it's on its last leg. I'm eating a small strawberry sundae, even though I was told that was the "most boring thing anyone could ask for at Dairy Queen." He's eating a hot fudge sundae with nuts.

"The Spanish kind, though," he told the counter girl. "I like my nuts with a bit of skin."

I'll never be able to set foot in this Dairy Queen again.

"The hot fudge sauce is too hot," he tells me. "You see how it's all run down the sides of the ice cream and pooled at the bottom of the cup? It should cling to the ice cream. Hot fudge should always cling."

"I'll make a note of that," I say.

"You have a very sarcastic side, young lady," he says, waving a finger at me. "I approve of that."

We eat in silence for a few moments. I watch some of the people going in and out. Parents. Kids dressed in sports uniforms. Elderly people. Young couples on dates. Everything seems so innocent.

"Do you know why I brought you to this Dairy Queen?" he asks.

"It's the same one you took my mom to," I say. "That night after your driving lesson in the cemetery."

"Not only are you sarcastic, but you're smart too. Do you

remember what I told you earlier? About how your mom said she'd never escape Tilden?"

"Yes."

"Your mom tried to kill herself that night. I don't know if it was the first time, but it was the first time since we'd been friends. She tried to cut her wrists. Kay was the one who found her, I think. They took her to the hospital. After a while, she was fine. But I understood then that Heather was dealing with something much darker than I'd believed. It seemed to me like she was trying to outrun her shadows, but she never could. Legs cramp up. Or the shadows are faster. I'm telling you this because whatever your mom was dealing with, Toby, was there long before you came along. She wasn't trying to escape you, in case you think that. She was trying to escape herself."

I look at the flickering lights of the OPEN sign. My mom had tried to kill herself before. When she was around my age. Why hadn't Grandma Kay ever told me this?

"In some ways, it was brave what Heather did," he says. "I don't mean it like it sounds, like it was an honourable act, but it takes a certain amount of bravery to know what you're leaving behind. She wasn't a coward to do what she did. That's what people think when someone commits suicide. They're cowards. But I don't think so. Sometimes, it's about facing something head on."

"I don't think that's true at all," I say. "My mom wasn't a coward, but what she did wasn't brave. It wasn't the only option." Even as I say the words, I know how two-faced I sound. A few days ago, I was certain suicide was the only option for me. I'm not sure how I feel now, only that Arthur has no right to talk about my mom and what she left behind when he's the one who left everyone in the first place. If he had stayed, she might not have killed herself. She would've had him for a husband. Or, if not a husband, then at least a friend. Someone she could confide in. Or laugh with. Someone who'd make her feel like less of a freak.

"You don't think it was inevitable?" he asks. "What she did?"

"I think my mom needed help," I say. "But she didn't get it. Not the kind of help she needed. I tried, but I wasn't enough. She needed more than me. But I don't think she knew how to find it. I don't know if she knew where to look. It's hard to find your way when you're surrounded by darkness."

He clears his throat. "I brought you this. Kay gave it to Shirley, who gave it to me."

He extends his hand. He's holding something square between his fingers. I take it from him. It's the photograph of him and my mom. That day at the carnival.

"This was with you at the cabin," he says. "Along with a stuffed parrot. I'm not going to ask about that one."

I feel myself blush. "My mom kept this in her dresser," I say, quietly. "She showed it to me after she told me about you."

"It's funny, but I have no recollection of that photo being taken. Or of that day."

"My mom said the two of you were at a carnival in a parking lot and that you were making fun of other people. You won a stuffed animal for her. A lion or a tiger. Something like that."

I look down at my half-empty sundae cup. I'm embarrassed by how much this story has been burned into my memory, how I imagined that day at the carnival over and over, the smells, my mom's laughter, the life underneath the flat photograph in my hand. I needed to know every detail, even if I had to make most of them up. And I realize, for the first time, something I never have before.

Everything I've lost makes up everything I am.

"I don't remember that day," he says. "But don't put too much emphasis on an old photo. We were just a couple of stupid kids. While Heather and I might have been your parents, we were never the mom and dad you should have had."

I start sobbing. I can't help it. It feels like there's an earthquake inside of me and the ground is splitting and hot lava is spilling out, and even though I'm trying to hold everything in, I can't. I just watch everything split and flow and crackle and burn.

I feel his hand on my back, rubbing it back and forth. My tears are falling onto my ice cream, and all I keep thinking is, *He's right. Strawberry is the most boring flavour.*

"You were the one who found her."

"Why didn't my mom make arrangements that day for Shirley to pick me up? Why did she do what she did, knowing that I'd be coming home from school? Knowing that I was just a little kid? How much did she hate me to do something like that? To her only child?"

"She wasn't in her right mind, Toby. You have to know that. She loved you."

"No, she didn't," I say through my tears. "You don't do something like that if you love other people."

"But you tried to do it too, Toby. The same as Heather. And you love people."

"No, I don't."

"I don't believe that."

"I don't." My words are wet and mushy.

"You're telling me you don't love your grandparents?"

"Not enough. If I love someone…" My throat won't let the words out, like it's trying to strangle them. "If I love some-one…"

"If you love someone, what?"

"I'll lose them." The words escape and fly into the air. Something breaks open inside of me and I fall onto the hard parking lot and bring my knees into my chest as an endless river of my tears flows across the black asphalt.

✳ ✳ ✳

We sit in the car in my grandparents' driveway.

"I'm sorry to tell you this," he says, "but you look like a raccoon. Had I known you were going to turn into Niag-ara Falls, I wouldn't have applied so much mascara at Sears."

I wipe under my eyes. Although my tears have stopped, I still feel their stain on my cheeks. "Are there any tissues in here?"

"I'm assuming Shirley has some lying around. No doubt she's shed her fair share of tears in here. It's a Chevette, after all."

He pulls a crumpled box of tissues from the back seat and passes it to me. "I'm guessing these smell like cheap perfume."

"You should be nicer to Shirley," I say, taking a tissue. "She's not a bad person."

"I never said she was," he says. "She's just fucking annoying."

I laugh before I can stop myself. It feels weird to do it, considering I was bawling like a baby just a short time ago. But maybe laughing and crying aren't so opposite. Maybe they're closer together than I realize.

He's right, though, about the tissue. It smells like perfume. Roses. Not real roses, but the fake kind with plastic dewdrops on the petals.

"Are you going to be all right?" he asks.

I nod.

"Are you sure?"

I nod again. "Yes."

"Do you want me to go inside with you?"

"No, that's okay," I say. "I'm fine. Thanks for the Chinese food. And the ice cream. And the makeup. And for the stories. About my mom, I mean."

"I know this is a lot to digest."

"What happens now?"

"What do you mean?"

"Is this the last time I'll see you?" I ask.

"Do you want to see me again?"

"Yes, I do."

All of a sudden, he's the one who's crying. He hunches over the steering wheel, his hands covering his face.

"What's wrong?" I ask. "You don't want to see me again?"

"It's not that. It's not that at all." His voice is muffled from behind his hands. His words come in spurts between his sobs.

"I was so…afraid to come…here. You don't know what it was like…for me, living here. How much I hated it. How…much everyone…hated me. Even my own family turned their backs… Except for your mom. You were the one… I was most afraid of. Because I let…you down. I wasn't there…for you when you…needed…me. And you want to see me again? Why would you…feel that way? I'm nothing. I'm nothing…but a piece of garbage."

"No, you're not." I want to reach out to him, the same way he reached out to me in the Dairy Queen parking lot. But I can't. My arms stay frozen at my sides. Instead, I just watch his back shake as he cries.

"I went to my house…to see my mother. I stood on the porch…and I knocked… I was so nervous. I haven't…spoken to her…in all these years."

Joyce. The woman from the grocery store.

"And when she opened the door… I said, 'Hi Mom.' And…she looked at me… Do you know what she did then? She…she…she closed the door."

My hand goes to his back as he sobs. I rub it back and forth, back and forth.

After a while, he lifts his head, sniffs loudly and takes a tissue out of the box.

"I never thought it would go like this," he says. "Not in a million years."

"Go like what?" I ask.

"Sitting here, with you. Getting to know you. After all these years. I don't blame you for being angry at me. I don't blame you for never wanting to speak to me again."

"I'm still angry," I say. "You can't undo fifteen years in a couple of days. But I don't hate you. I can't hate you. You're…"

He looks at me. The word is there, at the top of my throat. I have never said this word and even the thought of it scares me to pieces. But it feels right. So I let the word out before it gets buried deep inside me.

"You're my dad."

CHAPTER 44

Grandma Kay is waiting for me. No surprises there. She jumps up from her recliner as soon as I walk in.

"Well?" she asks. "How did it go?"

"Okay," I say.

"What happened to your face?"

My fingers go to my cheeks. "Oh. We experimented a bit with makeup. I'm going to wash this off now."

I start making my way down the hall toward the bathroom.

"Wait," she says. "Don't go yet. Tell me more. What did you talk about?"

"Things," I say, turning back. "A bit about my mom. About him. About me."

"And how are you feeling?"

"Okay," I say. And I realize it's the truth. "I'm feeling better now."

"That's good. When are they leaving?"

"The day after tomorrow," I say. Then I have a thought. "Can I ask a favour?"

"Sure," she says.

"Can we have them over for dinner?" I ask. "Just one last

family dinner? Things went so wrong the last time. But I don't think they would this time. I'm pretty sure about that."

"Okay," Grandma Kay says. "We can do that. A family dinner."

A family dinner. It sounds so strange.

"A family dinner," I say. I turn around before she can see my eyes starting to well up. My tears don't seem to have any end. "I'd like that a lot."

∗ ∗ ∗

I have to deal with Trisha. And Mike. I'm not really sure where to start. Both situations are very complicated.

I decide to start with Mike since he'll be the first one I see in the morning.

Same as the other day, I get up early and sit by the window to wait for his car to pull into the driveway. I wait for what seems like a long time, and I start to wonder if he's coming in or not, but then I see his car pull up in front of our house, slow down and turn into the driveway. I take a deep breath, get up from my spot and walk out to the front door.

I've changed out of my pyjamas and I've put some blush on my cheeks, making sure I followed Arthur's advice about blending. I almost stop before I open the door, but I remind myself I have to do this.

I need to take responsibility for my actions. There's no one else who can take ownership but me. I remember the psychiatrist saying that.

Mike looks up when he hears the front door open. He looks surprised to see me. Or maybe not. Maybe he's just surprised that I'm actually showing my face. I go down the front steps and walk over to him.

"Hi," I say.

"Hi," he says.

"I don't know where to start, Mike. But thanking you seems like a good place. So thank you. For rescuing me."

He looks down, making a line in the dirt with his boot. "You're welcome."

"And thank you for the drawing you did. It's amazing and I love it."

"You're welcome again," he says again. He's still not looking at me.

"I think the next thing I need to say is that I'm sorry."

He looks up then, biting his lower lip.

"I'm sorry for doing that to you. For lying. About why I wanted to go to the cabin. It was a shitty thing to do. And then to have you come back and find me like that..."

He shrugs and squints, even though the sun is just cracking the horizon.

"How did you know to come back?" I ask.

"Something told me," he says. "I'm not the smartest person, but something didn't seem right. The way you were acting. The things you said. Plus, your mom." He looks down again. "Knowing what I knew, I just stopped the car and turned back around. You remember anything?"

"No," I say. "Everything is a blur. Was I awake when you found me?"

"Sort of," he says. "You were kind of mumbling. Something about a mask. Or hiding. I didn't know what to do, but on TV they always make people puke, so I tried to do that. And you did. All over my hand."

"Sorry." I'm so embarrassed by all of this. "Again."

"Then I put you in the car and tore off for the hospital. I kept talking to you the whole way there. Told you jokes. Sang songs. Yelled at you. Anything I could think of to keep you from..."

Now it's my turn to look down. "I know."

"Can I ask you something?"

"Sure."

"Why did you do it? Was it something I said? Or did? I'm trying to understand, but it's not easy."

"It wasn't about anything you did or said. It was about me, Mike. That's all."

When I say the words, something goes off in my head. My mom's suicide. What my father said. It wasn't about me. It was about her. I think I finally understand that for the first time since her death.

"I was in a dark hole," I say. "And no matter who came to the opening of the hole and looked down or offered me a hand, it didn't matter. I didn't want help. I only wanted to stay inside the hole. It was comfortable. I guess I thought I deserved to stay in the hole."

He looks off toward the cows. I look over too. They're slowly coming in from the fields. Time for their day to begin. The way it does every day. It must be so boring for them. In the distance, I hear the long whistle of a passing train. I stop for a second to listen, remembering my plan, wondering if it's still the plan.

"You realize what could've happened, don't you?" he asks.

"Yes," I say. "I do."

"I would've been the one. To find you the next day. If you went through with it." He turns back to me. "Did you think about that? What that would be like? For me?"

I feel something cold, like an ice cube, run down my spine. "No," I say, but I'm not sure he hears me. My voice is more like a breath. How could I do that to him? The same as what my mom had done to me? But I'm not lying. I hadn't thought about Mike at all. Not about the consequences. What would happen after I died. I only thought about dying. How could I be so unfair to him? Why would I do that to someone I care about? Maybe it was the same for my mom. Maybe she wasn't even thinking about me coming home from school that day. Maybe she was too busy thinking about more urgent things. Not the future, not the consequences, just the moment she was in, blind to everyone else.

"I'm sorry, Mike," I say, fighting back tears. "I didn't think about it. I can't believe I'd put you through that. I don't know what was wrong with me. I wouldn't blame you if you never forgive me."

"I'll get there," he says. "At least I have a better understanding of why you broke up with me. Sort of. How are you feeling now?"

"Better," I say. "A little better each day."

"Maybe we can get together," he says. "When you're feeling up to it. See a movie. Go for a drive. Maybe we can just sit in the car and talk."

"I'd like that," I say, but I'm not sure what Mike means

by this. I don't want to get back together with him. I know this. But I owe him so much. And I'm not sure how *he* feels.

"I better get going or else your grandpa will have my nuts in a sling."

I lean over and give him a quick kiss on the cheek. "Thank you."

"I'm not saying 'you're welcome,' again, Toby."

* * *

When I get back inside the house, Grandma Kay is standing at the window. She's been watching Mike and me this whole time. I can tell by the look on her face.

"You're up early this morning," she says.

"I needed to take care of something," I say.

"And that something was Mike?"

"I haven't spoken to him since that day. At the cabin."

She asks me to join her in the kitchen. "I'm getting breakfast ready and I could use the help. Might as well put you to good use while you're up. Toby, can we talk for a minute about Mike?"

Oh, God. What does she want to talk about? I hope not sex. The last time Grandma Kay brought up the subject of sex with me, she hauled out an old illustrated health book with diagrams of people split in half. It was disturbing to look at the half-penises and half-vaginas.

"You're very young," she says, taking some plates from the cupboard. "And you have all the time in the world for many things. Love being one of them. Sometimes, girls feel that when someone likes them, they're obligated to respond. That's what men teach you, anyway. Like you owe him something when you never asked for anything in the first place."

She starts to crack eggs, and I watch as each yolk and egg white plops into the bowl.

"I'm sure Mike is nice enough, but I don't see much spark in his eyes. I don't think he knows what he's doing tomorrow, let alone the rest of his life. You don't want to end up here, do you? On a farm, cooking for hired hands that barely even acknowledge you? So chained by your day that every waking moment revolves around those stupid cows? Wishing and wondering if there was something else? Something better?"

She stops to wipe her eyes with her sleeve. I feel terrible watching her cry like this.

"It hasn't been a bad life, Toby. Don't get me wrong. I've had my share of hardships. Your mother tore my heart to pieces. She's a hole in my heart that I'll never be able to fill. But she gave me you. So how could I wish for anything else but the life in front of me?"

I do something I've never done before. I go over and wrap my arms around Grandma Kay. Egg guts splat on my arm, but I don't care. This is more important. I hear Grandma Kay make a sound, like she's surprised, and that just makes me hug her tighter.

"You live the life *you* want to live, Toby," she says. "Don't let anyone get in the way of that. And know that I'll always be here, cheering you on."

CHAPTER 45

I can't keep avoiding Trisha, so when I see her later at school, standing against the lockers with Claire and Angela, I gather up all my courage and walk over. I can feel their eyes on me.

"Hi," I say to Trisha.

"Hi," she says.

"Do you have some time to talk?" I glance over at Claire and Angela who are now leaning in, trying to hear everything.

"Now?" she asks.

I nod. "I won't be long," I say.

We walk off toward the far end of the hall and sit down on the floor in front of the Shop class.

"What's going on?" she asks.

I take a deep breath. "Trisha, I'm sorry about what I said the other day. On the phone. It wasn't right of me to go after you like that."

"No shit," she says. "You've never gone off on me like that before. I thought we were friends."

"We *are* friends," I say.

"Then why were you so angry?"

"I was feeling sorry for myself."

"Because of what you did?"

"That. And other things. Trisha, let me get this out because it's really hard for me to say, but it's important. I really appreciate everything you do for me, but you don't need to do it anymore. It's okay."

"What are you talking about?"

I sigh. "I'm talking about you feeling like you have to be my friend. You don't need to feel that way."

"I totally don't get what you're talking about. Of course I'm your friend. Why wouldn't I be?"

"But we're not friends in an equal way. I'm just someone who's been around in your life since we were kids. I don't fit in with your other friends. I don't belong. I see how they look at me."

"Claire and Angela? Uh, okay. So Claire has a phobia about public toilets and won't use them. And Angela is totally weird about food. I mean, she eats only iceberg lettuce every day for lunch. So they're just as weird as you."

"Not that weird," I say. "Not weird enough to try to kill yourself."

She places her hand on my knee. "I don't know if that's weird, Toby. Maybe sad. Not that I think you're a sad person. But you've had some shitty things happen in your life. Do you even realize how much I look up to you?"

I turn to her. "What are you talking about?"

"You've been through so much in your life. Between your mom and now your dad, growing up with your grandparents, living on a farm, which I could never do. I mean, the smell alone. You've overcome things that would make most people crumble. You think Claire or Angela could ever deal with what you've dealt with? Claire can't pee while she's at school, let alone deal with her mom's suicide. You're amazing, Toby. You're like this superstar in my eyes. That's why, when you did what you did at the cabin, it hurt so much. I just couldn't believe someone so strong would do that."

Me? Strong? Amazing? I've never thought about myself that way. Not even for a minute.

But maybe she's right. I *have* been through a lot. More than anyone else I know, anyway. And I'm still here. Standing. Or, really, sitting on the floor at this particular moment. But still here. Still Toby.

I've survived.

"You're my best friend," Trisha says. "My *only* true friend. I hope you know that."

"I do," I say, and I mean it.

I really do.

"Do you want to come for dinner tomorrow night?" I ask. "You can meet my father."

"Oh my God!" Trisha squeals, clapping. "Yes, of course! What will he be wearing?"

"I don't know. Clothes?"

"I can't believe I'm going to meet a real live drag queen. This is going to be the best dinner ever."

"I wouldn't get your hopes up too high," I say. "He's more normal than you might think. One other thing. I'm going to invite Mike too."

She rolls her eyes. "Why? Mike is totally going to ruin everything. He's going to be all weirded out by your dad."

"Maybe," I say. "But it wouldn't feel right not having him there, not after everything. He saved me, Trisha. I can't forget that."

"Maybe he's not as much of an asshole as I like to think," she says. "In some ways, I guess I'm proud of him for doing what he did. Never tell him I said that."

"See you tomorrow?" I ask.

"See you tomorrow," she says.

CHAPTER 46

Our guests arrive late afternoon the next day. Shirley's Chevette pulls into the driveway and when I hear the wheels on the gravel, I think of the previous visit and all the excitement I felt when he first arrived.

My father.

But it wasn't just excitement. There was fear too. It was like every single year of my life was wound up so tightly in that moment. Now, as I watch the passenger door open and Arthur step out, wearing a large pair of sunglasses, a blousy-type white shirt and a blue-and-red scarf tied around his neck, it's hard to understand what I feel. Not excitement. Maybe something more real. Something that lasts longer than excitement.

"Is he blitzed?" Grandma Kay asks from behind my shoulder. "Lord, tell me he isn't."

"Doesn't seem that way," I say, cautiously. "He's not being carried out, at least."

"That boy has made me nervous since the first time Heather brought him to the house," Grandma Kay mutters. "I don't think I'll ever get used to him."

"Smell the bouquet of cow shit," Arthur announces to

no one in particular, sweeping his arms wide and inhaling deeply. Bruno steps out from the back seat, carrying the same brightly wrapped box as last time. I don't think I'll be able to look him in the eye. The driver's door opens and Shirley steps out, looking stressed.

"I'm never getting into a car with you again!" she yells at Arthur. "You don't grab the wheel and honk at elderly ladies when they're crossing the street!"

"She was moving slower than a glacier," he says. "Besides, it got her heart beating again."

Looking at the three of them, I wonder what my mom would look like now. Would she dye her hair like Shirley, wanting to look younger? Would she complain about the beginnings of wrinkles? Would she still be working at Sears? Would we still be living in our apartment? Would my mom have fallen in love again?

I'd like that for her.

"Round three," Shirley says. She doesn't seem to notice how much her voice carries. "Remember what I said. This is your last shot. For the love of Christ and everything that's holy in this world, don't screw it up. Again."

"You don't have to worry about me," Arthur says. "I'll be so squeaky clean, you'll see your reflection in my forehead."

Bruno looks over and sees me standing in the window. He raises his hand. My first instinct is to duck behind the curtain, but I manage to stay in place. I feel self-conscious. Exposed. He must think I'm a total whack job.

"Hello, darlings!" Arthur calls out to us with a wave.

"Don't call them that," Shirley says, swatting his arm.

"Why not?"

"It's patronizing."

"What would you rather me call them?"

"How about by their names?"

"In that case, I'm going to call you by *your* real name: Miss Stick-in-Her-Ass."

Grandma Kay steps to the front door. "We'll get through this, Toby."

* * *

We sit on the porch instead of going inside. Everyone says the weather is too nice. Bruno hands the box to Grandma Kay and says it's for her. I feel a bit disappointed. Why is she getting a gift? I'm the long-lost daughter, after all.

"I don't know if you like," he says to her. "I'm no sure of your style, and Arturo, he was no help."

"I told you her taste was page 147 of the Sears catalogue," Arthur says.

"I'm actually more of a page 148," Grandma Kay says.

"Well, well. Good one, Kay. Nice to see you sass it up."

"Thank you for doing this, Bruno. You didn't have to."

"I want to," Bruno says. "I feel like I know you. And Heather." He looks down. "I'm sorry for what happened to her."

"Thank you," Grandma Kay says. "We all are."

There are a few seconds of silence. I look over at one of the empty lawn chairs, imagining my mom here. Maybe, in some ways, she is.

"Shouldn't there be a punch bowl out here?" Arthur asks.

"I've always felt strongly that porches and punch go hand in hand."

"I have some lemonade."

"Does it come with vodka?"

Grandma Kay's face turns hard. "There's not a drop of liquor in this house. You'll have to make do for one night. If you can stand it."

"Open your gift," I say.

She tears the wrapping and opens a small box. Inside there's a silk scarf that looks like a watercolour painting. Soft pinks and blues and reds.

"It's from Florence," Bruno says. "But you can find anyplace, I'm sure."

Grandma Kay runs the scarf through her fingers. "It's beautiful. I don't own anything like this. Where will I even wear it?"

"To the A&P," Arthur says. "You'll have the stock boys falling over one another."

"Wear when you like," Bruno says. "Even here, at your house. Even if no one see you."

"Thank you," Grandma Kay says. "That was very thoughtful."

I look over to see Mike's car pull into the driveway. I make out Trisha's shape in the passenger seat. I start to wonder if inviting them was a mistake. What was I thinking? But it's too late now.

"Well, heavens to Betsy," Arthur says, getting up from his chair. "Looks like we have company."

Mike and Trisha step out from the car. As soon as Mike

sees my father, his eyebrows shoot up high on his forehead. He looks Arthur up and down, taking in every inch. Trisha looks like someone told her it's Christmas and the biggest present under the tree has her name on it.

"My Lord, look at that red hair on the two of you," Arthur calls out. "It's the colour of wheat fields in the fading sunlight of a blazing autumn day."

Why is he talking with a southern accent? Why can't he just act normal?

"Y'all twins or somethin'?"

"Ew," Trisha says, crinkling her nose. "We're, like, barely related."

"They're brother and sister," I say. "Mike, Trisha, this is Arthur. My...father."

The word sounds so strange coming from my mouth.

"Trisha is my best friend," I say. "Mike is...also a friend." My face grows hot. I must be blushing. This is the most awkward introduction ever.

"And this is Bruno," I say. "My father's..." I don't even know how to introduce him.

"Manager," Bruno says. "I try to manage as best I can."

Mike looks skeptical. Maybe I should have told him. I was expecting Trisha might say something. Obviously, she didn't.

Arthur steps down the front steps and extends his hand toward them, but not in the way you do for handshakes. His hand dangles, a leaf about to drop from a branch.

"And how do you do, Michael and Patricia?"

Mike looks at Arthur's hand and I can tell he doesn't know what to do with it. He sort of takes the hand from underneath and moves it up and down. Arthur doesn't look impressed. He does the same to Trisha and she takes his hand and does this little curtsy, which is the most ridiculous thing ever.

"Pleased to meet you," Trisha says. "I've heard a lot about you. In the past couple of days, I mean. I didn't hear much about you before then. Given that you weren't around. And we knew nothing about you. I'm going to shut up now before I say anything more."

"I appreciate someone who exercises self-control," Arthur says. "It's never been one of my strengths. I suppose that comes as a surprise to no one."

"It's nice that you could join us for dinner," Grandma Kay says. There's a stiffness in her voice that I know is caused by Mike. She's uncomfortable having him here, not as a farm hand but as someone different. Not as my boyfriend, which he isn't, but not just a friend either. Mike is somewhere in between, which, when I think about it, is like a lot of people in my life.

My parents/grandparents.

My father/Arthur.

My boyfriend/Mike.

Maybe it's okay to have slashes between those people. Maybe it's not as confusing as I think.

"I hope you like roast beef," Grandma Kay says. "That's what Toby wanted. So you don't have much of a choice."

"Fine with me," Trisha says. "My mom never makes a roast beef. Or when she does, it comes out looking like something you'd use to scrub calluses."

"Don't get your hopes up too high," Grandma Kay says. "I can't guarantee mine will be much better."

"Well, it can't get any worse, believe me," Trisha says. "Here, my mom sent these."

She hands Grandma Kay a white Tupperware container. "Squares. There's cereal in them, I think. Peanuts too. Or walnuts. She told me, but I wasn't really paying attention." She turns to my father. "Why aren't you all dressed up?"

Arthur looks down at himself. "Am I naked and don't realize it?"

"I mean, you know, in your performer clothes. I was expecting you to be in a gown with a feather boa and tons of makeup."

"My dear child," Arthur says. "I don't dress like that all the time. How uncomfortable do you want me to be?"

"Oh." Trisha looks disappointed.

"Maybe later," he says, which causes me to panic. What does he mean by that? I don't want to see him dressed up. I wouldn't be able to handle that. It would be too weird. Especially in front of everyone.

"Gown?" Mike asks. "Makeup?"

Arthur walks over to him. "You look absolutely flabbergasted, Michael. I suppose no one bothered to tell you."

He takes a step back. "Tell me what?"

"He's a drag queen," Trisha says.

Arthur whips around. "You watch your tongue, missy. I am *not* a drag queen. Do you know what drag queens do? They lip sync. Badly. To the voices of other people. Female singers far more talented than they are. How pathetic. No,

Arthur Turner is not a dime store drag queen in a cheap wig. I am much more than that. I am one of, if not *the*, top female impersonators in the world."

His nose rises up toward the trees.

"What's the difference?" Trisha asks.

"The *difference*?!?" Arthur says with a snort. "Where do you want me to begin? For starters, I don't lip sync. I sing live and do all my own voices. All the glamorous stars you'd expect. Bette Davis. Mae West. Tallulah Bankhead."

Trisha blinks blankly back at him.

"Don't tell me you've never heard of them," Arthur says.

Trisha shrugs.

"This younger generation will be the death of me." He covers his face with his hands.

"How many impersonations do you do?" Trisha asks.

"Dozens."

"Is that like having split personalities?"

"That's close," Bruno says.

"Oh, you be quiet," Arthur says. "You can be as many people as you want to be in this world." He glances over at me. "Let no one tell you otherwise."

"I'm so confused," Mike says.

"Join the club," Shirley says, stepping down from the porch. "This one brings it wherever he goes. Confusion. Pandemonium. Mass destruction."

"Better that than a yawn," Arthur says. "I'll take pandemonium any day. At least that way you know you're alive. At least you're feeling something, rather than watching everything sail past your fingertips."

Grandpa Frank comes around the corner of the house. I see Mike stiffen. Grandpa Frank doesn't really acknowledge him but gives Trisha a nod.

"Nice to see you," he says, before looking at Arthur. "I take it you've met the newest addition to the family."

"I'm still waiting for my bassinet," Arthur says.

"Everyone, please come inside," Grandma Kay says. "Dinner is just about ready. Shirley, can you give me a hand? And Toby, can you set out the condiments?"

I'm grateful for any excuse to get away.

CHAPTER 47

The food is passed around. Roasted potatoes, shiny with the fat of the roast, carrots that are limp and sweet, canned corn and creamy coleslaw. Grandma Kay passes around tear-away buns that are soft as clouds and follows that with a tub of margarine.

"I'm sorry," she says. "I forgot to get butter. We don't use it much, anyway. You think we would, given the farm."

Everyone says Grandma Kay's roast is tender, especially Trisha.

"Honestly, this is the best roast beef I've ever had," she says, helping herself to another slice. "Can you come over and teach my mom how to make it? Not that she'll get it right or anything."

"There's nothing to it," Grandma Kay says, but I can tell by the way she's smiling that Trisha's words have made her happy.

"I haven't had a roast for years," Shirley says, smearing a wedge of meat with some horseradish. "Of course, who would I make a roast for? No point making one for myself. I made that mistake once. I wanted a turkey. So I went out and bought the smallest one I could find, which was, of course, too big. And I cooked it and ate it, but I didn't even make a dent in the thing, and there was so much left over, I almost cried. I froze whatever I could cram into the freezer and made stock. The whole episode just made me depressed."

"You could've invited us over," Grandma Kay says. "Or brought the turkey over here."

"I suppose." Shirley sighs. "But I never think that way. I don't invite people over very often. I always assume they don't want to come."

"You just let us know," Grandma Kay says. "We can come anytime. Frank loves turkey."

Grandpa Frank looks up from his plate. "Just the drumsticks."

"What's the food like in Italy?" Trisha asks Arthur.

"Heaven," he says. "Everything tastes better over there. I can't explain it. You can eat all the pizza you want and never get tired of it."

"I eat all the pizza I want now, and I don't get tired of it," Trisha says.

"But that pizza is shit," Arthur says. "Pardon my language, but it's true. You need to experience the real things in life. Not the carbon copies."

Mike is wearing cologne. He's sitting next to me and I can almost see the cologne winding its way toward me, a spice-scented river. The fact that he's wearing cologne makes me think that he's trying to turn me on. I'm not saying that it isn't working, but I'm more impressed that he's trying. He hasn't said much during dinner, and every time my father says something, Mike just stares at the salt shaker in front of him. I guess this is a lot for him to take in. I should've warned him. I should've told him what to expect.

"Are you Italian?" Trisha asks Bruno.

"Yes," Bruno says. "I was born in a small city outside of Rome."

"What do you think of Canada?"

"It's nice. Big. The streets are wide and smooth."

"I never thought about how wide our streets are," Grandma Kay says. "Or smooth."

"Come to Rome," Bruno says. "Then you see what I mean."

"You must think Tilden sucks," Trisha says. "There's nothing to do."

"There's plenty to do," Grandma Kay says. "You just have to go looking for it."

"If I have to go looking for it," Trisha says. "Then it's not worth doing."

As I listen to the conversation around the dinner table, I have a flashback to the day I tried to kill myself. I see the pills in my hand. I can hear the lake. I remember the way the morning light shone through the leaves.

Who was the girl at the cabin? She seems so far away, like an old photo that's curling around the edges and the colours are all faded to black and white. But I also wonder how far away she really is.

✳ ✳ ✳

Grandma Kay serves up my favourite dessert, even though the name of it always makes me feel awkward, especially those words coming out of her mouth.

"Who's up for a piece of Better Than Sex Cake?" she asks.

"Looks like things are finally about to get interesting," Arthur says, sitting up straighter in his chair.

Bruno swats him with a napkin. I see then, in that little moment, who they really are, what they mean to one another. They're partners. Boyfriends. Lovers. Any word I try to come up with feels weird, but what else would I call them? I try to picture them kissing, but I can't. I don't want to either. There are some things I don't need to know. But my mind can't help going back to it, wondering how they have sex, what they do in bed with their penises, how things fit together. I could ask Trisha, but she'd probably roll her eyes and say, "Tob-eee... ," as if I'm the dumbest person on the planet. Then she'd go on to explain it to me in a lot of detail, whether she actually knew what she was talking about or not. But I'm glad they're together, Arthur and Bruno. I'm glad my father has someone to take care of him.

I wasn't a husband or a boyfriend to my mom, even though I felt like that sometimes. But I took care of her, even if I wasn't always sure how. Even if I only wanted her to take care of me.

"Bruno, do you want a piece of Better Than Sex Cake?" Grandma Kay says, laughing. She seems a lot more relaxed now. Maybe she's relieved that dinner is over.

"He'd never turn down sex *or* cake," Arthur says, and everyone, even Mike, starts to laugh. Everyone.

Even me.

CHAPTER 48

Trisha starts begging my father to perform after the dessert dishes are cleared.

"Please," she says. "You have no idea. I'd kill to see anything out of the ordinary. A man dressed in women's clothes would do a lot for me."

"But I haven't prepared anything," Arthur says.

"All your things are in the car," Bruno says.

"You're telling me," Shirley says. "I could barely get the hatch closed."

"Good job you sat on it," Arthur says. "You're finally putting the big butt of yours to good use."

"You be quiet. My butt is not big."

"Maybe a couple of songs," he says. "But that's it. Now, where am I going to perform?"

"How about the barn?" I ask.

I'm surprised I'm interested in seeing him perform. I wasn't before. The thought of him dressed up made me feel weird inside. But now I want to see him. Because he's leaving to go back. And I'm not sure when I'll see him again. Maybe it's worth the risk.

And, in some ways, it feels like I'll be seeing the whole him. The real him. I want to see what makes him so talented. What made my mom fall in love with him that day in the gymnasium.

I want to see my father through her eyes.

"You mean perform with all those cows around me?" he asks, crinkling his nose.

"They're out to pasture now," I tell him. "And the farm hands would've swept it before leaving, right, Grandpa?"

Grandpa Frank nods. "As clean as it'll ever get, anyway."

"There's a concrete walkway that runs down the middle," I say. "Between the stalls. You can use that for the stage. We'll sit at one end."

"I don't know," he says. "The smell alone is going to make me gag. I mean, I've performed in some stink holes in my day, but this takes things to a new level."

But he finally agrees and goes to the car to get his bags. Bruno helps him.

"Shirley, can you give me a hand with my makeup?" Arthur asks.

"Why should I help you?" she asks. "You're always being mean to me."

"Yes, but I do it out of love, dear Shirley," he says. "I need an entourage. People around me in the dressing room. I love the flurry of it all. It energizes me. Say you'll help me, dear Shirley." He looks down. "Besides, it would be nice to get ready with you there. I need all the support I can get."

"You're so needy," Shirley says with half a smile. "But if you insist."

"Wonderful," he says. "And who would know how to cover up stubble better than you?"

"You're such a bitch."

"That's Ms. Bitch to you."

Grandma Kay tells them to stop using bad language.

"Say," my father says to her. "I could use an accompanist. How about it? For old times' sake?"

"Are you crazy? I can't play anymore," she says. "And there's no way on God's green earth that we're lugging that piano into the barn."

"I bet you're kicking yourself for not learning how to play the accordion instead," my father says. "Much more practical. And portable. Oh well. Suit yourself."

Grandma Kay tells Mike, Trisha and me to go to the barn and make sure everything is tidied up.

"I don't trust those farm hands," she says. "No offence, Mike. Just make sure there are no cow pies on that walkway. I can only imagine the holy terror we'll hear if he steps in something in his high heels."

So we walk there together, the three of us. It's the first time we've been alone, together, if that makes sense. With everyone knowing everything. Even though I'm not really sure there's much to know. I'm still not sure how I feel about Mike. Or what I want from him. If I want anything at all. I keep thinking about my conversation with Grandma Kay. About living the life I want to live. But how can I know the life I want to live when I didn't even want to live it a short time ago?

"If the two of you start making out, I'm going to vomit," Trisha says. "I'm warning you now."

"Stop being a frickin' moron," Mike says.

"This is still really weird for me," she says. "Knowing about the two of you. What was going on. Under my nose. I still can't believe it."

"No one meant to lie to you," I say. "We just didn't know what to say. Or how you'd feel about it. Sometimes, saying nothing is easier, even if it's a little bit like lying."

"*A little bit?*" Trisha says. "That's the understatement of the year. Anyway, I'll need some time to process this. You. My brother. It's still very disturbing to me, as you can imagine."

"You want disturbing?" Mike asks. "I'm about to watch a gay guy prance around in a dress in a barn. *That's* disturbing."

"Stop being so closed-minded," Trisha says. "No one's forcing you to do anything."

"And he's your *dad*," Mike says to me, shaking his head. "That's so fucked. Like, aren't you embarrassed?"

"I don't know what I feel," I say. "But embarrassed isn't the right word."

"Humiliated?" Mike asks. "Ashamed? Completely freaked out?"

"No," I say. "None of those."

"Well, you definitely have a weird way of looking at things," Mike says. "Because if that was my dad…"

"Our dad is boring!" Trisha yells. "He comes home from work and barely says two words to us. He eats his dinner and then lies on the couch until he falls asleep and mom has

322

to wake him up so he goes to bed. It's the same night after night."

"So what? He's tired. It's called working, Trisha. Nothing that *you'd* know about."

"I know a lot more than you, asswipe. The other day, Dad drove me to the mall, and the entire ride there, neither of us said anything. At all. Imagine being with your dad and you can't think of a single thing to say. And he couldn't either. We just drove in silence. And I kept thinking, 'Couldn't he just ask me about school? Or what I thought about something? Would it be the end of the world for him to pretend he was interested in my life?' And I'm telling you right now, if I end up marrying someone like Dad, I'll kill myself."

She stops. "Oh my God, Toby. I didn't mean that. I'm sorry."

"It's fine," I say. "Really. I know what you meant."

"It's just that I'm jealous. Of you."

"Jealous of me? Why?"

"Your life is so interesting. Your father is a famous female impersonator. That's so cool."

"It's not cool," Mike says. "It's fucked up."

"I'd give my right arm for someone interesting like that in my life. Just to have someone open a door like that for me. To show me there's something else. Something more."

"There *is* something more for you," I say, putting my hand on her back. "If not today, then soon."

"Do you really think that?"

"Yes," I say, and I want to believe it. I want her to be smart and not marry someone like her dad. I want her to leave Tilden, even if it's only for a little while, and do something she wants to do. Something that will make her happy, even if it makes sense to no one else.

I want her to have her more too.

CHAPTER 49

We set up some of the old milking stools for chairs at one end of the barn, next to the calves. Trisha can't stop fussing over them.

"It's awful they're taken away from their mothers," she says, patting one on the head.

"They survive," I say, before thinking, *We all do*.

"I don't have to watch this, do I?" Mike asks.

"It's not going to kill you," I say. "It's just a few songs. You're acting like he's going to murder children or something."

"I'd handle that better than this."

"You would not," Trisha says. "Stop being so stupid and immature. The world's not made up of people like you, you know. Thankfully."

Grandpa Frank and Grandma Kay are the next to arrive. They both look uncomfortable, especially Grandpa Frank, who busies himself by checking on the stalls and the equipment.

"Settle out," Grandma Kay says. "What do you possibly need to check on?"

"Force of habit, I guess," Grandpa Frank says. "Besides, you'd be surprised what you miss, even though you see something every day."

"You miss a lot of things," Grandma Kay says with a roll of her eyes. I think she loves Grandpa Frank, but I wonder how much. And I wonder what kind of life she expected to have, when she was younger. When she was my age.

"Here they come," she says, pointing out the window. We watch as the three of them make their way from the house. Shirley and Bruno are on either side of Arthur. He's wearing what looks like a black sequined top and a black skirt with black pantyhose and red high heels. He's wearing a blond wig. Even from here, I can see his red lips and fluttering eyelashes.

"Well, would you look at that?" Grandma Kay says.

"Do I have to?" Mike mutters. Trisha jabs him with her elbow.

"Who's he supposed to be?" Trisha asks.

"I have no idea," Grandma Kay says. "Some kind of celebrity? I'm horrible with those kinds of things. I can't keep up with Hollywood. Of course, nothing can compare to the glamour of dairy farming."

We watch in silence as the three of them make their way to us. I can hear Arthur talking to them and Bruno saying something back in a low and steady voice, like you'd use on a child if he was having a temper tantrum in the grocery store. At one point, my father almost slips on the gravel, but Shirley and Bruno grab him before he falls.

"These shoes were *not* made for the country!" he says loudly, and Trisha starts to laugh.

"This is the best thing that's happened in forever," she says. "Oh my God, right here, on your dairy farm."

"Farming life means you see all kinds of strange things,"

Grandpa Frank says. "I thought I'd seen everything. But then today came along."

They stop just outside the entrance. Shirley comes in first. "He told me I couldn't touch his face. I said, 'Why did you ask for my help, then?' He just wants to be fussed over. He's the most high-maintenance man I've ever met. And believe me, I've met my share in my day."

She takes an empty stool next to me and surprises me by grabbing my hand. "Are you nervous?" she whispers.

"A little," I say.

"Don't be," she says. "He's actually very good. I saw him perform once, in the early days. And I've read reviews of his shows. If there was ever a man born to play a woman..."

Bruno comes in next. "Ladies and gentlemen," he says. "Thank you for coming here tonight. We have a very special guest, someone loved all around the world. Tonight, he perform just for you. You will see the kind of magic that he bring to the stage. Please help me to welcome the one and only, man of a thousand women, Mr. Arthur Turner!"

We all clap, although it doesn't seem like much, and then my father appears in the doorway of the barn, hand on his hip, arm raised in the air. He has a goofy smile on his face, or it could be all the red lipstick. It's surprising because he looks so different. I wouldn't recognize him if he passed me on the street. He looks like a real woman. Well, as real as you can get with all that makeup. But real enough. And I think how he's so plain in his boy clothes. No wonder he dresses like this. He must feel beautiful right now.

"Thank you for coming to tonight's show, darlings," he

says with a dramatic bow. "I'm used to performing for animals, but never livestock. I'm so glad you could make it. It's wonderful to be performing for simple country folks. Please note that if you parked your horse on the street, you'll get a ticket after 9 p.m."

Grandma Kay starts to laugh. Even Grandpa Frank cracks a smile.

"I'm only going to do a few numbers for you this evening, as we don't have much time. But I do hope that will be enough. To show you a little of what I've got. I've played all around the world, in some of the biggest concert halls. But this show, this audience, means the most of any of them."

He looks at me and, for a second, I think I see a shimmer in his eyes.

"Tonight, I'll take you down some familiar paths and show you some familiar stars of days gone by. Let's start with one of my favourites, the gal who puts the dreidel in my bagel, Ms. Barbra Streisand."

He goes cross-eyed like he's looking at a bug on his nose and starts to sing. It's amazing, really. How much his voice changes. I don't know much about how Barbra Streisand sounds, but it doesn't really matter because his voice is so good. The song is something about people needing people. He starts to walk more into the space, spreading his arms out on either side of him, and as I watch, I start to see it. What my mom saw when she saw him. What she felt. I start to feel it too.

He. Was. Magic.

He ends the song and we all clap, especially Trisha, who sticks her pinkies in either side of mouth and whistles.

"What an enthusiastic crowd," he says. "I don't care what anyone says. Gentiles are good people too."

Mike leans over to me. "What's a gentile?" he asks, but I tell him it's not important. To be honest, I don't know myself.

"Now I'd like to bring on stage someone with pizzazz, razzle and a whole lot of sparkle. That's right, she's a lady dripping in diamonds. From the Broadway stage straight to the Goodman Dairy Farm, it's the one and only Carol Channing!"

He turns away, and I can tell by the look on Trisha's face that she doesn't know who Carol Channing is either. But Grandma Kay does, because I hear her say, "Oh, this should be good."

Arthur spins back around with his wig turned backwards. His smile stretches across his entire face.

"Ischn't thisch lovely?" he says in a raspy voice.

Grandma Kay starts to laugh. Shirley does too. Based on the way he's talking, I guess Carol had a weird way of speaking.

"I'm juscht in from Talahaschee," he says. "And the busch ride was an experiench I'll never forget. I'm juscht lucky no one tried to poach my…diamondsch."

Then he starts singing.

"A kisch on the hand might be quite continental, but diamondsch are a girlsch bescht friend."

I think I've heard the song before, but it doesn't matter. He's so funny to watch, his eyes wide and mouth wide open. Grandma Kay can't stop laughing. She keeps saying, "Oh, my goodness. That's her. That's exactly her!" to Grandpa Frank.

I catch Bruno looking at me, and he smiles in a way that

seems so warm and true. I think about what my dad said, how Bruno is his lighthouse. And I wonder what that would feel like, to know that someone is there, flashing in the darkness, guiding you to safety. Have I ever known that feeling? Even if I have, it was so long ago, I've forgotten what it feels like.

I smile back to let him know I'm having a good time. He nods and then turns his head back to Arthur, who finishes the song and takes another deep bow. We applaud, this time louder. Trisha is still whistling, but I think it's okay. I can see by the look in Arthur's eyes that he likes the sound. He wants us to like him. So we do. I clap a bit louder.

Then he takes off the wig and messes his hair. He looks more like himself, and I remember the letter he wrote to my mom, when he said he had a hairy octopus on his head. I wish I could've known him when he was younger. And I wish she could be here, with all of us. He says that the last number he's going to do for us is one that's very special to his heart.

"I'm hoping you all know the song," he says. "And the performer. I like to think of her as timeless, as someone who never falls out of fashion because her talent was so great. Some people have that ability, you know. To be larger than life. That's all anyone can hope for. To be bigger and better than you could ever dream. To make a difference. Even in the lives of strangers. Can someone get me a stool please? I usually do this one sitting down."

Bruno grabs a stool and takes it over to Arthur. He mouths the words "thank you" and Bruno nods back.

"This song is by one of the greats. Miss Judy Garland."

"Oh, I know her!" Trisha says, a little too loudly.

"Thank God for small mercies," my father says before starting the song. It's "Somewhere Over the Rainbow," which I've heard because I've seen *The Wizard of Oz* dozens of times on TV. Like in the two songs before this, my father's voice changes again. This time, it's coming from a deeper place; it's both stronger and sweeter, which is a strange mix when I think about it. But maybe not. Maybe strong and sweet can be side by side.

"Lord, I'm going to cry in this one," I hear Grandma Kay say, and Shirley passes her a tissue.

When he gets to the part about happy little bluebirds, I can feel something in my eyes, too, but I try to hold it back. It's his voice. The way that he's singing the words. I forget that he's my father, or a man. And I don't see him as a woman either—he's somewhere in between. It doesn't matter if he's a woman or a man, or if he's gay or not, if he's my father or not my father. It's his voice, a sound that comes from someplace deep inside of him. It doesn't matter what anyone thinks because he has his talent and no one or their opinions can take that away from him.

By the time he gets to the end, I'm crying. There's no way I can't. He's crying too. And when we stand up to clap our hands, he cries a little more. He says, "Thank you, thank you, thank you."

And then, just as quickly as he appeared, my father is gone.

CHAPTER 50

We're standing on the porch, although it's not big enough to hold us all, so some of us are standing on the steps and others are standing on the walkway leading to the stairs. I look at everyone around me: Grandpa Frank, Grandma Kay, Shirley, Trisha, Mike, my father and Bruno.

This is my family.

It's weird that this pops into my head, because this isn't my family, not in the way that families usually are. But it feels right. Even Trisha and Mike are part of my family, like my brother and sister, although if that were really true, it would mean that I saw my brother's penis, which is obviously disturbing, so I try not to think about it too much.

But it's true that I've known Mike and Trisha for most of my life. The same with Shirley. So really, they *are* like family.

There's only one person missing. There will always be one person missing.

"Well, my darlings," my father says. "I think the time has come. We have a plane to catch in a few hours and if you've ever been in a car with Shirley, you'll know the odometer needle rarely passes sixty."

"That's not true," Shirley says. "I was going at least eighty when I was driving you back here."

"I stand corrected," my father says.

"I'll be driving faster this time around," Shirley says. "The sooner I drop you off, the sooner I'll be rid of you."

"Do you really mean that, Shirley?" my father asks.

"Yes," she says, and then drops her head. "No. I don't. You're someone I dislike and love in equal quantities at any given time of the day."

"The feeling is mutual," my father says. "We have a past. We'll be forever joined, even if we're halfway across the world from each other."

Grandma Kay clears her throat. "Well, it's been nice having the two of you here, to our small corner of the world."

"I will bring back stories of Canada to Italy," Bruno says. "Of roast beef and Sex Cake."

"I can only imagine what people are going to think of us." Grandma Kay laughs. She touches the scarf around her neck. I was jealous when Bruno gave it to her. I wanted something for myself. But now I understand I got something much better. Something I needed a lot more than a piece of material.

"You come back anytime," Grandma Kay says. "Both of you. You can stay with us next time, if you like. Provided this one manages to stay clear of the sauce." She points to my father. "I won't tolerate any of that nonsense."

"I hear you loud and clear, warden," he says, giving a quick salute and tapping his heels together. "Although I'm never much fun sober."

"You've entertained us more than you realize," Grandma

Kay says. "You don't need anything to help you with that. Just be yourself."

"Easier said than done," my father says. "Especially for someone who makes his living pretending to be other people."

"Just because you're pretending to be someone else doesn't mean you're not interesting as you."

My father turns to look at me. He looks surprised. I am too. I said those words. I wasn't expecting that. They just popped out. But I'm glad I said them. They're true. I really believe that.

"Thank you for that, Toby," he says. "You're a very smart girl. Obviously, you didn't get that from me."

"No," I say. "But I did get these cheekbones."

Which makes my father laugh and laugh.

✳ ✳ ✳

He tells me to come visit him.

"The door is always open."

"Italy is far away," I say.

"Not as far as you think," he says. "You remember that."

"Will you come back here?"

"Absolutely! You can count on that. I'll need a stage assistant, though. Anyone you can recommend?"

"Maybe," I say.

He steps in closer. "If you ever get to a place that's full of shadows and you don't think you'll ever see the light, you call me. Collect. I'm only a phone call away."

He presses a piece of paper into my hand. I open it and see a long line of numbers.

"Promise me," he says.

"Promise," I say

Bruno steps over to us.

"It was nice to meet you," I say to him. I'm not sure if I should hug him or shake his hand, but he makes the decision for both of us and kisses me quickly on both cheeks. I feel my face go warm.

"That's what we do in Italy," he says.

"Will you take care of my dad?" I ask. I'm worried. I know about AIDS. I've seen men on TV who look like skeletons. What would I do if my dad got sick?

"I try my best," he says.

"Thank you, Zio Bruno," I say, and he smiles at me.

My father walks over to Grandma Kay and gives her a quick hug.

"Goodbye. Again."

She doesn't say anything but bites her lip. I can't look at her or else I'll start to cry, so I look at the bumper of Shirley's car.

"You take care of her," I hear my father say to Grandpa Frank. "She's been through a lot in her life."

He moves over to Trisha. "You are a fantastic whistler," he says before turning to Mike. "And you be good to my little girl." His voice is lower, like he's doing an impersonation of a cowboy. He punches Mike in the arm. "Or else you'll have Sheriff Turner to deal with. Understood?"

Mike nods but can't make eye contact.

"Oh, lighten up," my father says, his voice back to normal. "I'm just a guy in a dress. Trust me, there are people you need to be more afraid of in life than me."

336

He turns around. "Well, Dame Shirley? Shall we be off?"

"I guess," she says. "Do you think there will be many trucks on the highway at this time of the night?"

"The highway will be positively littered with them," my father says. "I'm expecting to hear your screams from the plane. On second thought, I'll never get any sleep that way. Why don't you let Bruno drive?" He adjusts the scarf around his neck. "The Italians are all stunt drivers at heart."

"I'm not letting anyone drive but me," Shirley says. "Are you crazy?"

They get into the car and start to back up. Everyone waves.

"Bye!"

"Bye, Toby!"

"Bye, Bruno!"

"Bye, Trisha!"

"Bye! Bye!

The car drives away, my father's scarf a flag in the wind.

"Do you think they'll come back?" I ask no one in particular.

"I'm not sure," Grandma Kay says. "It would be nice."

"At least they were here," I say.

"For a very small moment."

"Sometimes, that's all you get," Grandpa Frank says.

"There's still some Sex Cake," Grandma Kay says to everyone who's left. "Who's up for a second piece?"

"I'll have one," Mike says.

"Half for me," Trisha says.

"Me, too," I say.

"Going back to the barn," Grandpa Frank says, walking away. "Got some stuff to do in there."

"You've always got stuff to do in there," Grandma Kay says. Only, for once, she doesn't sound mad.

"I'll be there in a minute," I say.

I walk to the edge of the driveway and look down the road. My breath catches in my throat. Shirley's car is stopped. It's idling, the brake lights like angry eyes staring back at me. Why are they stopped? I step farther into the road. The car is sitting there, a low rumble coming from the tailpipe. The passenger door opens and my father steps out. What is he doing? He starts walking toward me. Not quickly or anything. Just a normal sort of walk. And maybe it's the way the breeze is blowing through his hair or the way I can only stand here, watching him, waiting for him to reach me in the middle of the road, but he suddenly seems so young and innocent.

"Did you forget something?" I ask when he reaches me. My heart is beating against my ribs.

He smiles and says nothing. Instead, he stares at me for a long time. I watch his green eyes move across my face, my own eyes, my nose, my mouth.

"No," he says after a while. "Just making sure I don't forget any last detail."

"Okay," I say.

He takes one step closer and places his hands on either side of my face.

"Let me be your lighthouse, Toby."

I realize that's the only thing I ever wanted my father to say, even before I knew him, even when he was just a story my mom would tell me. Not these exact words, but the feeling behind them. To know I was protected. That he was there, in the darkness, thinking of me, guiding me to safety. And now that I've heard my father say this, I don't know how I feel. I want to believe him, but how can someone be there for you when they're halfway around the world? How can anyone's light be that strong?

"Maybe," I say, because it's the only thing I can think of to say.

He looks a bit disappointed, but then he smiles. "You're a tough one, Toby Goodman. That will serve you well in this life. Just don't be afraid to be weak sometimes. Help is always here, even if you don't always realize it."

Before I can say anything else, he gives me a quick kiss, turns around and walks back to the car. He doesn't look back, but I watch him all the same. He gets into the car, the brake lights turn dark and the car starts moving again.

It gets smaller and smaller, the pings of gravel hitting its underside growing quieter and quieter. When I can't see the car and the cloud that had been following it, I know that they're gone.

I turn and walk back toward the house. The sky is turning navy. I can just make out the shapes of the cows in the fields. They look like dark anvils. Nothing changes for them, but I hope they have a peaceful night under the stars.

I come up the steps and stop at the screen door. My hand reaches for the door handle, but I hesitate. I listen to the voices, see the light coming from the kitchen.

I look to the right and see the lawn chair, the same one

I'd imagined my mom sitting in a few hours earlier. It looks so lonely. I want to go over and sit down in it. Just for a few moments. Just to see if I can feel my mom. To feel connected to her again.

I turn back to the screen door, to the soft light coming from inside, and I think about lighthouses. And how maybe there's not just one lighthouse in my life. Maybe there are many. Some lighthouses are close. And others are far away. Some are old and some are new and some have broken lights that barely flicker. But when the lights come together, when all the pieces join and become one, they burn bright.

I take a deep breath, open the door, and go inside.

AUTHOR NOTE

For many writers, research is an important part of writing books. For *Break in Case of Emergency*, I spent time on a dairy farm so I could capture the setting accurately. (I didn't milk any cows. I was too nervous. And, based on the way the cows were eyeing me, I made them nervous too.) But books are about more than just places—they're also about people. And getting your characters right is just as important. Maybe even *more* important. So much of my research was about trying to get inside the head of a character like Toby Goodman. I read accounts from people who experienced the death of a parent by suicide. I read about motherless daughters and about what it feels like when a father abandons his daughter, the same way Arthur abandons Toby. But the most important research I did was around the subject of mental health and young people.

I've gone through some dark chapters in my life, but I've never personally dealt with mental health issues. So I was a bit nervous about creating a character like Toby. I needed to get her character right, but I wasn't sure if I could. What was our common ground? There are a lot of differences between us, like gender, environment and family life. I'm also a few years older than Toby. Okay, maybe more than a few.

So that's why I wanted to do research about teens and mental health: I needed to understand what pushes teenagers toward suicide, why they feel so alone and why they don't always reach out for help.

In *Break in Case of Emergency*, there's a lot of talk about "pieces." The characters sometimes refer to the pieces of their lives or pieces of their personalities. Toby thinks about pieces when she's in the variety store, trying on a mask. Grandpa Frank talks about the pieces of his life after Toby's suicide attempt. Arthur mentions it when he does Toby's makeup in Sears. The theme of pieces shows up a lot because that's how I sometimes look at life and people. We're all made of different pieces that connect, in all kinds of strange and wonderful ways, to make us whole.

When I was a teenager, I kept my world private. Growing up in the eighties in a small southwestern Ontario city meant I wasn't surrounded by a lot of diversity. I knew I was different but didn't know who to turn to. I refused to let anyone know I was guarding a secret world inside—one that was full of shame. I felt like a misfit, a pervert, a monster. I thought that if people found out who I really was, they would hate me. This wasn't something I imagined. It was reality. I heard comments every day that confirmed it. Being gay meant being despised.

It turns out that maybe Toby and I had a few things in common, even though her situation was a lot more serious than mine was. We both knew about darkness and had feelings of never being good enough. We both thought we'd be rejected if we showed our true selves. We both thought that being vulnerable meant being weak and that no one, not even our best friends, would accept us if they found out who we really were behind our masks.

What I came to understand is that, while the research was important, some of the clues to figuring out who Toby Goodman was were already inside of me. I think there are pieces of other people inside all of us, and it's those pieces that help connect us to one another. To think twice before we pass judgment. To be a little kinder. The pieces remind us that, no matter how different things seem on the outside, we may not be all that different on the inside.

If you're struggling with anxiety or feelings of depression, or if other people are being cruel to you and you don't think you can face another day, please know there are other people who are going through similar experiences. You might not know their names or where they live, but they're out there. And there are people who want to help you and *can* help you. All you need to do is reach out.

At the end of *Break in Case of Emergency,* Toby stops and stands at her front door. She's still uncertain about opening it. To her, opening a door could mean something horrible and painful. And, after everything she's been through, can you blame her for feeling this way? But after reflecting on everything she's been through, she starts to see things a bit differently—that opening a door doesn't always have to feel scary. Toby comes to understand that there is light on the other side of that door. There are people waiting for her. People who love her. Who want to help, in whatever way they can.

There are people waiting on the other side of your door too.

RESOURCES

If you or someone you know is in crisis, feeling suicidal or in need of a safe, judgment-free person to talk to, crisis centers across the country offer assistance 24/7 via call, live chat or text messaging.

Suicide Prevention Lifeline
(800) 273-TALK (8255)
SuicidePreventionLifeline.org
The National Suicide Prevention Lifeline provides immediate free and confidential emotional support to people in suicidal crisis or emotional distress 24 hours a day, 7 days a week.

The Trevor Project—Saving Young LGBTQ Lives
Trevor Lifeline: 866-488-7386
TheTrevorProject.org
The Trevor Project provides crisis intervention and suicide prevention services to lesbian, gay, bisexual, transgender, queer & questioning (LGBTQ) young people under 25.

Your Life Your Voice from Boys Town
800–448–3000
YourLifeYourVoice.org
This service offers support for teens dealing with any issue, from suicidal thoughts to anxiety and low self-esteem, abuse by a family member, bullying, anger, concern for a friend, and more.

ACKNOWLEDGEMENTS

Thank you to Suzanne Sutherland. You were the best kind of editor—thoughtful, generous and this book's biggest cheerleader. Thanks for helping me take this book—and these characters—to where they needed to go.

Thank you to the awesome team at HarperCollins Canada, including Iris Tupholme, Jennifer Lambert, Deanna Norlock, Stephanie Conklin, Linda Pruessen, Patricia MacDonald and Alan Jones.

Thank you to Natashya Wilson and the team at Inkyard Press for bringing this book to American readers.

Thank you to my agent, Dean Cooke, and to Paige Sisley, for your support and feedback about this book over the years. And yes, it's been years.

Thank you to Salini Perera for your beautiful artwork.

Thank you to Samuel Engelking, Melanie Little, Jaclyn Price, Neil Smith, Katherine Vice, Deb and Ron Vice and Alison Wearing.

Last, but not least, love and thanks to Serge, my family and my friends for their continued support and encouragement. I've been very lucky in this life.